Dear Reader,

Being a writer frequently brings milestones—that
first sale, the launch of a series, gaining another fan,
listening to your first audio book, etc. There's a new
adventure around every corner, and that's equally true
for the characters in my stories. I love how characters
I think I'm familiar with—characters like Jase Tyler
and Carrie Ward, whom I first introduced in
Shades of Desire—can surprise and challenge me.
In *Shades of Temptation,* my biggest challenge was
to realistically explore the attraction between these
two cautious, strong individuals despite the horrific
circumstances forcing them to work together. I
wanted to dig deep, past what I thought I knew
about them, past the superficialities, past their fear
and insecurities, until I uncovered what was rich and
unique and flawed and perfect about them. I hope
I've succeeded!

One theme I explore in *Shades of Temptation* is how
appearances can be deceptive and can also contribute
to many of the emotional limitations we place on
ourselves. In my opinion, the strongest individuals
are those who attempt to see beyond the surface and
who understand nothing is wholly black or white,
good or bad, beautiful or ugly. Instead, our world
is enriched by each color of the rainbow, and life
is about exploring every one. Thank you for your
interest in the Special Investigations Group series.

Wishing you much love and happiness always,

Virna DePaul

**Also available from Virna DePaul
and Harlequin HQN**

The Special Investigations Group
Shades of Desire

And coming soon
Shades of Passion

VIRNA DePAUL

SHADES
OF TEMPTATION

HARLEQUIN®

entertain, enrich, inspire™

Recycling programs for this product may not exist in your area.

ISBN-13: 978-0-373-77674-0

SHADES OF TEMPTATION

Copyright © 2012 by Virna DePaul

Thank you to my writing buds
(including Susan Hatler, Cyndi Faria,
Rochelle French, Vanessa Kier and Joyce Lamb)
for your help on this one! Special thanks to
Michael Faria, who makes his mom proud
and I can totally see why. As always, I'm lucky
to have the support of my agent Holly Root,
my editor Margo Lipschultz and, of course,
my boys (love you!). Finally, thank you to
all the individuals at Harlequin Books for
spreading the word about me and this series,
and for showcasing us in such a wonderful way!

SHADES
OF TEMPTATION

CHAPTER ONE

SPECIAL AGENT CARRIE WARD entered McGill's Bar to break a dry spell, but there was to be no alcohol involved. She'd just closed another difficult case for SIG, the California Department of Justice's Special Investigations Group, a five-member state equivalent of the FBI, and she intended to celebrate by ending five years of celibacy. It didn't matter that she probably wouldn't achieve climax. She rarely did with a man. But pleasure wasn't what she was really after. She just wanted physical contact. Intimacy. To be able to pretend for a few hours that she belonged—on this earth, in this city, maybe even to a man who cared about her and saw her as more than a woman trying day in and day out to get away with doing a so-called "man's" job.

Less than thirty minutes later, Carrie exited McGill's alone. Her chest ached with loneliness far greater than any she'd ever felt before. And it wasn't because she hadn't found a man to seduce but because the one man she truly wanted to seduce—no, the one man she truly wanted to make love to, if there really was such a thing as making love—was getting ready to bed another woman.

She should never have come, she thought. It was a Friday night and she'd known Jase Tyler, a fellow SIG special agent, had a date. But she couldn't have known he'd bring his date to McGill's Bar, a favorite hangout of the San Francisco P.D. She'd seen him there with women before, of course, but they'd been women he'd picked up while he was there. She'd figured he'd take a date someplace swanky and more conducive to seduction.

She'd been wrong.

Her stomach contracted as she recalled her brief conversation with Seth Roberts, an SFPD cop. He'd said something that had made her laugh just before his friend had nudged him and said "Jase Tyler" in an admiring tone. With dread, she'd turned to look. Sure enough, she'd immediately recognized the back of Jase's elegantly dressed frame, his hand pressed against the slim bare back of the woman standing next to him. His date wore a black cocktail dress more appropriate for the opera than McGill's, but who was Carrie to judge? She hadn't even bothered dolling up for her manhunt. Instead, she was still wearing her standard office attire, which made her feel as feminine as usual—which was to say, not at all.

Now, standing outside McGill's, Carrie prayed Seth hadn't noticed the devastation she'd felt upon seeing Jase with his date. The way he'd looked at her, however—with slightly softened features and a hint of pity—told her she was wasting her time. But if he dared say anything to Jase about it, she'd make him sorry. If nothing else, she'd challenge him to another racquetball match and wipe the floor with him just as she'd done the last two times they'd played. Shoving her hands into her wool peacoat, she turned to walk to her car.

"Leaving so soon, Ward?"

She froze at the sound of Jase's voice. For a half second, she wondered if she was hearing things. If she'd made him materialize from sheer desire. The true question, however, was whether he'd appeared alone or with his date.

Slowly, she faced him. He was standing a couple of feet away, hands in his pockets, his ever-present tie loose, his suit jacket left behind. His sandy-brown hair was artfully disheveled, his tall, lean body showcased to full advantage by his tailored clothes. Although Jase would bristle at any suggestion that he was a metrosexual—and making him bristle used to be one of her favorite pastimes before the sexual tension between them had grown too dangerous—even Carrie wouldn't go so far as to label him as one. He cared about how he looked more than the average male. He dressed well. Looked good. Smelled good. But he was too intense and masculine to ever fit within that category.

It was no surprise, then, that Jase liked his women purely feminine. So why was he out here with her rather than inside with his date? She frowned, not because he was alone, but because of how damn relieved that fact made her feel. "What's up, Tyler? Did your date send you out here to retrieve the rest of her outfit? She getting chilly?"

He'd been watching her with a serious expression. Now, he grinned the same grin that always made women go weak-kneed and googly-eyed, her included. Thankfully, her slip with Seth aside, she was really good at hiding it.

"I'm pretty adept at keeping my dates warm," Jase drawled, his deep voice tinged with a hint of Texas twang. "I just saw you leave and wondered why you didn't stop and say hi."

She raised a mocking brow. "Didn't I? Sorry about that. Hi, Jase. How are you? Has anything interesting happened since I last saw you…let's see…" She glanced at her watch, a plain, simple design with a sturdy black strap. It was as fashionable and gender neutral as the rest of her. "Since I last saw you an hour and a half ago at the office?"

She looked back up at him. To her surprise, he'd moved closer and was practically looming over her. He hardly ever stood this close, as if he was trying to intimidate her with his sheer masculine presence. His body heat blasted her with the intensity of a raging fire. His scent, fresh and clean but with a hint of cologne, overpowered her. Desire rushed through her veins, making her dizzy, making her panic. Automatically, she took a step back and barely stopped herself from taking another.

She pushed a wayward strand of hair back over one ear and licked her lips. "Careful, Tyler. Your date might not like it if you stand so close to me. I mean, not that she'd view me as a threat or anything, but you know how silly most women can be."

Jase's fingers flexed. Absently, she noted he'd removed them from his pockets. He had big hands. Long, elegant fingers that belonged on some kind of artist rather than a cop. He had big feet, too. Although he had more than his fair share of height, he lacked the sheer bulk of some of their teammates, especially Liam "Mac" McKenzie and Simon Granger. And while he was handsome, Jase was more pretty boy than ruthless masculinity. It often made people underestimate him, shocking them when he transformed from dazzling charmer to dangerous badass right in front of their eyes. Sometimes even Carrie forgot how ruthless he could be. When that happened, he'd inevitably remind her by apprehending a dangerous suspect or responding to one of her snarky comments with a scathing retort. Tensing, she waited for such a retort now.

It didn't come. Instead, he lifted one of those big hands of his and lightly brushed her cheek with his fingertips. Her heart beat wildly. Immediately, she was tempted to close her eyes and lean in to him. As it was, she recalled the first and only time he'd kissed her, just a week ago, when Mac's girlfriend, Natalie Jones, had been assaulted and ended up in the hospital. Jase's kiss had been one of comfort, a light, brief touching of lips, over too soon. But its effect on her had been as forceful as a blow. Just as his touch was now. She couldn't help it. She trembled, and from the way his eyes heated and narrowed, he didn't miss her reaction.

"Regina should definitely view you as a threat," he said softly.

Her eyes widened. No. Surely she'd misheard him. She tried for a mocking laugh, but it came out breathless instead.

"I want to kiss you again, Carrie," he said before she could respond. "But this time I want to do it right."

The air completely left her lungs. She stared into his eyes, searching for signs that he was drunk but finding none.

His fingers trailed down to her jaw while his thumb lightly pressed against her bottom lip. When she gasped, he gave a shaky sigh and lowered his hand to shove it back in his pockets along with the other.

"The question is, are you going to let me? Or are we going to continue playing the same tiresome game, pretending we don't want to rip each other's clothes off and screw for days?"

His crude choice of words broke the hazy spell she'd been under. Jase was a lady's man. A bona fide charmer. He didn't use words like "screw" with women, at least not outside the bedroom. But she wasn't like the women he dated. She wasn't soft or feminine, and he obviously didn't feel the need to use his normal charm and gallantry with her. Or perhaps he was just being honest. He wanted to fuck her. Why waste his time with pretty words?

He was watching her carefully, with an almost predatory glint in his eye. Over his shoulder, through the windows of McGill's, she saw his date scanning the bar as if searching for him. She was just as beautiful from the front as she had been from the back. More so. So once again Carrie asked herself—what was Jase doing outside with her, pretending a desire that couldn't possibly be real? The only explanation was he was looking for some variety in his endless stream of sex partners, but she'd be damned if she was going to be the one to give it to him.

Deliberately, she softened her expression and bit her lip, hoping it made her look appropriately receptive. "Jase," she said shakily, keeping her gaze down.

Just as she hoped he would, he bent down to bring his face closer to hers.

"What is it, Carrie?" he asked, his voice deep and dark. "Tell me."

She peeked up at him through her lashes and lightly placed her hand on his chest. She could feel his heart thudding, strong and slightly erratic. She had him rattled, and while that should have made her feel triumphant, the ache between her thighs told her to tread carefully lest she be caught in her own trap. Ignoring the inner warning, she cupped the back of his neck and leaned up until her lips touched his earlobe. "Jase," she breathed again.

His hands settled lightly on either side of her waist, then tightened. He was getting ready to pull her against him. To press her body up against his hard, delectable length, and she knew if he did that, she'd be done for. She wasn't sure she'd have the strength to pull away from him. Turning her head, her gaze once more found

Jase's date inside. She'd homed in on them, and her posture told Carrie she'd be coming after him any second.

At that exact moment, Jase turned his head and brushed his lips against her jaw. A sizzling tingle shot up her spine before settling in her breasts and every other erogenous zone she possessed. She wanted to rub against him like a cat in heat. Not only that, but the temptation to fight Jase's date for the right to touch him—to *love* him—blindsided her.

Fool! What was wrong with her? She was teaching the guy a lesson here, not stamping her mark on him.

She kissed his jaw the same way he'd kissed hers. Then she clamped her teeth around his ear and bit him—hard.

"Shit!" Instinctively, he jerked. She immediately released him and took several steps back, this time not caring if it looked like a retreat.

Jase brought a hand up to rub his ear and glared at her. "Damn it, Carrie, what the hell was that for?"

"That," she replied breathlessly even as she continued to back away from him, "was to remind you that I'm no threat to Regina, but the same's not true for you. If you're bored with the bimbos you've been dating, then maybe there's hope for you yet. But don't waste my time by feeding me your bullshit. You don't want me. You want to beat me. Prove that you can make Special Agent Ward another notch on your bedpost. It's never going to happen."

"I don't want to beat you. At least, I didn't until you tried to take a damn chunk of my ear off, but—"

The door to McGill's opened. "Jase," a soft feminine voice called out. Regina held the door open and shot a look at Carrie, her expression one of obvious concern for Jase. "Do you need any help out here?"

Carrie actually snarled. The woman was acting like Carrie had cornered Jase and trapped him; after all, why else would he be bothering to speak with someone like her?

"Give me a second, Regina," Jase said. "I need to finish—"

"Oh, you're finished," Carrie said. She glanced at Regina. "Don't worry, I'm a cop. Jase and I work together. We were having a little disagreement, but he was just telling me how anxious he was to get back to you. So run along now, Jase. Have fun, you two."

"Damn it, Carrie—"

Ignoring him, she whirled around and walked in the opposite direction from her car. She'd come back for it later. After she'd calmed down.

After she remembered why she'd pushed Jase Tyler away rather than done what she'd really wanted to do— throw her arms around him and never let him go.

CHAPTER TWO

One month later

WITH THE WOMAN'S BODY still fully clothed, Dr. Odell Bowers placed two fingers on the carotid artery, then out of habit started to check for clouded-over corneas and rigor mortis. When he realized what he was doing, Bowers smiled, shook his head, picked up his shears and began to hum along to the strains of Mozart's "Requiem Mass in D minor" that floated around him.

"I've always loved this one. How about you?" He frowned down at the still-silent body. "I'll bring you around. Mozart was a visionary."

Carefully, he cut the woman's clothes off, then placed a modesty cloth over her genitalia. With slow, practiced movements, he washed her with disinfectant and germicidal solution, massaging the limbs the way his mother had often done for him. "Feels good, doesn't it?"

After settling eye caps over the woman's eyelids, Bowers began the slow, painstaking process of the preservation. Occasionally, he paused to wipe away the tears that trailed down the woman's face, then sighed when they flowed more freely and the woman's limbs began to twitch.

Even with her life force almost drained, the woman struggled to gain consciousness.

Bowers tightened the restraints as a precautionary measure. Then he picked up the syringe of Novocain and repeatedly plunged the needle into the woman's lips and cheeks. She quieted. He made a few minor adjustments until the woman's expression looked relaxed and natural. Soon, her features were set.

"I've picked out the prettiest clothes for you. And the makeup will complement your coloring. You'll be picture-perfect by the time I'm done."

Bowers resumed massaging the body's limbs as the mechanical pump injected embalming fluid into its blood vessels. A low groan, like an animal in pain, exploded from the woman's closed lips. Her limbs spasmed, and her fingers clenched before her whole body relaxed. The woman's final breath barely registered.

"Shh. That's right. That's perfect," Bowers whispered.

Bowers smoothed back the woman's damp hair, then finished the most complicated part of the procedure. Afterward, he rewashed and dried the woman's body, applied a moisturizing cream to her face then used his palette of cosmetics to camouflage her pale features. He smoothed on a very light pink lipstick, pleased with the realistic, translucent color called *Baby's Breath*. Next, he removed the eye caps and dabbed brown shadow on the eyelids for depth. Then a darker red along the cheeks, chin and knuckles to depict flowing blood. Finally, baby oil in the hair.

Bowers placed the clothing he'd selected on the woman's body, then stood back and studied his work. He shifted the arms that were crossed against the woman's chest back to her sides. Then he smoothed a stray hair down against her temple.

Finally satisfied, he picked up a scalpel.

Very slowly and very carefully, Bowers sliced off the woman's eyelids, then put them in a small box with the rest of his collection.

Over the next few hours, he completed his remaining tasks. He took some final pictures. Next, he wheeled the woman's body to her final resting place, but not before he pulled several teeth, and hair fibers from her and set them aside. Later, he'd send the ashes along with the photos, teeth and hair to the police. As he cleaned up his workroom, he actually giggled as he imagined the police scrambling to find her.

Ever since he was a kid, he'd loved planning scavenger hunts, giving the participants just enough challenging clues to make their task possible but by no means easy. With the cops, he'd virtually draw them a map so they could identify her, but that was because finding the victims wasn't the game. Finding *him* was. Of course, no one had ever been smart enough to do that. No one ever would.

After looking around and making sure things had been tidied up to the best of his ability, Bowers climbed the stairs that would take him from his basement to his elegant living quarters just blocks from the Golden Gate Bridge. He loved the juxtaposition of his different lives. How the upper floors of his home depicted his wealth and success, while the lower part evidenced his darker, private side. It never ceased to amaze him how the first so easily disguised the second. As if people truly didn't think they could coexist. Humming, he gathered his things, then double-checked his calendar on his smartphone.

His next appointment was at eleven. His patients rarely expressed appropriate gratitude for what Bowers did for them, but they certainly paid him well. Nonetheless, while he enjoyed the money he made, the perfection of Bowers's work was reward enough. Bowers took ugly things and made them beautiful again, just as he did with his girls.

Others might fail to acknowledge his mastery at first, but not for long. Bowers always opened their eyes to it eventually. All it took was strategy, time and discipline.

That, and a steady hand with a scalpel, of course.

CHAPTER THREE

THE SMALL ONES ALMOST *always ran.*

They figured they had the advantage when it came to speed, but few of them knew cops were trained to go the distance. It might take them a while to catch up, but they almost always did.

In this case, it also helped that Carrie was even smaller than the perp she was chasing, and, because she wore plain clothes, she wasn't hindered by a fourteen-pound belt loaded with a patrol officer's accoutrements. Instead, all she carried was her gun, which was securely holstered.

After all, despite what they showed on television, it wouldn't be smart to wave around a gun while chasing down a suspect. Especially not on a Friday night when the empty street might suddenly fill with people who'd just finished a movie, a late dinner or drinks at the local bar. A bar like McGill's. The bar where she'd left Jase and his date, Regina, despite the fact he'd wanted to kiss Carrie again. She'd turned him down and what had she gotten instead? A run-in with a petty thief. A fast one.

She pushed forward in a burst of adrenaline, won-

dering what the guy she'd caught burglarizing a local hardware store had on his rap sheet that was worth evading the police. The speed with which he'd bolted, when she'd only stopped to ask him a few investigatory questions, told her he probably wasn't a stranger to the justice system.

She was starting to gain on him when he veered toward a run-down-looking house off of Post Street and barreled inside the front door. Staying outside, Carrie immediately established cover, drew her weapon and called out, "Don't make things worse. Come out with your hands up."

"Fuck off, bitch!"

But the guy's words were slightly drowned out by the sound of approaching sirens.

"You hear that?" she shouted. "San Francisco P.D.'s on the way. Come out now."

He didn't immediately respond. To her surprise, less than a minute later, he walked out of the house, a gun held out in front of him.

He'd been in shadows when he'd started running, and for the first time she got a clear view of his face. He was just a kid. Surprise made her hesitate for a moment before she took a step closer, her own gun braced in front of her. "Put down your—"

He caught sight of her and aimed.

Danger! Protect yourself. Shoot to kill.

Her mind screamed at her to pull the trigger, but she didn't.

For one second, she hesitated to shoot him.

He readjusted his aim.

"Drop—" she screamed.

He fired his gun a second before she did.

Fire slammed into her leg, immediately making it buckle. She dropped to the ground. Then he was on her, hitting her and kicking her, knocking her weapon away. What followed was a blur of pain. Most of all, however, she was shocked. Stunned.

She'd missed him. How? She never *missed. But she'd been surprised by his appearance....*

He looked young. So young. How had he become so ruthless? So strong?

But despite the pain and her muddled thoughts, she continued to fight. To claw. To do her own damage. Until she managed to get to her weapon. Just as he raised his own and pointed it at her again.

Another gunshot.

Her attacker collapsed on her, crushing the breath from her body before she pushed him off and scrambled away.

She stared as a puddle of crimson immediately oozed out from beneath him.

For a second, relief made her dizzy.

Then relief turned into horror.

His still body twitched. Moved. Sat up.

He looked at her.

Raised his gun and pointed it straight between her eyes.

Grinned. And fired.

CARRIE WOKE AND SAT UP in bed. Her heart thudded in her chest, and her body was soaked with sweat. Her gaze skittered around her, searching for signs of danger. She saw only her grandmother's antique dresser. Various watercolors. Framed photos on her nightstand.

The familiar sights did little to calm her.

Panic wound through her, gaining speed and strength until it felt like a tornado. Black dots flashed in front of her, spinning around until they blurred together, making her feel dizzy.

She closed her eyes and concentrated on breathing, on repeating the self-talk she and Lana, a member of DOJ's Behavioral Sciences and Psychiatric Liaison Unit, had been working on.

She was safe. She was okay. It had just been a dream. She was okay.

When that didn't work, she imagined herself blowing into a balloon. Filling it up with her pain. Until it floated away. Until she was empty.

Finally, her heartbeat returned to normal. She leaned back, pulled the blankets closer to her chin and stared out at the dark sky.

As sleep continued to elude her, Carrie threw off the blankets, suddenly feeling suffocated and trapped. She threw out her limbs, stretching the length and width of the mattress to counter the feeling.

Accepting that her chance for sleep had passed, she got out of bed and went to the kitchen to start a pot of coffee. As she waited for it to brew, she leaned back against the counter and crossed her arms over her chest, rubbing her hands over the chilled flesh that was prickled with goose bumps. She wished she could crawl back into bed and hide under the warm covers, but she couldn't.

She looked at her refrigerator door and the piece of paper she'd placed there. A child's drawing, one made years ago by Kevin Porter and one his grandmother had mailed her, along with a note cursing Carrie to hell for killing the woman's precious grandson. She should have logged it into evidence. Instead, she looked at it each morning and each night before she went to bed.

Carrie closed her eyes and rubbed her hands over her face. No wonder she had nightmares. God, she was twisted.

She'd had no choice but to shoot Kevin Porter. She knew that. He'd already shot her once, had continued to assault her, and he'd still had his gun. But in the end, she'd taken a life. The life of a sixteen-year-old boy who'd been jacked up on drugs. One whose grandmother swore was a good kid who'd just happened to get involved with the wrong crowd at school.

She didn't keep his picture to torture herself but to remind herself that pain was often part of the job. Anyone could be a rapist or killer or other type of dangerous criminal.

Anyone.

Male or female. Old or young. Ugly or good-looking. Sometimes the ones she had to stop were just like Kevin Porter. Sometimes they had goodness in them, too. Sometimes they could have taken another path or were victims themselves. But it didn't matter. When they turned dangerous, she had to stop them in order to protect others. And, yes, to protect herself.

That's why she kept the picture.

To remind herself why she did what she did. And so she wouldn't be surprised, wouldn't hesitate to fire her gun again, simply because a perp didn't look the way she thought he would.

If guilt was a by-product, there wasn't anything she could do about it. Because guilt, too, was just another part of the job. And thankfully, after being gone for almost a month, she'd finally been cleared to return to SIG. Mac, SIG's lead special agent, had worked hard to get her back in rotation. He'd worked twice as hard to get her the assignment she'd requested. He'd questioned whether the case would be too stressful given that she'd just be returning to work, but ultimately he'd supported her, and she'd always be grateful to him for that.

She'd missed the team—Jase, in particular, though she refused to let her thoughts linger on him. Mostly, however, she'd missed the work. The challenge. Sitting at home recuperating was enough to make her want to scream with frustration. At least when she was working, she wasn't haunted by memories, both distant and recent, incapable of moving past them.

Having the job be challenging would be the least of her worries now. No wonder she was having bad dreams and doubts about her ability to perform. With the "welcome back" assignment that had prompted her to seek an early return in the first place, she could only hope she'd rise to the occasion.

She'd been passed over several times for serial-killer assignments and had been chomping at the bit for one. She had no illusions about how stressful they could be. How tough. But she wanted to prove once and for all, just in case there was any doubt, that she could handle any case the DOJ threw at her. Now, thanks to Mac, she had her chance.

She'd assured him she was fine, physically and emotionally. That she needed the rigors of an assignment like this one to get back into the game. Only she couldn't deny that things had changed since she'd shot Kevin Porter. *She* had changed. And she wasn't sure what to do about it.

Despite knowing Porter was armed, despite knowing it could mean her life, she'd hesitated to shoot him. And when she had finally shot, she'd missed. Granted, she hadn't missed the second time around, but that did little to reassure her.

It figured that it was only when she was at her least confident and most shaken up that the brass finally gave her the lead on a serial-killer case. They probably viewed the assignment as a damn medal of valor, not only a reward for her impressive closure record over the past year but a consolation prize for getting wounded on the job and having to make her first kill. She didn't want to get a choice assignment based on pity, but it didn't matter. It was hers.

So what if she'd hesitated to shoot a teenager? Even when she'd been on SWAT, she'd never actually shot to kill before. Her hesitation had been natural. Understandable. But she wouldn't make the same mistake twice. This was her chance to prove herself and move closer toward a management position with DOJ.

She loved being a special agent. Loved working the streets. As a female, however, she'd never have significant power there, no matter how good a cop she was. As upper management, on the other hand, she'd be able to wield the kind of power that would make a real difference when it came to making people safe. And somehow, being a powerful woman in a political position wasn't viewed as negatively as being a powerful woman on the streets. Who knew? Maybe she'd finally get some respect, as well as some downtime to concentrate on other things.

Like a personal life.

She snorted and walked into the dining room, where files were spread out across the surface. A personal life? Maybe someday, but right now she needed to focus on the job.

She'd started going over the files last night and had exactly one more day to get up to speed before she had to report to Commander Stevens and tell him her thoughts. Only once she'd proven her familiarity with the case and detailed her game plan would Stevens fully sign off on the assignment.

She glanced at the clock. It was barely eight in the morning. She had plenty of time to continue her research. But Mac had asked her to stop by McGill's Bar at around 6:00 p.m. He and his girlfriend, Natalie Jones, had up and eloped, and although Carrie had once had a crush on the intense SIG agent, she was genuinely happy for them. Didn't mean she wanted to celebrate their marriage in a bar, however. Especially the same bar where she'd last seen Jase Tyler and where he'd propositioned her despite the fact that his date was inside. Work would be the perfect excuse to bow out.

Except she'd feel like a coward. Even more than she already did.

It wasn't only the Porter shooting that had her second-guessing her gumption. Over the past year, she'd lost some of the passion for the job that had always fueled her. She'd started to become weighed down by the knowledge that no matter how hard she tried, there was always another victim waiting in the wings for justice. More and more it seemed the good guys were losing the battle. To make matters worse, she'd been distracted by more personal concerns, simultaneously running from her developing feeling for Jase and resenting that she even had to.

Would she let him kiss her, he'd asked her at McGill's. She'd wanted so badly to say yes, but there'd been too many reasons to say no.

Number one: they worked together.

Number two: Jase was a player. Even if she could compete with the women he dated, which she couldn't, she wasn't sure, once she'd actually had him, how she'd handle it when he chose to walk away.

Number three: she really couldn't believe that he wanted her for her, and not because of the challenge she presented or because he wanted to bring her down a peg or two. So she'd been the one to walk away instead. Ten minutes later, she'd caught Kevin Porter right in the middle of a B and E.

Full circle, she thought. Her back-to-back encounters with Jase and Porter telegraphed one thing—she might hesitate, wish for things to be different, but in the end she could never reconcile being a soft, desirable female with being a tough, ambitious cop. She had to pick. She'd always had to pick.

And since she was so much better at being a cop than a woman? Well, that's what she'd continue to focus on.

Shaking her head and blowing her hair off her face, she sat down at her dining-room table. Then the work took over. Hours went by. She took a short break to do her PT exercises and grab a bite to eat, and then she recommenced her review of The Embalmer's most recent murder.

The victim, Cheryl Anderson, had been found two days ago, but only after her killer had mailed the SFPD several gruesome pictures of her being embalmed—while still alive. He'd also left directions to a warehouse on Mission Street where police would find Anderson's ashes along with trace DNA sufficient to confirm her identity. The responding SFPD officers had processed the scene and entered the murderer's M.O. into the criminal database that could be accessed by all California law-enforcement agencies. It had taken only a few hours for SFPD to connect Anderson's murder with the murders of two women that had occurred over a year ago in Fresno, six months apart. The older cases hadn't been solved and had been well on their way to becoming cold. Importantly, the specifics of the murders had been kept out of the press, just like Anderson's had.

Now, with the Anderson murder, San Francisco appeared to have a serial killer on its hands. No other jurisdictions had reported murders committed in the same manner, which meant the killer was acting thoughtfully. Methodically. Taking his time picking out his victims and planning everything to the last detail to ensure his continued success and freedom, even as he tempted the police with evidence of his crime.

If he kept to his routine, which serial killers usually did, that meant they had some time to find him. And Carrie was almost certain the killer was a man. For one thing, serial killers were almost always men. But more specifically, the way The Embalmer had applied makeup to his victims' faces, as depicted in the photos, had a decided air of inexperience about it—like a kid playing with his mother's cosmetics, experimenting with colors and shadows. It might sound strange to a man, but chances were another woman would have used the enhancements more effectively, even on a corpse. Even Carrie, who rarely wore makeup and wasn't a girly girl by any stretch of the imagination, knew the basics. The Embalmer's heavy hand with lip liner and blush screamed "male" to her.

She wasn't sure she wanted to posit that theory to Stevens, however. It would only serve to remind him that she was, in fact, female, and that was something she strenuously avoided where work was concerned.

Unfortunately, it wasn't as if she had many other leads to report. It wasn't a reflection of her skill, simply what the evidence failed to show.

The only thing the victims had in common was that they'd all been teachers, but they'd taught at different schools and different grade levels. Johnson had taught seventh-grade biology. Steward had taught elementary school. And Anderson had taught English at a local college. It was a connection, true, but it was far from a solid one. Unlike the other victims, Anderson had lived alone.

Given the information they did have, the first thing Carrie would recommend was canvassing witnesses at Anderson's college. Talking to her students. Also checking out the facilities and who had access where. The man who'd killed Anderson had spent a lot of time on her. He'd needed the supplies, space and privacy to perform the embalming. It was unlikely he'd pick a busy college campus as his base camp, but she needed to make sure. After that, she'd have to explore other options. Places near the college. A mortuary? A hospital? And that was assuming he didn't have an embalming facility set up in a house somewhere. Maybe that's why there'd been a year-long gap between his second murder and his third. He'd relocated. Needed to set up shop someplace in San Francisco. That meant she'd need to check out businesses that sold embalming equipment. Track down individuals who might have stocked up on relevant supplies recently. And she'd have to speak personally with the detectives at Fresno P.D.

She already had their written reports. Of course, the Fresno P.D. had looked into a possible connection between Johnson and Steward, as well. They'd concentrated on questioning witnesses in neighborhoods near the victims' homes and businesses, but had come up empty. They'd interviewed the victims' families and friends, and SFPD had done the same with Anderson. But this was Carrie's case now, and that meant she'd probably reinterview everyone herself, just to be sure all bases had been covered.

It wasn't a matter of believing the other police officers had been sloppy or incompetent. It was a matter of speaking to the witnesses directly, being able to look them in the eye, study their demeanor and body language and tone of voice. In the same way that a jury needed to be able to assess a witness's credibility on the stand, Carrie needed to assess the credibility of the witnesses who might be able to help her or prevent her from finding a killer.

With each hour that passed, Carrie's "to-do" list got bigger and bigger. Long after she tired, she forced herself to keep working, reading police and psychological reports, looking at pictures, trying to draw links between pieces of evidence; even so, she was ever aware of the passage of time. At just before six, she couldn't avoid it any longer.

She had no good reason to miss Mac and Natalie's wedding celebration.

She'd been through the files multiple times and had compiled a detailed report of her findings for her meeting with Stevens. She was tired, mentally and physically, and she needed to take a break. Get a change of scenery and wipe her mind clear before diving in again. Was she going to join the other SIG members at McGill's the way Mac had asked? Or would she continue to hide?

Forty-five minutes later, she had her answer. Actually, she had several, not all of them good.

As she stood on the other side of the street from McGill's, staring into the bar through the front windows, she realized this was what she'd been dreading. More than she'd been dreading a reminder of her last encounter with Jase, she'd been dreading *this* feeling.

She'd been away from SIG for just over a month, but it had been enough. The passage of time had done more damage than Kevin Porter's bullet. She didn't even need to step inside McGill's to confirm it. She was on the outside looking in.

Not just outside a bar watching her teammates talking and laughing inside. But outside the team. At least, that's how she felt. Forget that she was the sole female on the SIG team. Or that she was one of only a handful of female special agents at DOJ, just as she'd been one of only a handful of female MPs in the army and the only woman on the Austin and SFPD SWAT Teams. She respected all her SIG team members and truly felt they respected her, but nonetheless her place within SIG had always felt tenuous, and tonight that seemed glaringly apparent.

She didn't fit in. She never had, not completely. Hell,

she wouldn't even fit in with the other people in the bar, regardless of whether they were law enforcement or ordinary citizens.

Automatically, she tugged at her already pressed-and-creased button-down shirt. It was a far cry from what Regina had been wearing on her date with Jase one month ago. It was nothing like what the other women in the bar were wearing now. Unlike her, they wore makeup and their hair down. They looked soft. Feminine. Touchable. Compared to them, Carrie probably looked as brittle as she felt.

Without meaning to, she searched for Jase.

He was sitting with fellow SIG agent Bryce DeMarco and talking with a couple of women who'd stopped by their table. They were stacked. Gorgeous. As confident in their femininity as Carrie normally was in her abilities as a cop.

Now she was just one jumbled mass of nerves and insecurity.

It was a hideous feeling, not because she didn't have her fair share of hang-ups, but because she was doubting her current ability to hide them. No one could see how vulnerable she felt. No one. Whether they were cops or criminals, strong personalities had a natural tendency to exploit weakness in others.

To prevent herself from becoming easy prey, she needed to act like nothing had changed. Like *she* hadn't changed. And that meant walking into that bar and congratulating Mac on his recent marriage.

She didn't want to. She didn't feel up to any of it.

Not congratulating Natalie Jones, Mac's new wife, a woman who, despite her blindness, seemed to have the kind of life that had never been an option for Carrie. Not seeing the faces of her teammates. Not bantering with Jase and pretending she didn't want him.

But she was going to go inside. She was going to pretend she was fine. And hopefully, soon, she would be. She'd have her bearings back.

Work was the thing that had always been her comfort. Her confidence. She'd never been the pretty one. Never fit in with the girls at school or understood their need to shop and primp and gossip. She'd been more interested in the things her brothers did. And she'd always been interested in helping others. Taking on those bigger and stronger than her and besting them through stamina and smarts.

That's what she'd always been good at.

That was her place in the world.

Trying to expand it would only bring her grief.

CHAPTER FOUR

JASE WAS IN A PISS POOR-MOOD, but he wasn't dead. That's why, when Carrie walked through the door of McGill's after a month's leave from SIG, his body responded the way it always did in her presence—at full aching mast. Time spun away, and suddenly he was back outside the bar with her body pressed against his, before Regina had come looking for him. Just as he had back then, he imagined taking Carrie in every imaginable way possible—with her standing up, sitting down, bent over or on her back with her legs spread wide and over his shoulders. He pictured her mouth doing everything but talking, while his own mouth got busy investigating the moist depths of her body.

In his mind, he took her with a ferociousness completely contrary to the way he'd actually kissed her before, when Natalie Jones-now-McKenzie had been hospitalized. Carrie had been trying so hard to comfort Mac, when in reality she'd needed comforting herself. And Jase had needed to be the man to give it to her. No, that brief, closed-mouth kiss on the lips had been nothing like the ones he currently fantasized about.

But knowing it was all he was likely to get, he cursed softly.

From beneath hooded eyes, Jase watched as Carrie headed toward Mac and Natalie, who were standing by the bar getting another round of drinks for the table. Except for Simon Granger, who'd be acting supervisor for the next two weeks, the whole SIG team was now present to celebrate Mac and Natalie's spontaneous trip to City Hall and their official new beginning. Tomorrow, they were headed to Africa for an unconventional honeymoon. Jase didn't doubt they'd be spending a lot of their time indoors and horizontal, but they'd also enjoy exploring the exotic locale. Mac had mentioned more than once that Natalie, who'd made her living as a photographer before she'd gone blind, was excited to try a new technique for blind photographers she'd recently read about. Knowing what Natalie had overcome in the past few months, including nearly being killed by a man nervous about some photos she'd taken, Jase couldn't be happier for them.

As Carrie made her way toward the couple, Jase rubbed his ear, the same ear she'd tried to bite off the last time they'd been here together. She wasn't like any other woman he'd ever known, yet he couldn't help comparing her to the women she passed. McGill's wasn't exactly a trendy pickup joint, but it wasn't a bad place to meet women, either. There were always a few trolling for men to spend some time with in and out of the sheets. Like the two friends who'd just been chatting with Jase. Like the brunette who was at that very moment eyeballing him from another table. Like the curvy blonde Carrie had just passed. They'd been painted, plucked and slathered with lotion until they radiated feminine allure.

On the other hand, Carrie looked just as out of place as she had the last time he'd seen her at McGill's. Her deep red hair was pulled back into her obligatory ponytail, any makeup she'd been wearing had long since faded and her pressed Dockers and starchy pinstripe shirt, while not quite disguising her femininity, definitely radiated business more than romance. The files she held at her side added to the professional image. Which was hilarious, considering she was on medical leave, and therefore business was the last thing she should have been dressed for. Hell, the woman obviously didn't know the meaning of the words *casual* or *fun*.

Didn't matter. She hadn't even looked at him, but he was already harder than an iron spike. His response to her was completely baffling, especially given how fervently she denied the attraction between them. Especially given she was a cop.

Professionally, Jase had no problem working with female cops. Some of them, including Carrie, were the best cops in the business.

Personally?

Jase liked his women simple, tarted up and willing to please. Carrie Ward, a former Army MP and now special agent just like Jase, certainly didn't qualify. So why did she get to him so much so fast?

It was barely noticeable, but he saw the slight way she favored her right leg as she walked. It had suffered significant trauma. Since the doctors had believed she wouldn't walk for at least six weeks, let alone that she'd ever walk without a cane, she'd obviously been doing her physical therapy and pursuing recovery the way she did everything else—head-on, at full speed ahead.

Well, that wasn't exactly true.

She pursued everything that way except her desire for him. That was the one thing she had no intention of facing. Ever. Her failure to even look at him simply confirmed the fact.

Hell, he should be glad. He'd fought his attraction to her from the instant he'd seen her. Had gone out of his way to avoid her since the night they'd shared that brief kiss. At least, he'd gone out of his way until that last night at McGill's. That night, he'd been standing next to Regina but studying Carrie's reflection in a mirror on the wall. He'd been watching her the entire time since she'd arrived. As such, he'd noticed when she'd turned and spotted him with Regina. For a split second, she'd looked hurt and then she'd left. Something—a flash of loneliness he'd seen in her eyes or perhaps the empty ache he'd felt in his own chest—had compelled him to follow her. To proposition her. But she'd rejected him quite thoroughly. Not all that surprised, he'd cursed himself for a fool and counted himself grateful that she'd ignored his little moment of weakness. Then she'd gotten shot, and the severity of her injuries had reminded him exactly why she was the kind of woman he needed to stay away from.

The kind that would eventually destroy him whether he kept her or lost her.

He'd almost gone crazy when he'd learned she'd been shot. He'd beat everyone to the hospital and had been hollering for an update before Mac had arrived and tried to calm him down. But even when he'd heard Carrie was going to be okay, he hadn't calmed down. He hadn't felt calm in over a damn month. No matter where he went, no matter who he was with, inevitably he thought of her. For a man who enjoyed women in all their infinite variety and had no problem moving on to the next great thing, it had scared the shit out of him. Afraid of what he might reveal, he'd forced himself not to visit her, at least not after that first time, and instead had settled for the occasional update from Mac and the commander. In the past few weeks, even though she was never completely out of his mind, he'd managed to think of her less often. It was an achievement he had to continue.

When she returned to SIG, things between them would be back to normal, with him dating his women and her... Well, he had no doubt she'd once again use her sharp tongue and another man to keep her distance from him. At one time, that man had been Mac. Now, it looked as if she'd be using several new men instead.

According to DeMarco, before she'd been shot, Carrie had been dating her way through San Francisco P.D.'s SWAT team. Was that why she'd gone to Mc-

Gill's that night? Had she been planning on bedding a SWAT officer only to be distracted by Jase?

"Jase, you dog. You've been holding out on me."

Jase reluctantly dragged his gaze from the sweet curve of Carrie's khaki-clad butt and turned to face DeMarco. "What?"

DeMarco grinned. "You were checking out Ward."

Rolling his eyes, Jase leaned farther back in his seat, automatically smiling when the brunette at the nearby table caught his eye again. "I wasn't checking her out. The last woman I'd be interested in is a whack job like Ward." Even as he spoke, he felt a twinge of guilt. Not for being dishonest but for being disloyal. He was attracted to Carrie and fighting it, but first and foremost he admired her. She wasn't a whack job so much as the one woman who was completely wrong for him but still managed to drive him crazy with lust. Somehow, it seemed wrong to disparage her just to disguise his own vulnerability, but he didn't have much choice, did he? Not with the sudden gleam in DeMarco's eyes that told Jase he wasn't going to let the matter drop.

"Come on. Fess up. You can't take your eyes off her, and with good cause. Ward is smoking hot."

Because Jase wanted so badly to agree, he forced himself to continue the charade with a bit more force than necessary. "She's a lunatic. An adrenaline junkie proud of her man-eater reputation." At least that last part was true. Carrie was tough and rarely showed fear. Not even to the team.

Probably, if he was honest with himself, the team

would be the last people she'd let see her afraid. It was true for him. Why not for her, too?

"Yeah," DeMarco continued, completely unaware of Jase's thoughts. "But she's still *muy caliente.* If it wouldn't be like kissing my sister, she could eat me up anytime."

Another image of long limbs, smooth skin and moist, pink secrets flashed before his eyes. He tried superimposing the nearby brunette's exotic features over Carrie's face, but it didn't work. "Different strokes, my man," he managed to drawl.

"You're protesting way too much. Why don't you just admit you want her?"

"Uh—because I don't." Lie. Such a big lie. "She's got a fine ass, but everything that goes with it is way too much trouble. Besides, I'm dating that model I met at the grocery store."

"You mean the blonde with big tits?" DeMarco tsked. "She's practically jailbait, man."

"Twenty-four is hardly jailbait," Jase said with a frown. Although it did sound a little young. "And talk about hot. The last thing I have time or energy for is Carrie Ward."

DeMarco stared at him for several long minutes but, even though her features were a blur, Jase didn't take his eyes from the brunette who now walked toward him.

"Well, shit. That's no fun."

Jase forced himself to grin. "I beg to differ. Lori used to be a gymnast, you know."

DeMarco snorted and shook his head. "For you, that's par for the course."

Jase stood when the brunette finally reached them. "Hi. I was hoping you were coming to see me and not my friend here."

She laughed, the sound low and just as sexy as her tousled curls and low-cut blouse. "Maybe I haven't made up my mind yet." Her gaze flickered to DeMarco. "You both look like you can show a girl a good time."

Despite his sudden weariness, Jase forced himself to play his part. He leaned toward the brunette. "Thanks so much, darlin'. But you need to know…"

Jase spoke with the brunette for several minutes. Before she left, she handed him her business card and gave DeMarco a flirty wave goodbye.

DeMarco just shook his head. "*Chica* doesn't know what she's missing out on," he grumbled good-naturedly, his massive ego obviously not in the least bit threatened.

Jase pocketed Kelly The Brunette's number just as Carrie turned and looked at him. She'd been chatting with Mac and Natalie, and had finally put down her damn files. She smiled tightly at Jase before turning back to the bartender, a tall, good-looking kid with dimples. Jase couldn't resist. "So have you heard when Carrie's starting work?" he asked DeMarco. "I thought she wasn't coming back for another few weeks, but she looks…good."

"She's meeting with Stevens in the morning. She's

got a shot at her first serial case. No way is she going to let it slip away."

Forgetting to feign casualness, Jase straightened. "She's getting the lead on the big one? Damn it, I told Mac I wanted that." And he'd thought he'd made his request early enough for it to make a difference. Serial cases were far more rare than people thought, but they were generally high-profile enough that solving one could do wonders for one's career. Besides, the connection between the recent victim and two cold-case victims, the same connection that had prompted the higher-ups to transfer the case to SIG, had only been made less than forty-eight hours ago. When had Mac and Commander Stevens made their decision?

"It's her turn. And after what she's been through— hell, after how hard she's worked—she deserves it."

Instantly, Jase recalled how pale she'd looked the only time he'd stopped by to see her at the hospital. She'd been groggy and trying to hide the pain she was in, but he'd seen it. Hell, yeah, she deserved it. She was a good cop. But so was he, and he'd wanted the lead on the case. He'd wanted the accolades closing it would win him.

But Carrie wanted them, too.

He swiped a hand across his jaw. "Yeah, I suppose." But he still didn't like it. His own ambition aside, Jase didn't like the idea of her working a case with a perp that was obviously as fucked up as this one. Which, considering what Jase and Carrie both did for a living, was a joke. Carrie would be the last woman to play it safe or let herself be coddled by a man. If she knew he felt the slightest bit protective of her, she'd kick his ass, then jump right back into the fray without a backward glance. And that was just reason number two to stay away from her.

Reason number one was what she made him feel. Too much. He'd spent his childhood witnessing exactly what kind of misery two strong-willed, passionate people could bring each other. Plus, his job was intense enough. He wanted a personal life that was indulgent and mellow. And if he followed Mac's lead and actually married someday? Well, he wanted a woman who was indulgent and mellow, too.

Jase glanced at DeMarco and, for the first time, noticed the dark circles under the man's eyes. DeMarco needed some mellowness of his own. He'd been working one difficult case after another. While he seemed social at the moment, he was moodily silent at work. Word around the department was the stress might be finally getting to him. "What about that witness in your Alvarez case? You get anything on that?"

"The neighbor with the rap sheet a mile long? She's recanted everything. Says the officer misunderstood and that of course that nice little boy from across the street would never have done something so horrible. Never mind that the little boy has gang tattoos on his face and packs more heat than a SWAT officer." He shrugged and, despite his obvious exhaustion and frustration, showed no signs of an imminent breakdown.

As usual, "the word" was likely all bullshit. "So," De-Marco said, looking at Jase askance. "Ward is a no-go?"

Jase automatically glanced up to see if she was still talking to the bartender. Instead, she was looking around her while holding a beer. She took a swallow before looking directly at Jase again. This time, he felt the fire in her wide-eyed gaze ignite sparks from his chest down to his toes. Color climbed her cheeks, suggesting that she felt the heat, as well. He told himself to look away, but he couldn't. His vision became so clear that he could see the flutter of her pulse in her throat as well as the slight chafing of her pouty lips, as if they'd recently been kissed raw.

In reality, they probably only looked at each other for a few seconds. Five at most. In that moment, he felt the world around him disappear. The pull between them was so intense that he actually stood up. Abruptly, she blinked. She said a quick word to the bartender, then turned on her heel and walked rapidly toward the restrooms. Jase instinctively took a step to go after her.

"Jase, stop!"

The command registered but was slightly muffled. He shook his head, trying to clear the lust-induced fog that weighed it down. "What?"

DeMarco looked at him incredulously. "Man, you can deny it all you want, but you practically staked your claim on her in front of everyone."

Every muscle still vibrating and at the ready to run

after her, Jase forced himself to sit down. He closed his eyes and took a deep breath.

"So was it just her ass you were admiring? 'Cause it looked to me like you never took your eyes off her face."

"Shut up, DeMarco," Jase growled while opening his eyes.

He could only stand DeMarco's cheery humming of "man-eater" for a few minutes. "I gotta take a leak," he muttered and stood. "Grow up while I'm gone, would you?"

BRAD TURNER WATCHED as the sexy brunette handed the good-looking man her card, then walked past the bar, smiling and hips swaying. Although the guy's dark-haired friend enjoyed the view, the woman's target absently pocketed her card without even looking at it. All his attention seemed to be on the plain redhead with a stick up her butt.

After several minutes, Brad watched the redhead walk toward the bathrooms. Unlike the other woman, there was nothing flirtatious or teasing about the way she walked. Despite her slight limp, which made Brad wonder what had caused it, her pace was measured and confident, though she'd seemed shaken by the way the guy at the other table had looked at her. Not surprising, that same man stood and followed her to the restrooms.

Probably to have sex, Brad thought jealously.

He'd never had sex in a bar. Hell, Brad had never had sex at all.

JASE ZIPPED UP HIS PANTS and washed his hands, then banged his way out of the men's bathroom. The door didn't swing wide and then slowly forward as he expected, but instead went to about midpoint before colliding with something with a muffled thud.

"Damn it!"

He couldn't know for sure, but somehow he knew the person behind that voice had red hair and blue eyes. Sure enough, Carrie Ward stepped around the door.

Her annoyed expression wiped clean the minute she saw him and was replaced by a studied blankness that he saw for what it was—complete and utter bullshit. She saw him, all right, and the knowledge made him feel randier than a seaman on leave. To cover, he tried something he rarely did with her—straightforward common courtesy.

"Welcome back, darlin'," he said. "I heard you're working your first serial case. Congrats. Let me know if I can help."

She narrowed her eyes, as if she wasn't sure whether he was messing with her. "Thanks, Tyler," she said simply. Then, with a satisfied smile, she asked, "How's the ear?"

He grunted. "How's the leg?"

"My leg is fine." When she moved to step around him, he automatically countered to block her. She frowned and said, "Is there something you need?"

His eyes shot to hers at the way she emphasized the word *need,* but her expression had gone blank again. Despite the prior rigidity he'd sensed in her stance, she was now all loose-limbed indifference. She was almost as good as he was at faking casualness. It made him want to drive a response from her even more, and, this time, he didn't even try to censor himself.

"You know what I need, Ward, and it's exactly what you need, too. If we weren't both cowards, we'd stop dancing around each other and just get to it."

Her eyes widened as her cheeks bypassed pink and went straight to scarlet. But she raised her chin and kept her gaze on his. "And by 'get to it,' you mean what? No, wait, let me guess. Me under you, right? Because it sure as hell wouldn't be me on top, would it? Well, in case it hasn't dawned on you, I'm not like the women you screw, Tyler. I've got a brain and ambition. Sorry if that equates to being a coward in your mind."

She'd been gone a long time. Having her sparring with him now, just like old times, caused excitement to sizzle through his veins. He leaned closer. "If we ever gave in to this thing between us, having you ride me isn't something I'd ever turn down," he said sotto voice to ensure no one overheard. In fact, at his words, his dick almost broke through his fly. *Down, boy.* "And I like your brain just fine, Ward," he said quietly.

"Ah," she nodded. "But not my ambition. Not the fact that I'm a big bad cop who can take you and any other man down? That's a little too much for even your ego."

"Anytime you want to take me down, or better yet, get down to more personal matters, I'm all in favor of it."

Her eyes rounded. Sure, they razzed each other constantly, but he rarely flirted with her. Not like this. Not in a way that immediately had them both picturing their naked flesh pressed together in glorious technicolor.

She swallowed audibly. "That's quite a change of heart," she croaked.

His brows furrowed. "I don't see how. I told you the last time we were here that I wanted you."

"You've been ignoring me the past month."

She didn't look very happy about it. And he was sure she'd rather cut out her tongue than admit it. "I thought we were busy ignoring each other," he said carefully. "The exact same way you've ignored that kiss."

She scowled.

Amazing that the expression didn't detract from how beautiful she was. She didn't advertise it, and he could see how easily it might be missed. But he worked with her and knew how passionately she fought for justice. She was dedicated and strong. Take all that and add her pleasing combination of features to the mix? She got to him on a gut level he couldn't ignore.

"That kiss meant nothing," she said. "It was the product of a weak moment on both our parts on a difficult night."

It pissed him off that she'd dismiss the kiss so easily, but since he wasn't surprised, Jase grinned and shrugged. "Sure. If that's what you want to tell yourself."

Carrie snorted, the sound feminine in spite of itself. "You want to tell me differently?"

He let several seconds pass while he stared at her.

Enough time to make her shuffle her feet. Enough time to be tempted to answer honestly. Which was why he kept his mouth shut.

When he failed to answer, she breathed a sigh of relief. "That's what I thought."

It was her sigh that did it. Neither of them was going to act on their attraction for each other. Fine. But she wasn't a coward. Neither was he. Why were they dancing around the obvious? He took a step closer, noting how her eyebrows winged up in alarm. "I want you, Carrie. I'm honest enough to admit it. The only reason I'm not pushing things is because we work together. I have no doubt that sex between us would be out of this world, probably the best either one of us has ever had, but given we both want to go places with our careers, I figure it's better to not get started."

"Maybe that won't be the case too much longer," she said lightly, then looked as if she wanted to cut out her own tongue. "The working-together part, not the no-sex part."

"Is that so?"

"Like you said, I want to go someplace with my career. I've got my eye on a much higher position. Once I break this serial-killer case, I think I'll be a serious contender."

She was gunning for another job? Whether he wanted to admit it or not, he'd missed her the last month. The idea of her leaving SIG troubled him and made him realize just how much enjoyment he got from seeing her. "You're not happy at SIG?"

"Come on, Jase. We both know that because I happen to have breasts, I'll never be taken seriously as long as I work the streets. It's why it's taken so long for me to get a serial case."

"Your breasts aside…" Though he wanted to, he didn't glance down. "I never thought I'd hear you play the gender card. We're all in rotation. We take the cases as they come and as the member with the least homicide experience, it makes sense you haven't been assigned one until now. Serial cases don't exactly pop up all over the place."

"So says a man who's worked two of them this year."

"I wanted this one, too," he pointed out.

"I know. I won't say I'm sorry."

"I didn't expect you to. Now, do you want to come join me and DeMarco?"

"I need to leave. I just came by to see Mac and Natalie. To wish them well before they left. But I have to work." With a bright, utterly disingenuous smile, she held up her files and said, "Looks like nothing's changed. You've got your pick of women to keep you company tonight, and I'm going to get up close and personal with my case. Tell DeMarco I said hello, okay?"

He didn't want another woman. And he certainly didn't want Carrie thinking about him with one. "Damn it, Carrie. You've been gone a month. What harm will having a drink with us cause?"

Her expression grew serious. Then she straightened. "I—I don't want to wait and find out. I can't afford to," she muttered. "What I mean is, I have a serial killer to find. Good night, Jase." With that, she turned on her heel and left.

CHAPTER FIVE

CARRIE EXITED MCGILL'S and took in deep breaths of air. She was a grown woman and had been attracted to plenty of men before. Why was Jase Tyler the only man who could throw her so off course?

Because he turned her on. And turned her inside out. Because a part of her wondered if, in a different time and place, without her baggage or her scars, they might have meant something special to one another. But that was ridiculous. Even without her troubled past, Carrie couldn't change who she was. What she looked like. She was strong and sturdy, not sexy and svelte. Jase flirted with her because they worked together, because she was there, and because he'd probably been coming on to females since before he could walk. It wasn't *her* he wanted, but the challenge she represented. Even so, she couldn't believe he wanted her at all.

Sensing movement from the corner of her eye, Carrie looked up.

"Murderer!" a voice yelled just as someone clasped her arm, jerked her around and threw her drink. Carrie felt lukewarm liquid splash all over the front of her.

Carrie stared in stunned disbelief at the short elderly

woman who stood aggressively in front of her, gripping
her with almost superhuman strength despite the fact
that her wrinkled skin was paper-thin and looked only
slightly more delicate than the frail bones of her body.
Her silver hair had a purple tint to it, giving her a comic
matronly appearance, but her eyes were a penetratingly
clear-blue, staring at Carrie with such hatred that she
automatically flinched back.

"Ma'am," she began.

The woman dropped her now-empty coffee cup and
shoved Carrie's chest with both hands.

Carrie barely moved from the impact, but a suspicious dread ignited in her stomach. She'd never actually met Kevin Porter's grandmother, but they'd talked
on the phone....

The door to McGill's opened, allowing some of the
noise from inside to drift out.

"Hey, lady," Jase called from behind her.

A quick glance confirmed he was walking toward
them, a concerned expression on his face. Carrie held
up her hand. "Jase, it's okay. Let me handle this."

The woman looked at Jase as if he was a dead snake.
"Who are you? Another dirty cop? You're all bastards.
Kevin's dead because of you. You should all be rot-
ting in hell!"

Carrie had been right—this was Martha Porter. She
kept her voice low and steady, trying to disguise the
anxiety seeping into her. Her breathing escalated, and
she felt a familiar suffocating pressure in her chest.

"Mrs. Porter, you don't want to do this. Please believe me, I think of Kevin every day—"

Anger and grief radiated from the woman's furrowed face, and she spit at Carrie with erratic aim, managing to hit her chin and collar. Carrie stood in stunned silence, wanting nothing more than to crawl into a hole and die.

"Jesus Christ!" Jase stepped in front of Carrie, forcing Martha Porter to step away. "Back off, lady. Now."

The woman leaned around Jase and pointed her finger at Carrie. "You don't have the right to say his name. My grandson. I raised him...my baby..." With her final words, the woman's face collapsed, and she started sobbing.

"Martha!" An elderly man rushed toward them and put his arm around her. He was being followed by a portly man in a navy suit whose briefcase bounced against his legs as he hurried to reach the elderly couple.

"Shh. It's okay, Martha. Let's go in now. Don't you worry now. It's going to be okay." The first man led Martha Porter away, shooting a deadly look over his shoulder at Carrie.

The man in the suit stopped to catch his breath. "I'm sorry. We're meeting someone here. She's upset.... I'm sorry." The man twirled around and followed the elderly couple into a building a few doors down from McGill's.

The street was eerily quiet. Acutely aware of Jase's gaze on her, Carrie raised a trembling hand to her chin and wiped the spit away. She couldn't do anything about the coffee staining the front of her until she got home.

Struggling to remain standing, she closed her eyes and took in several shaking breaths, trying to stave off the panic attack. The stack of files she'd been carrying slipped out of her hand, dumping papers across the sidewalk.

Jase cursed softly, but she was barely aware of him. Her breaths were loud even to her own ears, puffing in and out of her in quick, rhythmic bursts. With each breath, she felt her heart expanding. Growing bigger until it felt ready to explode.

Frantically, she looked for someplace to hide. *Please God, don't let this happen now.* She couldn't have a panic attack. Not here. Not in front of Jase.

But he wasn't looking at her. He'd bent down and was shoving papers back into their folders. "Who the hell was that?" he groused. "And why'd you let her go off on you? You should have arrested her! Hell, *I* should have."

When she didn't answer him, Jase looked up at her and stood. "Carrie?"

Carrie heard the concern in his voice. Knew she should answer him. But her vision tunneled until she was once again aiming her gun at Kevin Porter, then grappling with him on the ground. Trying to reach her gun before he shot her with it or his own. Shooting him. Killing the same kid who'd drawn the picture of himself with his grandmother, which even now was stuck on the front of her fridge.

"Carrie. Look at me." Tucking her files in the wedge of his arm, Jase grabbed her face between his palms

and brought his own face close to hers. "Look at me."
He smoothed his hands over her cheeks and jaw. Kept
murmuring words of reassurance.

She didn't know how long they stood there, but eventually she focused on his worried gaze. She concentrated on the feel of his touch on her skin. Felt her
breathing slow. Anxiety leaked from her like air escap-
ing a balloon. It was still there, but she no longer felt
as if she was about to burst.

"That's it. That's my girl. Good," Jase murmured,
and she took comfort in the deep rumbling of his voice.

Finally, she grasped his hands and pulled away, em-
barrassed by both the incident and her panicked reaction to it. "I—I'm okay. I'm sorry. I just... She surprised
me, that's all." Again, Carrie raised her hand, rubbing
her chin. Then she held out her hand for her files.

Reluctantly, Jase handed them to her. She felt his
gaze on her as she checked the ground around them to
make sure he hadn't missed anything.

Jase propped his hands on his hips. "She's a relative
of the guy who shot you?"

Carrie barely glanced at him. "It doesn't matter." But
God, it did. She'd almost melted down in front of him.
She couldn't afford to appear weak in front of anyone,
let alone Jase. He was the person who rattled her the
most, and therefore the person she had to be most wary
of. She rubbed her arms, trying to warm her icy skin. It
was a mild evening, and she was wearing a coat. Why
was she so cold?

"Carrie..."

At his worried tone, Carrie's gaze finally snapped to his. Licking her lips, she wished things could be different. That for just a second, he'd hold her. She hadn't had a lover in years. Except for the one brief kiss Jase had given her over a month ago, she hadn't allowed herself even the most casual contact with anyone, even a friend. A little human kindness. Was that too much to ask?

Yes, it was, she conceded as she remembered just how hard it had been for her to walk away from his kiss.

That kind of human connection always came with a price. Always.

She shook her head. Took a fortifying breath. Tried her best to give him a reassuring smile. "I'm okay, Jase. Honestly."

"What happened, Carrie? It looked like you were having some kind of panic attack. Maybe coming back to work tomorrow isn't such a good idea."

Her spine snapped straight, and she looked at him through narrowed eyes. "It might have looked like a panic attack, but it wasn't one. I told you, I was just surprised."

"The way you were surprised when Kevin Porter pulled a gun on you?"

"What's—what's that supposed to mean?"

He rubbed the back of his neck. "I don't know. God knows plenty of cops get hurt on the job. It doesn't mean you did anything wrong. But you—"

"But I what?"

"But your report says you took cover while he was in the house. If that's the case, how'd he shoot you?"

"I took cover, but I needed to detain him. I stepped out. I called for him to put his gun down. When he didn't, I fired."

"You fired and you missed," he said quietly. "Anyone could have. It doesn't make you any less of a cop. But maybe you haven't quite accepted that. Maybe that's what this is about. Maybe you need some more time before coming back to work."

He was so spot-on she almost panicked. Laughing harshly, she focused not on his concern, but on what he'd gain if her return to SIG was delayed. "Of course. I almost forgot. You wanted the lead on The Embalmer case. That's what this is about, isn't it?"

"I asked Mac for the case," he said. "But that's not why I'm concerned."

"No," she sneered. "You're just worried about me, aren't you? Afraid I'm going to get myself killed? Well, I don't buy it. You didn't visit me in the hospital, Jase. Not once. So don't act like you're so concerned about me."

Carrie almost groaned at the way his eyes widened with realization. Why had she said that? She should have been grateful he'd stayed away, allowing her to settle her scrambling emotions without having to deal with him, too. But she couldn't deny that part of her had been hurt by his seeming lack of concern.

He opened his mouth. Shut it. Finally spoke. "I came to see you in the hospital right after you were shot. You were higher than a kite on meds, but I didn't realize you wouldn't remember."

Biting her lip, she glanced away, not wanting him to see just how much his revelation meant to her.

"Look, I'm sorry. I didn't mean to question your competence. I didn't mean to make you mad. I just didn't like seeing that woman come down on you, and I know you well enough to know you don't reach out for help easily."

His words took the steam out of her. He seemed sincere. And truthfully, she was too appalled by her own words and loss of control to argue with him further.

He looked around. "Where's your car? I'll walk you to it."

She didn't bother arguing with him, and he fell into step beside her. Once they reached her ancient four-door, she unlocked the driver's side, saying, "I'll see you tomorrow."

"Carrie, wait."

Sighing, she looked up.

"You feel like getting something to eat? You can go home first. Change."

He'd just said he cared about her. Back inside Mc-Gill's, he'd admitted he wanted her but was ignoring that attraction because of their job. She was obviously doing the same. They'd rarely socialized as a team, let alone just the two of them. Why was he suddenly willing to change things? Because of Martha Porter? Because he'd sensed how much the woman's disdain had upset her? Or was it because he truly believed her to be emotionally unstable, and somehow that made her more attractive to him? More like the vulnerable women he dated and less like the cop he worked with? It didn't matter. "I really don't think that's a good idea, Jase," she said firmly.

"Why? Because you might enjoy my company too much?"

She shrugged. "Maybe. We've already established that getting involved won't do either of us any good—"

"Hold on. That's not what I said and you know it. I said getting involved with you could interfere with our careers, which is something else entirely. I have no doubt being with you would do us both a tremendous amount of good. But I agree, there are important reasons to keep things professional. So what? We can still be friends, Carrie, even if we can't be lovers."

She shook her head. "You were right before. We work together. You want the case I'm working. Whether you want to admit it or not, given what you said about Porter getting the drop on me, part of you obviously questions my competency as a cop. I'd say even being friends isn't a good idea. Besides, you don't have female friends, Jase. You're a serial dater. Hell, you barely even date. You please them and then you leave them."

His mouth twisted. "Hey, don't knock it. I'd love to please you. You'd never be the same afterward."

She smiled at his unrepentant arrogance even as her body throbbed at the thought of him pleasing her. Her response emphasized just how addicted she was becoming to his unique blend of confidence and sexy masculinity. "And part of me would love to be pleased," she conceded. His eyes flared, but she held up a hand, halting his step forward. "But it's not going to happen. I'm going home."

Jase leaned up against the other side of the car and planted his hands on top of the roof. "To do what? Think about the lady who spit on you? I'm talking an hour of your time, Carrie. Don't I deserve that?"

The question wasn't whether he deserved it, it was why he wanted it. Again, why the sudden need to spend time with her? Was this some kind of trick? He'd seen her in a weak moment and was hoping to see it again? Exploit it?

But he was right about one thing. Under ordinary circumstances, if she went home now, she'd just think about Kevin Porter and his grandmother. About her own inadequacy. Or about how empty her house seemed. Thankfully, she had something to distract her.

"I've got a big case I'm working, remember? That's all I'm going to be working on until he's caught."

She pulled her car door open and was about to get inside when he said, "So let me help you with it."

Straightening, she tilted her head inquisitively before narrowing her eyes. "Boy, you're on a roll here, Jase. What's wrong? You don't think I can do this alone?"

He pushed himself back so he was no longer leaning against her car. "Did I say that? It always helps to run things by a partner. That's why Mac asked me to help him with the Monroe murder several months back. Do you honestly think he couldn't have done it alone? You have a chip on your shoulder, Carrie. You might want to do something about it before it ends up getting you or someone else hurt."

His words struck home. He was right. She was overreacting and sounding more emotional than logical. She was making her decision for purely personal reasons and, even worse than that, out of fear. Even though she'd thoroughly reviewed the files and formed her own conclusions, why not run them past Jase? He had more experience than she did. She shouldn't dismiss his offer for help just because she was afraid of the sexual attraction between them. What kind of cop would that make her?

"I guess I could use your help."

There was no hint of triumph on his face, which enabled her to relax even more.

He nodded. "I'll follow you home."

As he walked away, she called, "No funny business. I mean it, Jase. This is purely one cop accepting another's offer for help on a case."

He turned to face her but kept walking backward with his hands in his pockets. "Of course it is, darlin'. You've made it clear you don't want to act on the attraction between us. As far as I'm concerned, you're just one of the guys now."

He couldn't know how much that statement hurt her, especially since she smiled brightly after he said it. "Great," she said. "Just keep that in mind and we should be fine."

CHAPTER SIX

WHEN THEY GOT TO CARRIE'S house, or rather, to her floor of a tri-level house on Divisidero Street, Jase was startled by how girly it was. He was used to seeing her at work, in the detective's pit with its straight-lined masculine furniture and her dressed in her button-down shirts and khakis. He knew she chose her clothes to appear androgynous, but he never thought of her as anything other than a woman. In fact, sometimes her professional facade had him salivating to unwrap the feminine package he knew lay underneath. Still, if he'd had to guess what kind of decor she preferred, he'd never have picked the shabby-chic stuff his frilly sisters were wild for.

Several soft watercolors, done in hazy washes of blues and purples, decorated the yellow walls. Her couch was covered with a faded floral slipcover, and her dining-room table was a polished cherry with curvy legs.

Cinnamon. The scent surrounded him as soon as he walked in.

Once inside, Carrie turned almost nervously to him. "Make yourself at home," she said while avoiding his gaze. "I don't think there's much in the refrigerator. I'm going to take a quick shower and change." She pointed to a nearby door. "Guest bath is right through there."

Jase nodded. She walked into another room and shut the door. He heard the lock engage and then the sound of the shower a few minutes later.

For a moment, he was overcome by images of her naked body. Her naked, wet body. Her naked, wet, slippery body. He groaned. He'd never been so sexually obsessed with a woman in his life. What was it about her that got to him? And what had compelled him to offer his help with The Embalmer case anyway? He had the next few days off. If he wasn't getting the lead on The Embalmer case, he should enjoy them. Visit the family. Play hoops with his cousin. Call Kelly Sorenson and see if the promise in her dark eyes turned out to be as good as it seemed.

Instead, he was going to put in extra hours helping Carrie on a case he'd wanted and that he wasn't quite sure she was ready for, while at the same time trying to control his attraction to her.

What the hell was wrong with him?

Sure, he thought she was attractive, but she wasn't the most beautiful woman he'd seen or been with. She was a cop, for Christ's sake. One who'd often claimed she could kick his ass and fully believed it. Instead of turning him off, the recurring threat had always conjured images of them rolling around on the floor together, their bodies touching and rubbing until they were ready to rip each other's clothes off.

Jesus, he had a one-track mind. Carrie wasn't just a cop, and she certainly wasn't a sex toy for him to play with and then toss aside. She was a complex woman, one he didn't know all that much about. Jase paced her small living room, looking for clues about the woman beneath the proverbial uniform.

Based on the books on her shelf, she was an avid reader, although she didn't read true crime. She either went for science fiction or historical romance. That surprised him. She was so pragmatic and no-nonsense at work. Like her taste in home decor, her reading preferences made him wonder what else she hid from the world.

He noticed some photo albums. Took one out and flipped through it. He smiled at the pictures of her in various stages of adolescence. She'd been all arms and legs, awkward. Despite the fact she was only five feet six inches now, she'd towered over her classmates at various stages, boys included. He imagined she'd endured some heavy teasing, especially because of her flaming hair that had been more orange than red when she was younger. Still, the Carrie he saw in the photographs appeared happy. Confident. Which for a high-school student was pretty damn unusual.

At some point that seemed to change, however. After high-school graduation, she grew more serious. Several photos were of her with an equally serious-looking man, sometimes wearing his police uniform, sometimes not. Others were of her with several men, all in uniform, all with the same red hair and blue eyes. Not many pictures of her mother. It looked as if she'd disappeared when Carrie was very young.

Jase put back the album and pulled out another one. This one was a scrapbook, with article clippings and little mementos and her full name written in scrolled lettering.

His eyebrows rose into his hairline. According to her scrapbook, she was a first-class markswoman. She'd competed in the Olympics when she was seventeen. She'd been the youngest member of the USA's shooting team and had won a silver medal. Several years later, she'd graduated from the police academy and joined the Army. And a few years after that, she'd become the first female sniper to join the Austin SWAT team.

She hadn't been kidding when she'd said she could kick his ass. He'd known she'd served a year on the SFPD SWAT before she'd joined SIG, but how come she hadn't told him she was a markswoman? And if she was such an incredible shot, it made the fact she'd initially failed to shoot Porter even more disturbing. Once again, he couldn't help wondering what had really happened that night. Or if his pushing things between them beforehand had played any part in it.

She hadn't given a whole lot of details in her report about that night, and Jase had gotten the distinct impression she'd been deliberately vague. Was she hiding something? Something she was ashamed of? Whether she wanted to admit it or not, she'd had trouble dealing with what that old lady back at the bar had done to her, and that didn't jibe with who he knew her to be. Cops met resistance and dealt with ugly confrontations all the time. Hell, he'd seen Carrie go toe-to-toe with guys twice her size and who had records that would make Al Capone look like a choirboy. Yet she'd freaked out because an old lady had spit on her and accused her of killing her baby boy?

Baby boy, his ass. Kevin Porter had shot Carrie, then tried beating her to death. If she hadn't taken him down, she'd likely be dead. She'd done what she had to do. So why did he get the feeling she was ashamed of what she'd done? Of killing Porter? Of being a good cop?

Jase heard the shower turn off and replaced the scrapbook. Yes, she had good reason to be proud of her accomplishments, but instinct told Jase the scrapbook had been compiled by someone else. Someone who was proud of her. It showed someone cared about her and that she occasionally lowered her guard with others. At least, she had at some point.

He ruffled his fingers through his hair and looked around again. Several files and stacks of paper were strewn out on her dining-room table, and she'd placed the files she'd brought to McGill's on the table, too. He shuffled through them, frowning despite himself when he saw the crime-scene photos. He'd heard about the most graphic aspects of the case, but it was always different when you had specifics in front of you. The Embalmer was a sick fuck, all the more sick because he was so organized and methodical. According to Mac, who'd talked to the Fresno P.D., everything The Embalmer did had a purpose. Special meaning. No one had been able to figure out exactly what, though.

Knowing Carrie would want to get started immediately, Jase used the hallway bathroom. It was just as frilly as the living room, with a lacy shower curtain, rose-colored towels and little flower-shaped soaps next to the sink. When he washed his hands, he once again inhaled the heady, sweet smell of cinnamon. He dried off with one of her rose-colored towels. She seemed fond of the color, which was odd. She never wore it. Always went with neutral colors. Nothing feminine.

Again, questions came to mind. Why was she ashamed of shooting Porter? Because she'd done it only after he'd gotten the drop on her? Or because he'd gotten the drop on a female cop? Now that he was here, seeing how ruthlessly she separated the two parts of herself—the woman and the cop—he was sure he was right. It also made him wonder if it was the real reason she fought him so much. Because he made her feel like a woman when she was on the job, and it was the last thing she could handle.

When he came out of the bathroom, Carrie was in the kitchen with her back turned to him. For a second, he simply enjoyed the sight of her looking as casual as he'd ever seen her. She wore a loose T-shirt and sweats. Her hair was still damp and hung loose around her face. Her feet were bare.

He could only see the faintest hint of her heels below the hem of her sweats, but those few inches of pale creaminess were enough to make his mouth start watering. Just like that, he wanted to remove her clothes and kiss her from bottom to top, but he knew he couldn't. He'd offered his help, and that was what he would damn well give her. All he was going to do tonight was work the case with her. He wasn't going to flirt with her. Wasn't going to try to kiss her again. Certainly wasn't going to wheedle his way into her bedroom and prove to her that no matter what she did for a living and no matter how hard she tried to deny it, she was first and foremost a beautiful, desirable woman.

He didn't care. He was looking forward to a few hours talking shop with her far more than he'd anticipated any of his dates or bedmates in…well, he didn't know in how long.

He cleared his throat, and she turned to face him.

She was wearing glasses. Sexy librarian glasses that reminded him of a favorite fantasy of his.

"So did you have a chance to look at any of this?" she asked.

He thought of the album and scrapbook he'd viewed. Wanted to express his admiration for her. Wanted to ask her about her life. All the things he didn't know about her. Instead, he said, "I sure did. Looks like you've got your hands full with this one, Carrie." And maybe because he was trying so hard to ignore his desire for her, he said the worst thing possible. "Now more than ever, I'm surprised Mac and the commander agreed to give you the lead."

As soon as the words left his mouth, Carrie could see Jase regretted them. Briefly closing his eyes, he shook his head and groaned, "Way to go, Jase."

It was the only reason she held back her instinctive urge to gouge his eyes out.

He held up his hands surrender-style. "Look. That came out wrong. You're a good cop, Carrie, but even as far as serial cases go, this one looks complicated. And we both know you've never worked a serial case before, that's all I meant."

"There's a first time for everything," she said mildly.

"Sure, but this one? With a killer who's this organized? This methodical?"

"Most serial killers are. That's how they're able to get away with multiple killings before they're caught. Also, I might not have actually worked any serial-killer cases, but I've taken advanced courses on them. Assisted on plenty. I know how they work. I can find him."

"If you were at the top of your game, I'd have no doubt about that. But that's not what we're talking about here. You've been gone for a month. Don't you think you should ease into things a little more slowly?"

She crossed her arms over her chest and snorted. "Ease in by giving you the case? Forget it. And if you're done, you can leave now."

Instead of leaving, he leaned against the wall and crossed his legs. "Why? Because I'm questioning you? That's how you're going to handle things? By avoiding them? I'm not the only who's going to be questioning your assignment to this case."

"Because I'm a woman," she said.

"No. Because you're still learning and you're in a shaky frame of mind."

"We're not robots, Jase. Cops have to deal with personal stuff all the time and still do the job. I can find this guy just like anyone could. Mac knows that and that's why he gave me the case. He believes in me."

"Damn it, don't pull that bullshit. I believe in you, too."

"Then act like it. You offered your help and I wasn't too proud to accept it, Jase. I know I have less experience with serials and that you've worked these kinds of cases before. Stop trying to convince me that I'm not the right choice for this assignment and help me catch this guy instead."

He worked his jaw for a second before straightening. "Okay. Let's sit down." He sat on her couch.

Slowly, she did the same. "That's it? No more badgering me?"

"I won't say another word about it. Not tonight anyway. Tell me what you've come up with."

After a moment's hesitation, she did. She told him about the victims all being teachers and her plan to interview witnesses at their various schools. She'd also made some guesses as to the serial killer's actual profession. Teacher? Administrative staff at a school? Mortician? Medical student? Doctor?

When she mentioned her plan to track purchases for embalming supplies, he nodded.

"That's good. You should definitely make that a top

priority. Also check with nearby hospitals and have them do inventory checks. See if any relevant supplies have suddenly gone missing. Same with local mortuaries or crematoriums. He burns the victims after he's done with them, which means he's got to have access to a kiln. If he installed something like that in his house, someone should have noticed it. I'm banking on the fact he has access to one professionally, though. It would make things easier for him."

She made notes. "That's good. I didn't think about the kiln." Swiftly, she looked up at him. "But I would have."

Jase smiled. "I know. No judgments from me. Like I said earlier, working these cases is always better when you've got two minds to look over the evidence. Did Mac or Stevens mention assigning you a partner?"

"No. But I assumed that would be coming. I figured they'd send someone over from SFPD. DeMarco is heavily involved with his caseload. Granger is acting supervisor. And you…"

The air was suddenly too thick to breathe. *You,* she thought, *I wouldn't want to work with. Not day in and day out. That would be too much. Too distracting.*

"You've got your own caseload, right?" she said instead, looking down at the envelope in her hand.

"Yeah," he said simply.

Something in his tone suggested he was holding back, but she didn't push it.

She held up the manila envelope in her hand. "So what about the letters he's sent?" she asked. "Fresno

P.D. didn't get anything from them." She picked up an identical envelope and handed it to him. "These contain The Embalmer's first two letters. He mailed them in Fresno. Generic self-sealed envelopes, generic stamps, no forensic evidence left behind."

Jase opened the envelope she'd handed him and carefully pulled out two plastic baggies, one that contained the letter and one that contained the envelope it had been mailed in. "The envelope and letter went through a printer. Any idea what kind? Laser or ink jet?"

Carrie frowned. "Would that matter?"

"Ink jets are much more common now. If it was printed on a laser printer, which is more rare and involves buying expensive toner cartridges, it wouldn't hurt to check Fresno supply stores to see if anyone purchased them or toner around the times of the murders. Little needle in a big haystack, but we're tossing out all possibilities, right?"

She grinned. All of a sudden, she didn't feel as if she was an outsider. Even when Jase had been questioning her, she'd been pissed, but she hadn't felt out of place. She supposed that meant something, right?

"No other links between the victims?" Jase asked.

"They ranged from late twenties to early fifties. Nothing in common except their careers and hair color. Brown."

"One of those is likely significant, then. Maybe he's choosing them because they remind him of someone. A teacher he had."

"That's what I thought. Or his mother. A girlfriend.

But where's he picking them from? The schools? Don't you think a stranger hanging around at schools would be noticed?" She chewed her lip, then said, "So maybe he's not a stranger. Maybe his job gives him access to a variety of different schools. Maybe he delivers school supplies, so it doesn't matter what the grade level is. Everyone needs paper and pencils, right?"

Jase nodded. "That's exactly the kind of thinking that'll close this case. You're digging deep for the microdetails, but what about the broader things? Why's he killing them the way he is?"

She sat forward, wincing a little when pain shot up her injured leg. Automatically she rubbed it. "There's two things that are obviously significant. He embalms them and photographs them in that state. And he cuts off their eyelids, which isn't part of the embalming process. The eyelids are probably some kind of trophy. Something he takes with him, along with the photographs, to replay the murders in his mind. But we also have to assume they have symbolic significance, don't we?"

Jase's attention had been on her leg, which she'd continued to rub. When she stopped talking, his gaze returned to hers. "Maybe not. Does he take the eyelids when the victims are alive or dead?"

"Let me check." She turned back to her table and pulled out Steward's autopsy report. Scanned through it. "It says here she was already dead when he cut off her eyelids." She checked Johnson's autopsy. "Same thing for the first victim."

"If he cut off their lids while they were alive, I could see the lids meaning something. For example, that the victims had vision problems. Or that he was fixing their vision. But what kind of problems? You might want to confirm whether the victims wore glasses."

"Got it." She began to pace. "Now, about the embalming. He does it when they're still alive, and at some point during the process, they die. He gives attention to every last detail. He's trying to preserve them. At first, he's preserving their bodies and then their images on film. But he doesn't pose them. Which seems to suggest it's the embalming itself that is the important thing rather than how they actually look in the photographs."

Jase leaned back on her sofa, legs sprawled out in front of him, arms stretched wide. He looked comfortable. Right at home. And somehow, despite the gruesome facts they were talking about, having him here felt right to her, too.

"But then he burns them," he pointed out. "Why?"

"The preservation is symbolic. Or a task he needs to complete for his own satisfaction. Maybe the burning suggests that preservation isn't deserved."

"Not deserved? Or rejected?"

"Right." She closed her eyes, took off her glasses and rubbed the bridge of her nose. Not only did her muscles ache, especially those in her leg, but she'd been working the case for so long today, her mind was beginning to feel muddled.

"You don't wear glasses at work," Jase said, his voice closer than she'd expected.

She looked up. He was now standing several feet from her, his gaze intense. "No, I wear contacts."

"I would have expected you to wear glasses. To add to your professional, back-off image. But I understand why you don't. It would highlight a weakness, wouldn't it? One you want to hide. Just like you're trying to hide that your leg is bothering you right now."

"And you're trying way too hard to psychoanalyze me, Jase."

"Maybe, but am I right?"

"My leg is healing and I have P.T. exercises to do. That'll loosen things up before I go to bed. As far as why I don't wear glasses to work, it's so I don't have to worry about misplacing them. You and Lana should get together if you really want to delve into the workings of my subconscious mind."

"So you're still seeing Lana? Did she sign off on assigning you this case?'

She glowered at him and opened her mouth to shoot off a sharp retort, but he shook his head.

"Never mind," he said. "It just slipped out. Like I said before, I care about you."

She wanted to believe him. Badly. But his increased interest...his desire to help her... Both competed with the knowledge that he'd wanted the lead on The Embalmer case. That he probably still did. As far as Jase was concerned, she'd always be part and parcel of the job. She had to remember that. Still, that didn't mean he couldn't care about her, too. Even just a little. "Thank you, Jase," she said simply. "I don't take that lightly."

He glanced down at her leg. "You were starting to limp. Why don't you let me help you with your P.T. exercises and then rub you down before you go to bed? That way you'll be ready for your big day tomorrow."

She burst out laughing and he grinned. "What? Too obvious?"

"Just a little," she said. "Besides, you've spent enough time helping me. And I don't want to keep you. It looked like you had better options for where you were going to spend the night than with me, working a case."

"You like throwing up my dating habits to me, don't you, Carrie? Why is that? Personally, I think it's because I scare you and talking about me with other women gives you a convenient shield."

She shrugged. "I just noticed the brunette you were talking to was pretty, that's all. She looked like your type."

"And what, exactly, do you know about my type?"

"The same thing everyone else does. Gorgeous. Sweet. A good time in the sack and not a whole lot of problems out of it."

"And you think less of me because of that? Because I want my personal life to be as simple and pleasurable as possible?"

"No. I understand why you'd want simple pleasures on your off time. I just define simplicity a little differently and choose to focus on my work instead."

"Hmm." He glanced around, walked back to the sofa and sat down again. When she just stared at him, he patted the cushions beside him. "So, if you're not scared and you know you're not my type, sit beside me and let me rub your leg out for you." His gaze held a distinct challenge, one she immediately wanted to run from.

Instead, maybe because of all their talk about his women and his type and her not being either one, she was feeling ornery enough to do what he said. "Fine. I already told you, I'm not too proud to accept your help. Let's see what these magic fingers of yours can really do, Jase." Casually, she dropped onto the sofa hard enough that she bounced, then swung her feet onto his lap. Lying back, she folded her hands behind her head and stared up at the ceiling, trying to control her escalating heartbeat and erratic breathing.

For the longest time, Jase didn't touch her. When he finally did, when he cupped his big palm over the arch of her right foot, she closed her eyes. And prayed like hell she'd be able to hide just how very, very much she wished she was his type, after all.

TODAY WAS TURNING out to be Jase's lucky day.

Not only had he spent the past hour talking shop with Carrie, in her private sanctum no less, but now she had her bare little feet in his lap, obviously willing to let him put his hands on her to prove that he didn't scare her.

But he knew that wasn't true. And she sure as hell scared him. Even so, he wasn't a fool. He might never get the chance to touch her like this again, so he planned to enjoy it while he could.

She had small feet, and her toenails were painted a soft pink, the color so subtle he'd thought they were bare. He cupped his fingers around one of her arches and began to massage the bottom of her foot, alternating between kneading and pressing deep with his thumbs.

Her involuntary moan of pleasure made him swell, and he shifted her feet slightly away from his erection. Despite the massage he'd started, she was tense, her limbs rigid. To distract himself and her, he murmured, "You said you were concentrating on your career. So DeMarco was wrong? You haven't been dating your way through SWAT?"

The foot he held jerked slightly, but he held on and moved to massage her toes. They were adorable. Perfectly shaped. He'd never paid much attention to feet before, but he could see himself quickly becoming enamored with this woman's toes.

"I—I still date occasionally," she breathed. "I'm not a freak. I have needs just like anyone else." When Jase's hands stilled, she snorted. "Sorry, I set myself up with that one, didn't I? But this feels good. I could—" She yawned. "I could almost fall asleep. I think you have magic fingers, after all."

"Close your eyes."

To his surprise, she did. He worked on her feet for several more minutes, then pushed up the hems of her sweats. Her eyes flew open.

"It's okay. I'm just going to massage your calves. Close your eyes, Carrie."

It took longer this time, but eventually she did as he said. With firm pressure, he squeezed her slender calves, working the muscles there. Though she was strong, she wasn't at all bulky with muscle. She had the lithe limbs of a dancer, muscled but not overblown. When he was done, he gently skimmed his fingers over her right thigh.

"This is where he shot you," he said.

Her eyes were still closed, but she'd gone still. Her breathing quieted. She nodded.

"How firm should I be when I massage it?"

"The pressure you've been using is fine. It'll help tomorrow, and I won't be so sore. But if you're tired—"

In reply, he began stroking her thigh through her sweats. Using a firm but gentle pressure, he kneaded the tight muscles before moving to her other thigh to do the same. He kept alternating his attention between them. Each time he shifted his attention from one thigh to the other, his fingers trailed near the juncture between them and she sucked in a breath. He became hypnotized by that intoxicating rhythm: kneading her flesh, stopping to move to her other leg, but only after she gave him that soft, sexy inhalation.

At one point, he pulled her thighs farther apart to get a better grip, and she whimpered. His eyes shot to hers. She was watching his hands just the way he'd been. Her face was flushed and her eyes dilated. Her mouth trembled.

Shit. He was breathing hard.

He wanted to push her thighs even farther apart to make room for his hips. Wanted to press his aching flesh into hers and confirm that she was warm and wet the way he thought she was.

For several shaky seconds, he wasn't sure if he'd be able to stop himself from doing exactly that. Maybe she sensed it, because she moved to swing her legs off him. He automatically held on so she couldn't.

"Jase," she said softly. "Thank you for my massage. But I think you should leave now. Please." She smiled up at him, and he saw it then. All her desire. Her regret. She wanted him just as much as he wanted her. But she'd never let herself have him. Not without putting up a damn good fight.

With a sigh, he released her. Quickly, she got to her feet and tugged the hems of her sweats down. She glanced at the clock on her wall. "Not too late," she said brightly. "Who knows, maybe the brunette is waiting up for you." She walked to the door and swung it open.

Slowly, he followed. He didn't bother responding to her blatant attempt to push him away. "Tragic circumstances aside, this was fun. Working with you. It's been a while since we've talked shop together."

"Thanks for all your help. I appreciate it."

"I'm always here if you need another opinion. Or another massage."

She smiled slightly. "Good night, Jase."

Just before she shut the door behind him, he caught the edge of it, stopping her from closing it. He leaned closer. "Hey, Carrie?"

"Yes?"

"Despite what I said earlier at McGill's, I think it's only fair to tell you I've changed my mind."

"Changed your mind about what?"

"About whether it's worth pursuing this attraction between us. Like you said, you've got needs, and I've got a need for you that's been building since the first moment I saw you. So long as commitment isn't what you're asking for, we can have some fun in the sack, too. If you thought a leg massage was good, you should see what I can do when you're spread out and naked. I'll show you a better time in bed than anyone on SWAT can, I promise you that."

For a second she hesitated, as if she was considering his half-assed offer. Then she smiled tightly and said, "I have plenty of fun, Jase. You're free to do the same. Just do it without me."

CHAPTER SEVEN

BRAD COULDN'T BELIEVE his luck. He'd never been the kind of guy to leave a bar with a girl, let alone one as classy and beautiful as this. Tonight, not only did he have a pretty girl on his arm, but she was going home with him. And according to her, she was willing to do whatever he wanted when he got there.

The possibilities were endless. There were so many things he wanted to do to her. And with her. So many things that he wanted *her* to do to him…first.

Before.

Before he took advantage of the information he'd overheard at McGill's.

Before he proved that he was better. Smarter. More creative than even *him*.

After all, it was *his* fault Brad had never left a bar with a woman before. And it was his fault Brad now had the courage to do so. Being able to blame him for both seemed not just fortuitous but destined.

Like there was a higher power at work, telling Brad that after all the pain, the mockery and the rejection, his time had finally come. If only he was willing to seize the opportunity.

Still, in the back of his mind, a gnawing feeling of guilt ate at him.

He glanced at the woman beside him.

It would be wrong to sleep with her. Wrong to use her. After all, he didn't love her.

He loved Nora.

It was Nora he really wanted to make love to.

But she'd never seen him that way. And she never would.

Not now.

Not when she had him in her life. *Him*—who was perfect. Handsome. Popular.

All things Brad could never be.

That knowledge wasn't new, but it stung as if it was.

Pain was the last feeling he'd ever wanted to associate with Nora, but it was there. Erasing his guilt. Prodding him on.

If he couldn't have Nora, he decided, then this girl would do.

She'd do for now.

CHAPTER EIGHT

"WE CAN HAVE SOME FUN," Carrie mimicked the next day as she walked into the building that housed SIG Headquarters. "Fun my ass," she breathed, more to push away the images the phrase brought to mind—all involving her and a very naked, sweaty Jase Tyler—than anything else. "He's exactly what you thought," she told herself. "He respects female cops, but God forbid he ever become involved with one for more than a quick screw."

She snorted and shook her head. Quick screw? Right. As if. From what she knew about Jase Tyler, he wouldn't be a quick lover. If his slight Texan drawl and his deceptive habits of lounging and ambling weren't proof enough, all she had to do was remember the slow, firm strokes he'd used to massage her legs. He'd had all the patience in the world, teasing both her and himself with carefully controlled touches when it had been damn clear they'd both wanted more.

When he'd tugged her thighs farther apart, it had taken everything she had not to grasp his hand and guide it between them. She'd been aching for his touch, his penetration. Wanting to be filled. Wanting to lose herself in pleasure in a way she never had before. It was one of the things that drew her most to him. Her life demanded constant energy from her and that's the way she liked it. Most of the time. She knew that once Jase got a woman in bed, he'd make sure they stayed there for a long time. While he did all kinds of wonderful things to her.

Too bad that woman was never going to be her.

So forget about him already. You've got a job to do.

Sighing, she rubbed at her eyes, which felt covered with grit.

She'd been doing her job all night. So much so that she hadn't gotten any sleep.

After Jase left, she'd kept working just so she wouldn't give in to temptation and call him. Thankfully, after looking at the crime-scene photos again and going over the notes she'd made, she'd forgotten about Jase and their turbulent relationship. All she'd been focused on was trying to come up with a lead. Any kind of lead.

Her mind still on the case, Carrie took the elevator to the lower floor that contained locker rooms and a small workout room. She hadn't done her P.T. exercises this morning, so she'd do them now. That way, she could work uninterrupted through the rest of the day. After meeting with the commander, she'd start setting up interviews. Then she'd—

Turning a corner, she didn't even see the man coming toward her. She ran right into him.

She actually bounced off Jase's hard body before he grabbed her arms to steady her. Instantly, she took in his half-dressed state. He wore shorts, socks and sneakers, but nothing else. His chest was bare, his muscles defined and bulkier than she'd have expected, his skin a smooth surface sprinkled lightly with the perfect amount of hair. He was sweating and breathing hard, and she realized he must have just finished working out, either running on the treadmill or lifting weights or both.

She gulped in air, trying to steady herself, but all she ended up doing was inhaling his spicy, musky scent, all hint of cologne gone and only the wonderful subtle aroma of man left behind. His grip loosened, but he didn't let go of her. Instead, he smoothed his palms against her arms in a gentling motion. From just that slight touch, from just seeing him, she was ready to take. And to be taken.

It pissed her off, but...

Big deal. So her response proved she was human, female and breathing.

Despite his southern charm and snazzy clothes, he exuded that bad-boy quality that made grown women turn into simpering fools. She'd seen that herself last night at McGill's when one woman after another had propositioned him.

But he didn't want them, a voice taunted her. *He wanted you. Only not for a commitment—for a roll in the sack.*

Story of her life.

But she was stronger than the bolt of chemistry that hit whenever they were together.

She had to be.

Didn't she?

She wasn't so sure anymore. They stared at each other before his gaze dropped to her mouth. She sucked in a breath, wondering if he would kiss her. Hoping he would.

Instead, he frowned and took a step back. "Good morning. Did you sleep well?"

She immediately tensed but there was no hint of taunting or innuendo in his expression. To the contrary, he looked subdued. Tired. As if he'd done the exact *opposite* of sleeping well. Because of her? Had he replayed their time together as much as she—

"Listen, Carrie. I need to talk to you about something," he said, his expression growing even more solemn.

She cleared her throat and tried to look anywhere but at his bare body. "Did you have more thoughts about the case? Because it really helped me to talk things out with you last night, Jase. After you left, I thought about—" She couldn't help it. Her attention had strayed to his naked chest. Then his six-pack abs. Her gaze would probably have continued its downward path but for the fact that she caught sight of a crisscrossing network of raised scars on his smooth, slightly tan skin. She sucked in a breath. "Jesus, Jase, what happened?" Without thinking, she reached out to touch the scars that riddled his left side. Before she could, he caught her wrist.

"It happened a few years ago," he said, still holding her. "When I worked for Dallas P.D."

"They look like knife wounds."

"They are. I got called to a domestic situation. Met the woman outside. She was beaten pretty bad but she told me her husband, the guy who'd done it to her, had left. When I walked her back inside, he ambushed me. Sliced me up six ways to Sunday before I could get to my gun."

"She let you walk in there knowing he was going to do that? Knowing that you were just trying to help her?"

"I don't think she knew what he was going to do. She thought he was hiding in the bedroom. Waiting for me to leave."

"So he could beat her up some more," she snapped.

He shrugged. "You know the reality of domestic abuse, Carrie. He probably apologized before I got there and that was enough for her to believe that maybe, just maybe, this time he'd change. Anyway, it was touch-and-go for a while, but..." He shrugged.

Her mind reeled at his words. She shouldn't be so surprised to learn he'd been hurt on the job or that he'd almost died, but seeing the proof of his wounds, hearing him describe the incident that had almost taken his life, rattled her so much that she shocked them both.

With him still holding her wrist, she bent awkwardly and pressed her lips against the worst of his scars.

He sucked in a hissing breath and went perfectly still.

Straightening, she swallowed hard. "I'm sorry you got hurt. I'm really—"

He curled his arm around her and yanked her against him. Then his mouth slanted over hers. This time, she knew he kissed her with absolutely no thoughts of comfort in mind. Instead, he seemed to care only about possessing her. And despite where they were, who they were, she wanted to be possessed by him.

JASE SLIPPED HIS TONGUE into the heated cavern of Carrie's mouth and groaned at the pure pleasure of it. Despite her prickly demeanor whenever they were together, she was as soft and warm as he'd always imagined she'd be. As soon as her body touched his, their individual components locked together with ease, as if every part of her had been created for the sole purpose of complementing every part of him. At work, they were equals; by nature, they were opposites, but opposites of the best sort. Where he was hard, she was soft. Where he was male, she was fabulously female. Her plump breasts gave to the pressure of his torso. Her graceful hips cradled his. And her scent? God, her feminine scent wound around him the way he knew her hair would if it was loose.

With his free hand, he reached up and carefully withdrew the band from her ponytail. Her russet curls spilled over his hands like molten lava, and he buried his fingers in the tangled mass. Cradling the back of her skull, he tilted her head to give him better access to her mouth. He explored every sweet corner with his tongue, lingering over the smooth sharpness of her teeth. She rose on tiptoe, trying to gain control of the kiss by sucking on his tongue. With a groan, he ripped his mouth free to take in desperate bursts of air.

His hands didn't know what to do. They wanted to stay in her hair and around her waist, but at the same time it wasn't enough. He wanted to touch her everywhere, all at once, to cup breasts and buttocks and, yes, that sweet hot core between her thighs before one of them came to their senses and realized they shouldn't be doing what they were doing.

He licked the hollow beneath her ear just as she gasped, "Jase. Jase, stop. We can't."

He rested his forehead against her shoulder, and although he wanted to howl in denial, he took several deep breaths, released her and stepped back.

She looked like an erotic fantasy, her lips bee-stung and her hair a wild cloud around her face. Most of all, her blue eyes glittered with a fierce desire that he'd never forget, no matter how much she denied it later. She raised her hand and gingerly touched her mouth, and he remembered the sting of pleasure that had bolted through him when she'd pressed that mouth against his scars. Automatically, he lifted his hand and touched the scars at his side, as if by touching himself he was touching her, too. Her eyes followed the movement before darting back to his.

With a whimper, she turned and walked away.

ODELL BOWERS'S SMILE disappeared as soon as the door to his office closed. He'd just finished a consult with yet another woman willing to pay thousands of dollars for elective cosmetic surgery that she really didn't need. It was the bread and butter of his practice, and enabled him to live in the manner to which he'd grown accustomed, but he was so damn bored with boob jobs and tummy tucks. Even the face-lifts, which he'd always viewed differently, weren't challenging him any longer. All he could think about was his girls. The magnificent results of what he'd done to them. How proud Laura would have been of him and his work.

Unlike the women he saw day in and day out, Laura had been comfortable in her own skin. She'd made it her duty to help Bowers become the same. She hadn't cared that he'd liked to borrow her clothes or play with her makeup. In fact, she'd reassured him that he looked better in them than she did.

Laughing affectionately, Bowers rose and locked his office door. Then he buzzed his receptionist and told her he needed an hour of privacy. Using his private bathroom, he washed his hands thoroughly, the way Laura had taught him. By the time he was done, and he retrieved his briefcase from under his desk, he was trembling with anticipation.

He always had his briefcase with him. Always.

The snick of the lock as he disengaged it made him jerk.

The smooth glide of the lid as he slid it up made him gasp.

The sight of the small box inside, an intricately carved ivory container Laura had given him for his birthday, made him moan.

Lightly, he brushed his fingertips over the surface and imagined he could still feel the warmth from her having held the box so long ago.

But he knew it wasn't real.

That was okay. Because the contents of the box were very real.

Each time he added more items to the box, he paid homage to Laura and repented for the way he'd failed her. He was good at his job, the best, but what he did with his girls was the work he was most proud of. He'd give up everything—his practice, his money, his social standing, everything—for the time with Laura that he'd been denied. But since that couldn't happen, he took comfort in the ones that he could help.

He closed his eyes and recalled the last one. How smooth her skin had looked. How creamy. He'd overplucked her brows, just the tiniest bit, but he was confident the brow corrector had done its job. Even if the police had enlarged the photos he'd sent them, he doubted anyone would be able to pinpoint his mistake.

Grimacing, Bowers reached down and cupped his growing erection. He hissed and let go. Hand shaking, he touched the ivory box once more, then picked up the shiny tube next to it. As he popped off the lid, he strode to the gilded mirror on the wall across from his desk. He layered the lipstick—the same baby's breath color he'd used on his girls—on his lips.

He studied himself from first one angle and then another. Not satisfied, he added even more color.

Yes. That was it.

Lovely. He was lovely.

His gaze strayed back to his briefcase and the ivory box inside.

It was almost a shame that he had to limit himself. The urge to speed things along, to show off his artistry, was increasing. It was getting to the point that whenever he caught sight of a woman that reminded him of Laura, he could barely stop himself from approaching her.

But he had to. And he did.

Because Laura had been in a hurry when she'd been killed. She'd taught him the dangers of impatience.

He wouldn't make the same mistake.

CARRIE BEAT JASE to the SIG office by a mere ten minutes, yet when he strolled in, he'd already showered and changed into his work clothes. He looked calm and composed, but the searing heat in the gaze he directed at her told another story. She, on the other hand, was feeling anything but calm. She tried to look anywhere but at him. Although she'd once more pulled her hair back, twisting it into a strategically tucked knot because he'd pulled the band free and tossed it on the floor somewhere downstairs, she imagined that everyone could see how his lips and hands had been all over her.

What on earth had compelled her to kiss his scars the way she had? She hadn't even been aware she'd been thinking about it until she'd already had her lips pressed against his naked skin. Who could blame him for taking her up on such a blatant invitation by kissing her the way he had? As if he truly desired her. As if she wasn't a convenience or a challenge, but a woman he wanted to sink into and stay inside for a good long while.

But that was silly, she told herself. He was Jase Tyler, playboy cop extraordinaire, and she was Carrie Ward, cop, plain and simple. Maybe he always reacted that way when a woman expressed sexual interest in him.

Nervously, she glanced up, hoping he'd have mercy on her and let things be. But instead of ignoring her the way she'd been hoping and, yes, half expecting, he came right up to her desk. "I told you, I need to talk to you about something."

She lowered her gaze to the paperwork in front of her. "I've wasted enough time with you, Tyler. I have work to do before I meet with Stevens."

"Damn it, Carrie. That's what I want—"

"Hey, Ward. Tyler," DeMarco called from his desk. He was leaning back in his chair and flicking a small green card between his fingers. "Commander Stevens wants to see the two of you."

Since she wasn't supposed to meet with Stevens for another two hours, Carrie frowned. "Did he say why?"

"Just that it had to do with the serial-killer case you're working."

She turned to look at Jase. "But why—" Confusion melded into a dreadful suspicion, one reinforced by his guilty expression. Standing, she sucked in an enraged breath as betrayal swept through her. "Did you go running to Stevens about me? Did you tell him your little theory that I don't deserve this case?"

Jase's mouth tightened. "I never said you didn't deserve it, Carrie. And I didn't come in to talk to Stevens. He came to me, asking whether I saw any problem with you working the case on your own. And I gave him my honest answer. That I did."

"I can't believe I trusted you," she whispered. "I should have known better."

"This isn't a matter of wanting the case for myself, Carrie. But from what I saw outside McGill's last night—"

The crack of her palm against his cheek echoed wildly in the room. Everything went quiet.

"Hey, guys—" DeMarco began.

Jase held up his hand. "Keep out of this," he gritted out.

"Yes, DeMarco," Carrie said. "Keep out of this. It's between me and this lying, slimy worm who stabbed me in the back. What, I didn't take you up on your offer for a roll in the sack, so you interfere with my career?"

"This has nothing to do with you having sex with me, Carrie. The job never will. When it happens, it's going to be because you want it just as much as I do." He whispered the final words, obviously not wanting DeMarco to hear.

She didn't have such compunction. "Read my lips," she said loudly. "The day I sleep with you, Tyler, is the day I quit the force because I know for sure I've lost my mind. Until then, keep your pop-psychology opinions to yourself and don't you ever try to 'help me out' again. In fact, stay as far away from me possible, you got it? Next time, I won't just slap you. I'll show you that my faulty aim with Kevin Porter was a complete and utter fluke."

"Oh, I have no doubt about that. After all, you're an expert markswoman. A silver in the Olympics, right?"

Her eyes widened. "So what? I wasn't hiding it. But what did you do? Go snooping through my things last night? Were you digging for information to relay to the commander? Sorry I couldn't offer you something more damaging than my skills with a rifle."

"Bullshit you weren't hiding it. You've never had a problem tooting your own horn when it comes to your skills as a cop. So why didn't you tell us you were an expert markswoman?"

"You're deranged. The commander and Mac know. So does DeMarco."

They both looked toward the man in question, who kept his gaze on his paperwork but nodded. "Yep, I knew, but keep me out of this, okay?"

Carrie turned back to Jase. "I don't go around advertising my talents. Unlike you, I don't need to flaunt what I'm good at. Too bad taking desperate women to bed is the only thing you're good for."

Jase shook his head. "Don't go there, Carrie. Not after last night. Not after…" He paused, and she knew he'd barely stopped himself from mentioning their encounter downstairs. "Don't play dirty."

"Or what? You'll play even dirtier than you already have? Bring it on, Jase. I dare you."

He grabbed her by the arms for the second time that morning and jerked her forward. "You should think twice about that. Damn it, I'm not a saint, Carrie. One day you're going to push me too far."

She shoved away from him. "And one day, I'm going to be gone, Jase. I'm sick of having to prove myself to you. To the commander. To everyone."

"This isn't about having to prove yourself, damn it. If you'd just listen…"

"Go to hell," she snapped. She twirled around and headed up the stairs that would lead to Stevens's office.

HIS EXPRESSION GRIM, Jase turned to DeMarco, who was staring at him in amazement. Slowly, DeMarco shook his head and whistled.

"I didn't rat her out to Stevens," Jase said. "He asked me for my opinion. I told him. That's all."

DeMarco nodded. "I'm not questioning you, Jase. Just wondering how you're going to get anything done if you have to watch your back every second. Ward isn't just pissed, I've never seen her so incensed."

"Yeah, incensed—as in emotional. Maybe even unstable. So what does that tell you?"

"It tells me things are going to be mighty interesting around here for a while."

Interesting, Jase thought as he turned away. Hell, with that kiss downstairs, things had bypassed interesting and skyrocketed to extremely complicated in less time than it had taken for Carrie to press her succulent lips against his skin.

Why had she done it? Her actions had taken him so completely by surprise that he hadn't stood a chance of controlling his instinctively primitive response. He'd forgotten they were at work, that he'd just been using exercise to physically exhaust himself so he'd be too tired to think of her for even one more second, and that she was going to be extremely pissed at him, and with good reason, once Stevens had a chance to meet with her. He hadn't been able to form a rational thought except to kiss her and do any other damn thing she'd let him do to her body as soon as possible. And she'd wanted him to do plenty. She'd pressed her breasts against him as if they ached for his touch. Her mouth had opened willingly for the penetration of his tongue, and her own tongue had come out to play, as well. And her hands? Her hands had attached themselves to his ass with a demanding need that had practically blown his mind.

She'd done all that for the same reason that she'd kissed him. Out of sheer desire. But as soon as he'd pulled away and she'd had a chance to think again, to rein in her desire the way she always did, she'd done just that. Leaving him jittery and aching and plain fucking confused.

He wanted Carrie. He'd wanted her for a long time now.

He just didn't know what to do about it anymore.

Because what he had been doing? Ignoring it? Taking his lead from her?

He wasn't doing anymore.

CHAPTER NINE

CARRIE TOOK SOME TIME in the bathroom to get herself composed. By the time she walked into Commander Stevens's office, she had things under control. She didn't take the offensive. She didn't start peppering him with questions or jump to defend herself. Doing so would only put her in a more vulnerable position. If Stevens had doubts about her competency, let him say them to her face. Then she'd handle them calmly and professionally, shooting down his concerns as if they were clay pigeons.

She and the commander made small talk for a while before someone knocked on his door. When Jase walked in, Carrie barely looked at him. He took the seat beside her. None of them said a word.

Stevens sighed. "Well, I can see this is going to be a whole lot of fun. Agent Ward, I want you to know that when Mac came to me with your request to lead up this serial-killer investigation, he did so with some hesitation."

Carrie couldn't disguise her surprise. Honestly, if she'd been alone, she'd have grasped for her chest because she felt like she'd been stabbed in the heart. All along, she'd thought Mac was supporting her, but that wasn't true at all. "Agent McKenzie never said anything to me about having any reservations," she finally said.

"That's because he didn't feel his concerns warranted keeping you off the case."

"I'm afraid I'm not following, sir."

"I know. I'm going to be completely honest with you. Even though it might leave me and this whole department open to yet another lawsuit."

Another lawsuit? Carrie thought. What did the commander—?

"Mac admitted he had reservations about assigning you The Embalmer case," the commander continued, his unexpected words displacing all other thoughts from Carrie's mind. "But he also couldn't say with certainty that he'd have the same concerns if you were a man that had been on leave for a month and requested this assignment. That troubled him. It troubled both of us. You've worked hard here at SIG. You have an impressive case-closure record. The best in the department, in fact. You've earned the right to prove yourself with something more challenging."

"I agree with you," Carrie said slowly, then looked at Jase. But he didn't look at her, and he remained silent. "Then why am I here, sir? With Agent Tyler?"

"Two reasons. First, you've never worked a serial case before. There will be plenty of people wanting to take you down a peg or two, including Martha Porter."

"The old lady who…"

Carrie glared at Jase, who stopped talking midsentence. "What does Kevin Porter's grandmother have to do with this, sir?"

"She's filed a wrongful death suit against the state. It's nothing I'm worried about, necessarily, but it won't hurt to have a more experienced agent work The Embalmer case with you."

She stiffened, her mouth tightening. "What you really mean is that if Martha Porter's claims of incompetence against me prevail, the state will have a defense against future allegations that The Embalmer case was mishandled, too. Because a more senior detective would have supervised my every move. Isn't that right?"

Stevens didn't even flinch. "Let me worry about the politics of the job, Ward. Just know that if I didn't believe in you, you wouldn't be going anywhere near The Embalmer case, partner or not."

Staring at him, she could see he was being honest. Her shoulders relaxed slightly. "Assuming that's going to be Agent Tyler, then which one of us is going to take the lead? Because I was under the impression it was going to be me. Has that changed?"

"Not necessarily. Earlier, I asked Agent Tyler his opinion about whether you should work this case as the lead. He, too, expressed doubt. But he, too, confessed he couldn't say with one hundred percent certainty that his doubt wasn't the result of the fact you are a woman, and one he cares for on a personal level to boot."

Carrie's eyes rounded. It took everything she had not to glance at Jase again and to just listen to what the commander was saying.

"The problem is, Agent Ward, as enlightened as we all want to believe ourselves, you are the only female on this team and we are naturally protective of you. But I can't let that stop me from giving you what you need in terms of your career. So I'm not going to. You'll continue to be the lead agent on this case. For now."

"For now?" Carrie automatically bristled. "Does that mean you're simply waiting for me to fail? And let me guess. Agent Tyler here will be waiting in the wings to take over?"

Commander Stevens held up his hand. "Hear me out. As I already said, I want Jase to team up with you on this case. It's a complicated one."

"It was complicated two days ago and you never said anything about having me work with Agent Tyler. I anticipated having a partner, of course, but I don't need to be babysat."

"No, but Jase has worked several serial cases before. And he told me you've already discussed several theories about the case with him. Is that right?"

She gritted her teeth. It was her own fault for accepting his help, she thought. "Yes. But this serial killer is a slow-moving one. I have all kinds of notes prepared for our meeting later today—"

"He *was* slow-moving. That might not be the case any longer. As such, things have just changed."

"Sir?" she asked. Both she and Jase straightened and leaned forward in their chairs.

"We've just gotten word of another possible victim in the case."

"Another—?" Carrie couldn't help looking at Jase now. He looked as surprised as she felt. "But it's only been three days since SFPD discovered Cheryl Anderson's remains. Most serial killers wait months before striking again, and that's certainly been The Embalmer's M.O."

"I'm not certain this latest murder was actually committed by The Embalmer. That's going to be one of the things you'll be focusing on. Both of you. You'll have the lead for now, Agent Ward, but if it turns out we're dealing with a copycat, it becomes a whole different ball game. There's no way we have the manpower to handle a serial killer and a copycat. And if it's a copycat, he won't be satisfied with just one victim. More will surely follow. I won't have any choice but to call in the FBI. They'll have jurisdiction on The Embalmer case, leaving you and Jase free to work the second case. That is, if you're willing to abide by my orders. Otherwise, I'll put Tyler on the case with another officer assisting right now."

"I understand why things will change in the event of a copycat. I can take the lead, sir. And I can accept the FBI stepping in if that turns out to be necessary."

"Good. SFPD got a 911 call an hour ago from some hikers over at the Marin County Water Preserve. The hikers found a mutilated female. Patrol officers have secured the area and are waiting for you to examine the body."

"So there's actually a body this time, not just photos? Was the body embalmed?"

"I don't know that. But the body was eviscerated. Mutilated."

"If we don't know whether the victim was embalmed, how are you linking this victim with The Embalmer's victims?"

Stevens sighed and swiped his palms over his face. For the first time, he looked truly troubled. As if he really questioned their ability to catch a killer. "Upon being interviewed by the patrol officer, one of the witnesses said he found a woman's head. One whose eyelids had been cut off."

CHAPTER TEN

STANDING IN FRONT of his bathroom sink, Brad washed his hands. Unlike last night, the water ran clear, but his imagination filled in the color that was now missing. The woman's blood and his shaking hands had combined with the water to create ribbons of pink liquid and splashes of crimson against the dingy white bowl.

The woman...

As soon as he'd killed her, he'd been flooded by a sensation so foreign he almost didn't recognize it.

Power.

And pleasure.

Emotional and physical. So much so that he'd barely had to touch himself before he'd had the most powerful orgasm of his life.

Hours had passed. Hours to dispose of her body. Smartly. Fastidiously.

Dramatically.

But the rush of power still ran gloriously through his veins. Raising a steady hand, he ran his fingers over his neck and face, feeling the cobbled texture underneath the dark purple stains. Still there, but definitely better.

He'd done that. Simply by killing her. A prostitute. A whore.

He'd made her see his power. His strength.

His beauty.

And he had Dr. Bowers to thank for it. After all the bumbling and unsuccessful treatments he'd put Brad through, Bowers had finally earned his salary by leading Brad onto the right path.

No amount of power the other man had experienced as a doctor, even one with the ability to save others' lives, could compare to the feeling of so ruthlessly ending one. It was a heady rush unlike any other. One that couldn't be duplicated by alcohol or drugs, and God knew Brad had tried both at various points in his life to numb his pain.

He'd always felt slightly foolish afterward. Guilty. As if he'd been weak to rely on a foreign substance rather than his inner strength.

But what he was feeling now was all him. Nothing artificial. Nothing meant to stifle or disguise, but rather expose. Clarify. Magnify.

It wasn't the violence or actual killing responsible for the change in him. He'd killed animals when he was a kid. Raped that one girl two states away before he'd graduated high school. And last year, he'd killed a girl. Not on purpose. By accident. After she'd laughed at him. Mocked him. But those acts hadn't made him feel like this. Because he hadn't been focused. Hadn't realized the extent of his power and what he could gain from it.

It was selecting the right victim for the right reason that was the key.

The one last night had simply been a small taste of what he could have.

Just imagine what he could accomplish if he actually killed someone who mattered.

Maybe then Nora would notice him. Maybe then she'd desire him. Maybe then she'd finally see him for who he truly was. Imperfect by birth but not by will.

I'll prove myself worthy of her. Prove I can change. For her.

His angel.

CARRIE NAVIGATED her government car around a skeletal-like screen of trees surrounded by the tall marsh grasses of the Marin County Reservoir. Pulling to a stop next to a county ambulance, an old pickup truck and a city squad car, she noted the vehicles were positioned just fifty feet from the concrete pillars of the causeway. Traffic whizzed steadily above her as commuters rushed to get home, oblivious to the fact that a woman's body parts lay strewn beneath them.

Uniformed officers identified by dispatch as Tracy Fitzpatrick and John Gordon approached as she opened the door. The unusually warm weather immediately prickled Carrie's skin, rushing into the car and clinging to her before she completely exited it. Her feet sank a little into the damp dirt.

The paramedics talked to a heavyset man and a teenage boy, presumably the two hikers who'd found the body. Carrie turned to Gordon, the senior officer. Gordon had kinky black hair and weighed about three hundred pounds, a perfect foil to his young partner who probably didn't weigh one hundred pounds sopping wet. "Was one of the witnesses hurt?"

Gordon shook his head. "Precautionary measures. Special Agent Tyler called. His ETA is about five minutes."

Carrie nodded, keeping her face blank even though her stomach tightened. When they'd been talking to Commander Stevens, Carrie had clung to her self-control by a thread. She was still reeling from the knowledge that Jase had talked about her with the commander, not to mention the escalation of murders in this case.

Once Stevens had given her the pertinent information on the latest call, Carrie had gotten ready to go. To her surprise, Jase had said he had other things to discuss with the commander. She'd known those things would have something to do with her. With the case. And she hadn't liked it. But she'd simply said, "See you at the scene," and left. As soon as she'd closed the door, she'd heard him arguing with Stevens. Jase's words still echoed around her.

"If she's not good enough to handle the case alone then she's not good enough to handle it at all. Give it to me and let her work on another case. Our backlog is getting too big as it is."

Bastard, she'd thought, then and now. He knew how long she'd been waiting to head up her first serial case, and he wanted to take over? No way. If she had to work with him, fine. Maybe the more time she spent in his company the faster she'd get rid of the ridiculous feelings she'd been harboring for him for far too long.

"Special Agent Tyler asked that you wait for him before viewing the body," Gordon continued, jerking her out of her thoughts. He swiped an arm across his slick forehead, his breathing slow but labored. "Hope we didn't interrupt anything exciting to get you out here."

Carrie, who'd turned to study the surrounding area, froze at his words. Slowly, she faced him again. His comment might have meant nothing but for the way his gaze dropped to her chest. Carrie narrowed her eyes and stared the officer down until his grin disappeared. "What were the witnesses doing here?"

Gordon shrugged. "Tim Larson and his son Ronald were searching for plants for some kind of school assignment. The kid saw a woman's foot sticking out of a mound of dirt behind some bushes. The, uh, foot wasn't connected to a body. Then he saw the woman's head, propped on a tree stump, facing the trail. Freaked him out. His father came running, stumbled across the body just a few feet away. Literally."

"And they probably trampled all over the crime scene." Carrie didn't blame them, but it would still wreak havoc with the recovery team's ability to process the scene. "Have you seen the body yet?"

The officers glanced at one another, guilt and relief in their eyes. For a split second, Carrie saw a look pass between them—a look of encouragement and comfort—that shocked her. Gordon's lasciviousness obviously didn't negate a genuine respect and caring for his partner.

"No, ma'am." Fitzpatrick answered, all bravado. Her posture was so erect and her speech so precise Carrie half expected her to salute. "We knew you and Special Agent Tyler were on your way. We figured we'd wait and make sure we didn't contaminate the scene any further."

"Good thinking." Carrie looked around again and noted the road she'd taken to get here. The only way in. "Block the access road at the turn from the main highway," she told the officers. "Try to keep the press out as long as possible."

"But that's almost a mile from here," Gordon said, his voice perilously close to a whine. "That's a pretty large area to contain. Shouldn't we just focus on the immediate area where the body was found? Perhaps Special Agent Tyler—"

"Special Agent Tyler would agree with my assessment." And he would. Because unlike Gordon, Jase knew his stuff. Carrie shook her head, trying not to show her impatience. Ignorance or laziness? Neither was acceptable. And besides, whether Jase agreed with her or not, she was the detective in charge of this case. "From the limited information we have, it's possible this murder is connected to another recent one, as well as two that occurred almost a year ago. I'm here to confirm or dispel that possibility. To do that I need a clean crime scene. The crime scene includes not only the burial plot and adjacent areas but any area the victim and perp moved through to get to the burial sight." She held up her hand to stop Gordon from interrupting her. "If he transported the body in a vehicle, the only way he could have gotten here was on that one mile of road. We need to contain as much of the area as possible."

She glanced up at the darkening sky, and both officers' gazes followed hers. Despite the warm weather, Marin County was known for fog and rain. "The recovery team's going to have to work fast. The weather could change at any moment." She looked at her watch. "Damn it. What's keeping Jase?"

Gordon's eyes narrowed when she used Jase's first name, but she ignored him. It had been a slip. One she wouldn't make again.

She studied the dense foliage separated by pits of mud and residual water. Would the recovery team use a helicopter to take a full panoramic picture of the scene? More likely they'd rely on current GPS technology to establish a blueprint to mark down whatever evidence they found. And preserve exact measurements. Problem was, with the body having been exposed to the elements for an unknown amount of time, chances were its condition, even its placement, had already been compromised.

Carrie turned to Gordon. "Where's the body?"

"They said it's through those trees right there. Just to the edge of the water and under the causeway. Back and to the left." He hesitated. "You want me to come with you?"

"No," she murmured, wondering if he was trying to be gallant or insulting. "Thank you, Officer Gordon."

As she edged into the shadows cast by the hulking highway overhang, the vibration of rush-hour traffic shook the saturated, fetid ground sticking to the soles of her Rockports. Nervously, she eyed the dark crevices between cement blocks and knew she wasn't imagining the flutter of movement she saw inside. Automatically, her right hand hovered near her weapon.

Bats.

Within the cavernous hollows of this highway lived thousands upon thousands of bats. Each fall, students were brought here to observe their twilight exit pattern, the group migration painting the sky in a massive shadow reminiscent of eels slithering in low water.

Carrie swallowed hard and looked over her shoulder. Twilight was hours away. She took a deep breath, trying to prepare herself.

But nothing could have prepared her for the sight of the woman's bloody remains. The first thing she thought when she saw the tilting dirt-stained head resting atop a tree stump was—she'd been beautiful. With long brown hair other women would envy. The victim's eyes stared garishly back at her, completely devoid of eyelids. Carrie's chest tightened and she instantly visualized the autopsy photos of The Embalmer's three victims. They'd stared back at her from the photos, as well.

Accusingly.

Pleadingly.

Even if she hadn't been able to save them, Carrie

could help solve their murders. Find their killer, whether it was the same man or not. Bring their families—maybe even their spirits—some semblance of peace.

Moving closer, Carrie saw hundreds of maggots and other insects feasting on the woman's remains—her ears, her mouth, her wounds. Flies flew around her, landing periodically as if to direct the baser wingless insects from one spot to another. The department's forensic lab would collect specimens. Classify the insects and even dissect them to determine the time of the woman's death.

One thing Carrie did know, however. The woman had been killed someplace else and her body transported here later. Otherwise there would be more blood. Signs of struggle. And except for several vehicle tracks and some muddy footprints, there was no other indication of recent human activity.

Carrie took several shallow breaths before returning her gaze to the woman's unnatural one. Somehow, she felt looking away would be disrespectful. This woman deserved to be recognized as more than the individual body parts she'd been reduced to. Given the state of her body, even once they identified her, her family wouldn't get the chance to see her again before she was buried. The monster who'd killed her shouldn't be the last person to truly see her.

When she couldn't stand it anymore, she scanned the adjacent area. The woman's torso lay about ten feet away, still clothed in a sleeveless lace top. The ragged cloth covering the woman's lower half, or at least what was left of it, was dark and crusted over with dirt and blood. Her limbs were gone and, based on the discovery of her foot, would likely be found nearby.

The dismemberment hadn't been done by an animal. At least, not the kind with four legs. Carrie could only pray she'd already been dead when the guy had mutilated her.

The sounds of footsteps made Carrie turn. The recovery team was carefully working its way toward her. Joe Mansfield, one of DOJ's forensic examiners, met her first. Walking beside him was Jase.

"Hey, Carrie," Mansfield said.

Carrie nodded but Mansfield kept talking.

"I haven't seen you at McGill's in a while. Did you get a jealous boyfriend or something?"

Carrie forced herself to respond in the same casual tone Mansfield used. "Something like that. But hopefully I'll see you guys soon. How's Marcie?"

"She's pregnant again." He raked a hand through his thinning auburn hair. "We're having a boy this time."

"That's great. A little brother is just what Lucy needs." Carrie thought of Mansfield's little girl, whom she'd met at a department barbecue only once. The spitting image of his petite, dark-haired wife, right down to matching dimples. Did Mansfield know how lucky he was? The light in his eyes said he did. "Congratulations."

"Thank you, ma'am."

Mansfield put on a pair of latex gloves and took out

his evidence collection kit and a camera. "I hear it's pretty bad."

"You could say that."

She looked at Jase. "Did Officer Gordon fill you in?"

"Yes. Let me take a look at the body and then we can compare notes."

"Fine," she said. "I'll be by the car. Just yell if you need me, okay?" Carrie started walking back toward the road.

Less than a minute later, she heard Mansfield's gasp. Then cursing. "Jesus!" he exclaimed. Then retching sounds filled the air as the veteran law-enforcement officer emptied the contents of his stomach.

She was several feet away when she heard Mansfield say, "She must be made of steel or something. Nothing gets to her, does it?"

If Jase replied to Mansfield's question, Carrie didn't hear it. But she did hear Mansfield ask, "Jase, what's wrong? You look—you're looking at her like you knew her."

Carrie froze and waited tensely for Jase to respond. Nothing but a heavy silence followed Mansfield's question.

Then Jase said, "I didn't know her. But I talked to her. Last night at McGill's. Her name is Kelly."

CHAPTER ELEVEN

A COUPLE OF HOURS LATER, Carrie and Jase arrived at Kelly Sorenson's home. Sitting on the couch to Jase's right, Carrie watched him closely. His expression gave nothing away. No hint of any inner turmoil he might be feeling. But she suspected he'd be feeling plenty, and she didn't like the grim blankness that had settled on his face ever since he'd matched up the grotesquely beheaded female they'd found with the same woman that had flirted with him and DeMarco the night before in McGill's Bar.

The young woman sitting across from them sobbed, drawing Carrie's attention away from Jase. While she was technically a person of interest in Kelly Sorenson's murder, it was only because she was Kelly's roommate, not because they had any real reason to suspect her. Even so, the fact that she had a solid alibi—at the same time Jase had been chatting with Kelly at McGill's, Susan had been in the middle of an all-night cramming session with several other students—wouldn't necessarily get her off the hook. Although Kelly was a few years older and had already graduated, she'd attended the same college as Susan did now—the same college where Cheryl Anderson, The Embalmer's third victim, had taught English. While Susan might not have killed Sorenson or even Anderson herself, that didn't mean she hadn't hired someone to do it. At least, that was one theory they had to explore, even though it ranked low on Carrie's list of possibilities.

Most homicide victims were slain by someone they knew, but Carrie's instincts told her that Susan wasn't involved. Not only did the woman's grief seem completely genuine, there was also the fact that Kelly's killer had shown the same strange fascination with removing his victim's eyelids that The Embalmer had. There was no way that was coincidental. In addition, what had been done to Kelly Sorenson hadn't been the distant workings of a hired killer. It had been personal. Viciously symbolic. Given that, it was less likely that Susan was a killer and far more likely that The Embalmer was picking victims he spotted on campus, but had changed his M.O. in order to throw off the police or, more likely, just for kicks and giggles. In all probability, Kelly had simply been a *mushroom,* a term used by law enforcement for a person who just happened to pop up in the wrong place at the wrong time so as to catch a killer's attention.

"We have a few more questions. Do you feel able to continue?" Jase asked gently.

Susan raised her red-rimmed eyes. After taking a deep shuddering breath, she nodded. "Yes. Whatever it takes to find the bastard who killed Kelly."

"Thank you. You didn't report Kelly missing even though she didn't come home last night. Why is that?"

"I knew she was working, and it wasn't unusual for her work to extend into the morning. I was worried when she didn't show this morning, but I figured I'd give her a couple of hours. Kelly is—was—a free spirit and didn't like to be tied down."

"You said she was working. But I saw her at McGill's around seven. She—uh—" Jase rubbed the back of his neck and looked decidedly uncomfortable for a moment. Then he plowed forward. "She intimated she was free for the rest of the evening. Granted, I could have gotten my signals crossed but she even gave me a card with her phone number."

Jase's tone was slightly apologetic. He didn't want to imply Kelly had loose moral standards simply because she'd flirted with him.

Susan studied Jase, but she didn't appear to take offense. "Can I see the card she gave you?"

Interesting request, Carrie thought, but Jase flushed. "I didn't keep the card. I actually tossed it before I left the bar. But I glanced at it. It was purple. Simple. With a name and phone number, I think."

Susan smiled slightly.

"You find that amusing?"

"No. I mean, yes. Not amusing, but… If Kelly gave you that card, it meant she liked you. For you. Not because she saw you as a potential customer."

Even more interesting, Carrie thought.

"A potential customer?" Before Jase finished his

query, his face lit with understanding. "You mean she was a…?"

He deliberately let his words dangle so that Susan would finish the sentence for him.

"A professional escort," Susan said.

"Forgive me if this seems like a rude question, but why?" Carrie asked. "Kelly doesn't fit the profile of most sex-for-pay professionals we run into. She's college-educated." Carrie waved to their surroundings. "She had a nice place. A nice life. Why go that route?"

Susan hesitated, and Carrie sat forward, urging, "She's dead. To the extent we're interested in anything illegal she was doing, it's only because we want to find her killer. Before he does this to some other girl."

At Carrie's gentle but frank words, Susan's eyes overflowed with tears once again. She sniffed, blew her nose then said, "To put it bluntly, it was the easiest and fastest way to make the most money. College loans are ridiculously high these days. She had her own. And she wanted to help her little sisters go to college, too. It's just too bad you weren't interested in her." She glanced at Jase with a rueful smile. "If you'd gone home with her last night, she might still be alive. Instead, she settled for another job."

Jase frowned. "What do you mean by settled?"

"She called and told me she'd picked up an unexpected job from McGill's, although she said it was more a charity case than anything else."

"What time did she call you?" Carrie asked.

"I—I think it was about nine o'clock. I can double-check caller ID on the phone."

"Maybe in a second. A charity case? Those are the exact words she used?"

"Yes."

"And did you know what that meant?"

"Not really. I know this is going to sound funny considering what Kelly did to make money, but she was pretty discriminating about who she hooked up with. She wasn't stupid. She was careful. And she had her standards. Only lately..."

Susan's voice broke, and she started crying again.

Carrie and Jase looked at each other but said nothing as Susan composed herself again.

"I'm sorry," she said as she swiped at her eyes with a tissue.

"It's okay," Jase murmured. "We know this is extremely difficult for you and we appreciate the fact that you're willing to talk with us right now. Time really is of the essence in these types of situations."

Susan nodded, took a deep breath then said, "Lately, I got the feeling Kelly was being a little less exclusive when it came to the jobs she was taking. What she told me last night confirmed it. When she said she was taking a charity case, she meant that someone was getting lucky because she needed the money. But for that, it wasn't anybody she'd ever sleep with."

Carrie met Jase's gaze again, then looked back at Susan. "There's some indication that the person who killed Kelly might have killed other women, as well.

Can I show you some pictures of the women? See if you recognize them?"

Susan looked panicked, and Carrie rushed to reassure her, "Just regular photos. Nothing gruesome, I promise."

Reaching into the files she'd brought with her, Carrie took out the "before" photos of The Embalmer's first three victims. She handed them to Ingram one by one.

When she got to the picture of Cheryl Anderson, Ingram gasped. "I know her. That's Professor Anderson. I had her for American Literature last year. She's dead?"

"She's the latest victim. We've tried to keep her name out of the paper so the press doesn't interfere with the investigation, and we need you to keep her identity as a victim in this case a secret. Can you do that?"

Susan nodded vigorously. "Yes. God. Kelly and Professor Anderson. I can't believe it."

"You had Cheryl Anderson as a teacher. Did Kelly?"

"Not that I know of."

"As far as you know, had the two of them ever met?"

"Again, not that I know of."

Of course, Susan could be lying. It was entirely possible she'd had a score to settle with Cheryl Anderson and Kelly, too.

God, things were getting messy. Even messier than they already had been, and that was certainly saying something.

"Do you work, Susan?" Jase asked.

"No. I just go to school. I'm lucky. My parents pay my way. It used to make Kelly so jealous...." Susan covered her face with her hands as her body began shaking with sobs. "Oh, God…"

Again, Jase and Carrie waited helplessly, silently, as the woman grieved. Instinctively, Carrie wanted to offer the other woman some comfort, but because she wasn't sure how to do that or how such a gesture would be received, she hoped their respectful silence was enough.

When Susan once again raised her head, Jase asked, "What about her car? Would it still be parked near McGill's, or would she have driven to her client's house?"

"She biked around campus. Used public transportation or got rides from friends when she needed to."

"Okay. Almost done here. In addition to Professor Anderson and Kelly having the college in common, we need to explore any other places they might have both frequented. Did Kelly spend time at a particular mall, gym or restaurant?"

"No. She—she liked McGill's, but you already know that."

Carrie looked at Jase. At his slight nod, she stood, as did he.

"I'm sorry for your loss," he said. "We're going to do everything we can to find out who did this. I need to ask you just one more thing. Do you have extra copies of Kelly's cards? The purple card and the other one, the one she'd use for more professional reasons?"

Susan nodded and slowly, as if it was very difficult for her, got to her feet. "Yeah. I'll get them for you right now."

LATER THAT DAY, the mood in the SIG office was grim. Maybe that's because Carrie and Jase were the only ones there, and they certainly had no reason to be anything but. After their interview with Susan Ingram, they'd stopped by McGill's. They'd talked to the manager and gotten a list of employees who'd worked the night before. Several employees, including the manager, noted that Sorenson had been a regular, and though she often left with someone different, she was rarely drunk when she did. Their observations seemed consistent with a professional working girl who was, just as Susan Ingram had said, active but at the same time somewhat discerning.

When they'd gotten back to the office, Carrie and Jase had made a list of everyone they could remember being present that night, whether it was someone they knew or simply someone they'd seen before. All in all, they had about fifty people they needed to interview. Although Jase hadn't seen Kelly Sorenson after she'd given him her business card, Susan Ingram said she'd called her from McGill's several hours later. Chances were someone they knew—maybe even DeMarco, Jase pointed out—had seen her between the time Jase had left and the time Kelly had left with her client.

DeMarco, however, had left town for a family emergency, and they hadn't been able to reach him.

They were waiting for a call from the coroner, hoping he could lock down the exact means and time of Kelly's death. With her body in so many pieces, Carrie suspected it was going to present a unique challenge, and they'd be waiting a while.

They hadn't found Sorenson's hands at the scene. Their absence suggested the killer had disposed of them separately, maybe because Sorenson had fought back and had scratched him. If that was the case, the killer was smart. Ruthless. Exactly what she would expect from The Embalmer.

Yet what he'd done to Sorenson's body? It was so different from what he'd done to the others. The change seemed to indicate a sudden increase of personal investment and loss of control. The kind of loss of control that came with mental deterioration? Even if that was the case, he'd still had the wherewithal to take Kelly's eyelids. Compared to everything else that had been done to the victims, it was a small detail but a hugely important one. A serial killer's modus operandi could evolve over time, but rarely would he change his signature, an act that often had nothing to do with the way the victim actually died but had more to do with fulfilling some kind of need the killer had. As she'd told Jase the first night they'd discussed the case, she was betting the eyelids served as some kind of memory prompt for the killer.

Carrie pushed back from the photos she'd been looking at and rubbed her temples. She glanced at Jase, who'd also been staring at photographs of the latest murder scene. For the first time since seeing Kelly Sorenson's body, Carrie allowed her thoughts to veer toward the personal. Hours ago, she'd slapped Jase because he'd tried to rip her case out from under her. Even after Stevens had confirmed he was giving her the lead, Jase had tried to talk the commander out of it.

Granted, much of her anger at Jase had been replaced by concern the moment they'd realized he'd had recent contact with Kelly Sorenson. He was usually such an open book that she'd immediately noticed when he'd pulled inside himself. For one of the first times since she'd known him, she hadn't been able to guess at what he was thinking. Feeling. He wouldn't be blaming himself, would he? It seemed ridiculous to think so, but as she well knew, sometimes logic had nothing to do with the emotions that came with the job.

Yet she wasn't going to intrude and ask questions. If he needed to talk to her about it, he would. And besides, now that they were back at work, now that he seemed to be handling everything okay, some of her anger toward him had resurfaced.

She still respected him. Still cared about him. But she didn't trust him. Not anymore. And she was supposed to work with him?

It seemed too much to ask of her, but he was acting as if nothing unusual had happened between them. So, fine. She wouldn't be the first one to cave. No way. She wasn't going to give Jase the chance to complain she wasn't a team player the next time he saw Stevens. So she tried focusing on the evidence and only the evidence. She was so absorbed in her task, in fact, that she jumped when Jase suddenly shoved back his chair, stood and said, "Damn it, Ward. Let's get it over with. I know you have something to say to me, so just say it."

Although her gaze immediately flew to his, she looked away just as quickly. Staring at her file, she responded coolly, "I don't know what you mean. We've been talking about the case ever since we were at the preserve. Have you had any new thoughts?"

To her amazement, he reached out and flipped the file she was reading shut. Slowly, she looked up at him. Crossing his arms, he leaned against her desk and stared down at her.

"I know you're pissed because of what I told Stevens, but I can't change how I feel. I could have lied and said I had absolutely no concerns about you taking the lead on The Embalmer case, but I didn't. Forgive me if I don't want to be responsible for you getting yourself or someone else killed simply because you're more worried about proving what a badass you are than giving yourself the time you need to recover."

Now it was she who shot to her feet. "Recover from what? My leg is healing just fine."

"It's not your leg I'm talking about and you know it. Are you seriously going to tell me you're not shaken up by the fact that you were almost killed? By the fact you shot and killed a sixteen-year-old? Because I'm not buying it."

"You don't have to buy anything. You admitted to Stevens you can't separate my gender from the job, so you don't have the right to ask me that question."

She could feel her control slipping. And she didn't

like that. When it came to Jase, she needed every ounce of control she could muster. She tried to walk past him, to put some breathing space between them, but he stopped her with a gentle grip on her arm.

"Listen to me. I can't separate your gender from the job. Not completely. Am I sorry about that? I'm not sure. It has nothing to do with equal rights, but what we all bring to the table, good and bad, and frankly, gender is a factor. It might make me a caveman and an asshole, but I'm hardwired to protect women. Cherish them. But it's my issue and I told Stevens that."

"Yeah, and so did Mac," she said bitterly as she wrenched her arm out of his grip. "Mighty big of you two."

"Damn it, don't you get it? It has nothing to do with thinking you're less capable, Carrie. My question about you being shaken up is legitimate. And it's a gender neutral question. The fact you're a woman might mean I'm more willing to ask you the question, but a guy would be shaken, too. I was shook up the first time I killed someone. And the first time I almost died on the job. You've seen the scars yourself, but there were emotional scars, too. It's nothing to be ashamed of."

She didn't like the reminder of those scars or his near-death experience. She wondered if he'd brought it up on purpose, not just to make his point, but to worm his way a little more into her head. Into her heart. Raising a hand to her temple, she tried to think. To concentrate and give his words the serious consideration they deserved before answering. "I'm—I'm not ashamed," she finally said. "Even if you're right, even if I'm still dealing with what happened with Porter, it's not going to affect my performance. I won't let it."

He reached out and pinched her chin. "Because you're Superwoman, right?"

She barely stopped herself from flinching. God, she hated that moniker. How many men had called her that in her lifetime? How many men had said it in the same sarcastic tone? Only she had to admit, Jase's tone when he'd called her by the dreaded nickname had sounded more exasperatedly affectionate than sarcastic. Because she recognized that, she smiled tightly. "Something like that. Now, can we get back to the task at hand and focus on the case?"

"Fine." Once again, he took his seat, spinning it to face her. "Let's assume Kelly Sorenson's killer is The Embalmer and not a copycat. What he did to her doesn't make sense," he said. "Except for the eyelids, he completely changed his M.O. Why?"

"It's not uncommon for a serial killer's M.O. to change, as you know," she replied. "It's not the method they use to kill the person that's the signature, it's usually something completely separate that has special meaning to them. So in this case, the eyelids are the common denominator. The most important, in my opinion. Of course, that doesn't rule out that this is a copycat killing."

"No. It doesn't. Plus we can't forget the killer could be a woman. Not common with serial killers, but still something to consider."

She couldn't help herself. "By all means, let's remain gender neutral so long as we're talking killers, not coworkers."

He didn't laugh and she hadn't expected him to. Although she kept her head down, she could feel his gaze on her. "When are you going to accept you're not just a coworker to me, Carrie? I was being honest when I told Stevens your gender was an issue for me. I was also being honest when I told him I couldn't be certain my personal feelings for you weren't clouding my opinion of whether you were the best person for this assignment. Or are we just going to keep ignoring that, in addition to the fact you slapped me this morning?"

"Can we?" she said, still not looking at him.

When he didn't reply, she sighed and finally met his gaze. "I thought you were ready to talk shop and let the other stuff go."

"You're the one who gave me the opening," he pointed out gently.

She sighed. What could she say? He was right.

"This isn't just about me wanting the lead on the case for my own professional reasons, Carrie. I care about you."

He *cared* about her. Such an innocuous word to sum up his feelings for her, when she knew her feelings for him were far more complex. "Yet you *did* want the lead. And you admitted you still do." When he just looked at her, she blew out her breath and nodded. "Okay, fine. You care about me. I—I care about you, too. There. I said it. But you can't protect me, Jase. That's not how this works. Not when I've worked just as hard as you have for my badge. Not when I've worked just as hard for the opportunity to lead this type of case."

"And after seeing what you did today, you still want it? It has nothing to do with you being a woman, either. I mean, even I'm having doubts, Carrie. I've seen some sick things in my time, but what was done to Kelly Sorenson…"

"Of course I've had doubts. I've had them throughout my career. About whether I'm good enough. Whether I can handle it. But one thing I've never doubted is that I'm going to try. I can make a difference in catching this bastard, and I'm going to. So don't worry that I'm going to break down and cave on you. I won't."

"I know that. Mansfield seems to think you're some kind of supercop when it comes to dealing with the bad stuff."

"And you?" she asked, not sure why she did. Only certain that his answer mattered. "What do you think?"

"I agree with him. I also think there must have been some super bad shit you had to deal with to make you so good at it."

"Some deep dark history of abuse that toughened me up, you mean? Careful, you're stereotyping again. Would you assume that if I wasn't a woman?"

"I was actually referring to the job, Carrie. But now that you mention it, I can't help but wonder. So did you?"

"Did I what?"

"Have a deep dark history of abuse?"

"I had an ideal childhood, Tyler. You should have figured that out yourself when you were looking at my photo albums. Normal teenage angst and all, but nothing out of the ordinary."

"You smile a lot in those photos. Up to a point. So what happened? What made you so much less willing to smile?"

It shouldn't surprise her that he'd seen so much in the short time he'd looked at her albums, but it did. She shook her head. "Unless you're willing to share some personal information about yourself, I suggest we stop the 'delve into Carrie's psyche' questioning. I remember what happened the last time I let you in, Jase. I'm not going to fall for it again."

Leaning farther back in his chair, he clamped his hands behind his head.

She tried, unsuccessfully, of course, to keep her eyes off his straining biceps.

"So delve into mine," he said.

"Excuse me?"

He shrugged. "You're right. I've been privy to personal information about you and I've used it to make judgments about you. About what makes you tick. It seems only fair that you get to do the same."

"You already told me about the perp who almost killed you. What now? You're just going to give me free and total access to your secrets?"

"I honestly don't have many secrets. If you come across one I'm not interested in sharing, I'll tell you. But I know you're still pissed at me. If we're going to work together on this case, we need to work on getting you to trust me again, too. I figure if I make myself a little more vulnerable to you, that will make us even."

"We won't be 'even' unless Commander Stevens asks me about you and I use whatever information you give me to argue you aren't capable of handling a particular assignment."

"Gotta start somewhere, right?"

"We need to work—"

"We've worked so long our eyes are crossing. If you're going to chicken out, come up with a better excuse than that, Ward."

Hand on her hips, she stared at him. When it was obvious he wasn't going to relent, she threw up her hands and took her own seat. "Fine. You want me to ask you something personal? Hmm, let's see…" She tapped her forefinger against her chin in an exaggerated manner, then held it up. "I know!" Despite her joking tone, she felt her expression become serious. "Why do you date the women you do? Why do you want the easy personal life, the way you mentioned yesterday? Because in every other aspect of your life, you seem to be bored with easy."

He stared at her until she squirmed.

"What?"

"Nothing. You just seem to know me a lot better than I thought you did." He shifted in his seat. "You know the debate about nature versus nurture? People disagree on whether biology is more important to one's behavior as an adult or if it depends more on how a person was raised."

"Yeah. So?"

"Well, my parents fought a lot."

"That's it?" she asked when he didn't elaborate. "Your parents fought a lot? So you were nurtured to date a lot? That doesn't even make sense. Great way to open yourself up and show your vulnerabilities, Jase. Next time, don't waste my time."

She started to get up, but he held out his hand. "No wait. Hold on a second and let me explain. I'm serious here."

Slowly, she lowered herself to her seat.

Leaning forward, he clasped his hands together. For a long moment, he stared at them, as if their discussion literally had him remembering a scene from his past. "My parents fought a lot because they both had strong personalities. Strong passions and opinions. But they disagreed a lot, and neither one of them liked to back down. It seemed like everything was a fight. From what to eat for dinner to what route to drive to a particular destination. It wasn't until I was older that I realized my parents actually enjoyed fighting. That they got off on it, in a way."

"Both your parents are cops, aren't they?"

"That's right. But I haven't sworn off relationships with cops so much as strong women, and strong women generally tend to become cops."

She smirked. "So rather than risk fighting with a

strong woman your whole life, you date women you can dominate. I guess it makes sense."

"In a sick way, yeah."

"Misguided, maybe. I wouldn't call it sick."

"I would."

"Why?"

"Because with the way I was raised, I don't entirely trust my nature."

"I don't understand."

"I know you don't. My dad—he slapped my mom around."

It was the last thing she'd been expecting him to say. "What?"

"It didn't happen very often, but once in a while, when I was little, he'd lose control and hit her. And she'd forgive him. Saying that she baited him."

"Oh, my God. That's twisted. As a cop, she would have known better."

"She did. But she loved him."

"And you're afraid you would hit a strong woman?" She shook her head vehemently. "That's ridiculous, Jase. You have more honor and integrity than that. I practically bit your ear off and you didn't raise a hand to me. You'd never hit any woman." She thought of the way she'd slapped him in anger. "But I hit you. I'm so sorry."

"I know why you did. I understand. Which isn't license for you to do it again, by the way."

"But you heard what I said, right? About you being nothing like your father?"

"I know it's wrong, but so does he. And he doesn't do it anymore. He hasn't for a very long time, certainly not since I became old enough to do something about it. But he used to do it, Carrie, and I'm like him in a lot of other ways. I even look like him."

"So they're still together?"

"Yes. They're still in Texas. My mom stood by him, and he got help. And part of me is glad. Despite everything…I'm glad. We've never talked about it. Any time I tried, they both denied it. But I know what I saw. I've always known."

"I imagine it would be hard to bring up. But I meant what I said, Jase. You don't have to date passive women because you fear you'll lose your temper and become your father."

"No, I don't have to, but it sure makes things easier that way. The job takes so much out of us. I never want to worry about how I'll act in my personal life because of it. So what about you?"

"What about me? You wanted to open yourself up to me, not the other way around. Besides, I have nothing to share."

But even as she said it, she knew she was lying. And she could tell that he knew it, too. Before he could call her on it, however, her phone rang.

"Special Agent Ward," she answered.

"Detective Ward? This is Officer Ian Bellows at SFPD. There's been some trouble at your house."

Her eyes widened and she glanced at Jase, who was frowning. "Trouble?"

"Vandalism, ma'am. Or more specifically, arson." As she listened to Bellows recount the details, Carrie felt the color slowly drain from her face. She reached out a hand as if to steady herself, which was odd given she was already sitting down.

"Carrie—" Jase began.

"I—I'll be right there," she told Bellows. Shakily, she hung up the phone. She tried to get in enough air, but she suddenly felt as if she was suffocating.

Immediately, Jase was at her side. "What is it?"

"My house," she said, still stunned. "Someone threw a Molotov cocktail through the window. It was fire-bombed. The fire department's there but, according to the officer who just called, it's bad."

CHAPTER TWELVE

As Jase stood nearby, Carrie spoke with Officer Ian Bellows and the lead firefighter outside her house. From the street, the place looked fine, but the inside was a different matter. The fire department had gotten there in time to stop the fire from spreading, but Carrie's living room was charred and smoking. Ironically, the files spread out on her dining-room table had been spared, while the photo albums and other personal items in her bookshelves had been lost.

"It was definitely arson," the firefighter said. "We have witnesses who saw a group of boys enter the building just before the fire began and your front door's been kicked in. From the descriptions we have of the boys, it looks like gangbangers are involved."

"Did they mention any particular gang?" Carrie asked.

Jase instantly understood. "Porter was in a gang." It infuriated him that even in death, Porter continued to put Carrie in danger. If she'd been home when—

"Yes," she said. She was pale, but her voice was calm. Still, he'd seen the devastation on her face when she'd stared into her damaged home. It had reminded him of her expression when Martha Porter had railed at her. And though he knew she was tough enough to take it and recover just fine, he resented the fact that she had to. If he could, if she'd let him, he'd do almost anything to protect her from feeling pain again.

"Afraid not. And I'm sorry, but you're not going to be able to stay here for a while," the firefighter said. "Not with this amount of damage. I'll give you the number of a good cleanup crew, but until they're done—"

"She'll stay with me," Jase interrupted.

Carrie started. "What? No, I can't."

"Why not? It's late. You don't have anyplace to go. And we'll be seeing each other early tomorrow morning to get started on the case again. It makes sense."

She said nothing until the firefighter walked away, an amused glint in his eye. "Sense is the last thing it makes, Jase, and you know it."

"Why? Because of what happened this morning after I worked out?"

"That and other things."

"Afraid you can't keep your hands off me?"

"Honestly? Yes. A foot massage is one thing. I'm not stupid enough to think I can stay with you at your house and not have anything happen between us."

Her bluntness startled him, then filled him with pleasure. He wanted to crow at her admission that she wanted him so badly, but he knew that wouldn't be wise. Instead, he said, "Let's at least have dinner, then. We'll drive separately. You can go wherever you want after we're done. How's that sound?"

He expected her to resist again, but she was obviously more stunned by the evening's events than she wanted to let on. With a sigh, she said, "Fine. I guess I could eat. But first I need to finish up here."

He waited while she got the number of that cleanup crew and finished filling out some paperwork. It took about an hour, but then she was ready to go.

"I'll work on getting the place cleaned up beginning tomorrow. They said it shouldn't take more than a few days. Where do you want to eat?"

He suggested Ernesto's, a Mexican restaurant with the best salsa and guacamole in town, as well as a full bar. Since it was still early, the normally packed restaurant was quieter than usual, but still busy enough to provide background noise and soothe Jase's raw nerves.

They ate their meals in relative silence. Part of it, he knew, was because she was still in shock from having her home burn down. The other part, however, was because she was distancing herself from him. Seeking solace from the day's incredibly disturbing events. He wanted to give her that comfort, but at the same time he wanted to break through her protective walls.

More than once, Jase started to ask her about the panic attack she'd had after the Porter woman had gone off on her. Somehow, he knew it hadn't been her first one. She'd been too controlled, both during and after it, as if she'd had a lot of practice dealing with them. That thought didn't sit well with him.

He didn't like to think of her in pain, emotional or otherwise. But with what they did for a living, how could she not let it affect her? With all the pain and tragedy she saw on the job, it was bound to seep into her on some level. And whether she liked it or not, it had to affect her differently because she was a woman. Didn't it? Hell, he truly didn't think of himself as a chauvinist, but while he indisputably viewed her as a strong cop, he never forgot she was a strong *female* cop. If that didn't make him a chauvinist, what would? Still, he wondered if she had anyone to talk to. If she had a friend to confide in. To cry with or laugh with. Somehow he didn't think so.

For the first time, he truly saw how isolated Carrie's life must be. He felt a stabbing pain in his heart and re-alized what it was. Sadness for her. And for him. Be-cause he knew she deserved more. And he wasn't sure if he was capable of giving it to her.

He didn't want to think of Carrie as sad or lonely. Understandably, however, she still looked troubled. Hell, she'd just had the mother of all bad days— something he'd unintentionally contributed to—and she'd just been evicted from her home. Sure, she was handling it, but he could tell by her distant expression that his plan to distract her from her troubles with din-ner hadn't quite worked.

He wasn't giving up, though. He wasn't about to ask her about her panic attacks or anything else that would make her retreat from him even further. So he'd stick to the safest topics possible. For now.

He leaned back in his chair and smiled teasingly

at her. "So what's your favorite color, flower and TV show?"

Startled, her gaze met his. "Are we going to play twenty questions now?"

He shrugged. "What I know about you personally I only know from sneaking a look at your photo albums. I need to do some catching up."

She smiled just slightly, but it was enough. "Red, peony and I don't watch TV."

"Not even cop shows?"

She shook her head and took another sip of her wine. "Are you kidding? Sometimes they're good for a laugh but that's about it."

"Tell me about it. It's so much more complicated than TV portrays. But you can give me the inside scoop on something. What was it really like being on SWAT? Did you learn any cool SWAT secrets?"

"SWAT secrets? Like...?"

His plan was working, he thought. For the first time since learning about the fire, her gaze seemed clear. Focused only on him. "I don't know. Anything us lowly special agents might not already know."

She snorted. "'Lowly' is the last thing I'd describe you as, Jase."

"Good to know. But let's be honest here. I'm a badass, sure, but SWAT? That's a whole other game altogether. So spill."

Leaning forward, she crossed her arms on the table. "Well, they gave us advanced training on hostage situations. Not only how to escape a potential kidnapper, but how to work as a team. That's one of the things I liked about SWAT. That team feel that even being a part of SIG doesn't satisfy."

"So how would a team work to escape a kidnapper?"

"Let's say a suspect takes me hostage and you're there. He orders you to drop your gun. We both know you can't give it up, right?"

"Right. If the hostage is a civilian, it might be a different story. But when another cop is involved, if it's a choice between letting a dangerous suspect get away to hurt others or saving a fellow cop, well, there's no choice, really."

"But every department should have a signal for such a situation. Something they can use against the bad guy."

"And SWAT had such a signal. What was it?"

"Saying the captured officer's middle name. We all knew that if another cop said our middle name in a crisis, that was our signal to duck and cover."

"And what's your middle name?"

"What's yours?" she asked.

"Tit for tat?"

"Something like that."

"David."

"Jase David Tyler. That's so…I don't know…*normal*. That's not fair," she pouted. "Certainly not worth telling you mine."

With that exaggerated pout on her lips, he could almost convince himself she was flirting with him. He decided to play along. "Why? You have a strange middle name?"

"Maybe."

Of course she wouldn't give it up that easily. What would be the fun in that? "You should tell me. Otherwise, how will I be able to give you the signal if I need to?"

"I can always just give you a made-up name for that."

True. But she also could have done that already. The fact that she hadn't pleased him. It was almost like she *wanted* him to pry the information from her.

But he didn't have to. He already had it. And it was darn good information. "But you won't. Will you? Katherine Katrina Ward."

Her eyes widened. "How do you know my full name?"

"It was on a page in your scrapbook. Kitty Cat. I like it."

She crinkled her nose at him in an adorable gesture that almost knocked him off his seat. "Yeah, well, that's exactly why I never tell anyone my real name. Carrie's much more respectable."

He cleared his throat and tried to remember why they were here. *So you can distract her from her troubles, Tyler, not so you can get your hands all over her.* Yet that's exactly what he wanted. He wanted to get down and dirty with Katherine Katrina Ward, but she was talking about being respectable. Or, at least, choosing a respectable name. "Carrie's not just respectable, is it? It's androgynous. Which is what you would have wanted when you joined the military. And the police academy. Right?"

She shook her head and finished her wine in one long swallow. "Carrie was a nickname given to me by my brothers. Appearances to the contrary, denying my femininity had nothing to do with it." She stared at her empty wineglass, the light mood they'd achieved evaporating.

Smooth move, Jase. But before he could answer, the waitress refilled Carrie's glass. She took another sip of wine and then leaned her chin on the palm of her hand. "You row, right? Why? Is it just for the physical challenge?"

Instead of answering her, he took a sip of his own drink and asked a question of his own. "Why did you decide to become an MP in the army?"

She shrugged. "That's easy. I wanted to help people. Serve my country. Make a difference."

He swirled the wine left in his own glass. "Yes, but you could have done that a number of different ways. Become a teacher. Or a doctor. Why a military cop? I mean, I know your dad was a cop and so were your brothers, but shouldn't that have made you less likely to become one, given you knew what a tough job it was? And joining the military took things up a notch, didn't it?"

Seconds passed before she answered. When she did, her words were slow and measured. "I knew I had a special gift with my shooting. It's what people seemed to validate the most. The fact that I was good at something that most women weren't. I guess I got used to that kind of adulation. Wanted it to continue. And I'd always been more comfortable around guys. Things seemed less complicated with them. I always knew where I stood. It seemed natural to pick a male-dominated career. To prove that I could do that as well as any man."

"Did the guys in the military respect you?"

She nodded. "For the most part. But it wasn't until I made SWAT that I thought I found my place in things."

"Why's that?"

"Because I felt like an invaluable component. We were truly a team, combining our strengths and watching each other's backs."

Her eyes lit up as she talked. It made him a little jealous of what she'd shared with her SWAT team. SIG was a team, too, but a slightly fractured one. They didn't typically enter dangerous situations where the only thing standing between them and possible death was their ability to rely on their partners.

Despite the misgivings he still had about Carrie working The Embalmer case, he had no qualms about her having his back. Ever. She'd give everything she had to protect someone on her team, just as she'd give everything she had to working a case.

He leaned forward. "What was the most challenging aspect for you? When you tried out for the SFPD SWAT, I mean."

"Physically?"

"Yes."

She blew her hair out of her eyes. "I suppose it was

the solid six foot wall we had to climb over to pass the physical exam. I couldn't do it at first. Wasn't sure if I ever could."

"But you did." Of course she had. He could picture her training, determination stamped on every inch of her face as she worked on overcoming anything that could be perceived as weakness on her part.

She nodded.

"And how did that make you feel?"

She didn't hesitate to answer. "Powerful."

Her answer didn't surprise him. He'd felt that same power on many occasions, too. It was part and parcel of being a cop. He could only imagine how intense that power would feel when you were talking about the kind of situations SWAT put you in. "So why'd you leave? You weren't feeling powerful anymore?"

She hesitated a few seconds before saying, "No. That wasn't it."

"Then why?" As he waited for her to answer, he couldn't help but feel a bit of dread. Deep down, he knew why she'd probably left.

She shrugged. "Let's just say that in the end, SWAT, especially SFPD SWAT, wasn't any more ready for female members than the military was."

Her answer confirmed what he'd thought. It made complete sense that her gender would have provoked others to challenge her. Still, the fact that she'd actually allowed that to influence her... "I never would've pegged you for a quitter. Not because someone was trying to run you off."

"Maybe that's because you're a man and it would be harder to run you off, right?"

"Is that a snippy retort meant to remind me that I'm a chauvinist or a hint of exactly how men tried to run you off?"

"It's neither, Jase," she said tiredly. "Come on. I thought we were trying to get to know each other better, not cut each other down. If that's what we're going to do, we might as well get back to work, don't you think?"

She had a point. "Fine. You asked me why I row. For the same feeling you felt when you got over that wall. To get past that moment when I don't think I can go on any longer. For that rush when I make it across the finish line. Knowing that, despite the struggle, I was strong enough, determined enough, to do it."

She lapsed into silence, teasing the rim of her glass with her finger, touching it in a soft, undulating circle that hypnotized him. She cleared her throat and looked up at him through her lashes. "You're certainly strong."

He quirked a brow at her, wondering if she was tipsy.

Then, unable to resist, he reached out and caressed the hand she'd rested on the table. Her skin was smooth and warm, yet tempered by a strength that was sexy as hell. "Yeah, but as you know, being good at a sport isn't necessarily about physical strength. It's about knowing your body. How to move it. How to reposition it in space. It's about creativity, learning to adapt and to reserve your energy for when it's most important." He lifted her hand and twined their fingers together.

Her eyes seemed to heat when he brought her hand to

his mouth and kissed it. "It's a whole body exercise. It's about being still when you have to. Moving when you have to. It's about overcoming your fears of the world."

His kissed her hand again, this time using his tongue to swipe at the tender valley between her thumb and index finger. He felt her pulse skitter against his fingers, making his own heartbeat skip.

WHEN THEY'D FIRST SAT DOWN for dinner, Carrie had thought she'd simply have to endure Jase's attempts to distract her from her troubles. Distraction had seemed impossible given everything she was dealing with. Death. Serial killers. A lawsuit. Her living room being torched.

Not to mention her attraction to Jase and his growing willingness to do something about it. Given everything else, however, she'd assumed their sexual chemistry would fade into the background.

It hadn't. Which simply proved how dangerous Jase was to her.

Even with her world falling apart, he had the uncanny ability to make her forget all the bad stuff and yearn for the simple pleasure of his company. His touch.

As Jase kissed her hand, Carrie had the feeling they were no longer talking about sports. His words and touch had started a throbbing in her body. The words slipped out before she could stop them. "You're so easygoing most of the time. You don't seem afraid of anything."

Jase's brows rose in surprise. "Everyone's afraid of something, Carrie. Especially me."

He trailed his fingers up and down her arm, the strokes getting progressively longer until he was caressing her from shoulder to wrist. His legs tangled with hers under the table, and she felt him nudge her legs apart with his foot.

She gasped. "What…what are you afraid of?"

He hesitated, looking at her with serious eyes that flashed first with tenderness, then with heat. "Let's just say I don't like leaving things undone. Personally or professionally."

Was he talking about her? Maybe. But she also knew that wasn't all of it. He'd dropped the mask he'd donned at Kelly Sorenson's murder scene a little, but not completely. It had been weighing on him all day. And for some reason, after drinking wine and talking with him tonight, she wasn't so reticent to ask him about it.

"So, Kelly Sorenson," she said softly as she smoothed her fingertips over his hand. "You and DeMarco talked to her. It would have been troubling for you to see her today. Is that what you mean about finishing things professionally? Things like that?"

He kept his gaze on her fingers as they trailed over his darker skin. "Yes. Justice is one of the most important ways to finish things, don't you think? And the fact that I met her?" He looked up now and met her gaze with his troubled one. "Yeah, it's weird. She was a stranger, but she had a pretty smile. A bold spirit. No matter what I think of the personal choices she made, she was living her life the way she wanted to, and as far as I can tell, she wasn't hurting anyone. She had a right to that life."

"Did it bother you? What Susan Ingram said? That if you'd left McGill's with Kelly she'd still be alive?"

"I can't blame myself for something like that. Just because a woman tried to pick me up in a bar doesn't mean I had any duty to take her up on what she was offering."

"No. You like a challenge too much for that, don't you?" She didn't mean the words to sound critical, but they did. Still, he took no offense.

He swept his hand up to her shoulder again and then cupped her nape. "I like *you,*" he said softly.

The simple words made her heart leap. They made her feel more powerful, more worthy, than she'd ever imagined. Given everything she'd accomplished in her life, it seemed silly that Jase "liking" her could matter so much. Didn't it?

Even as she struggled with how to respond, he massaged her neck with a strong grip, making her eyes close in ecstasy.

"Anything else I can get for you?"

Carrie's eyes popped open when the waitress stopped by their table. She looked amused and didn't wait for Jase or Carrie to say anything before placing the bill on the table.

Jase released her neck and hand, breaking the spell he'd cast over her. "Do you want more wine?"

She looked at the empty glass in front of her and

shook her head. He paid the bill, and they exited the restaurant. He put his hand on the small of her back as they walked to their cars.

The street was bustling. The night air should have been cool and comforting on her overheated skin. Instead, it acted as an unwanted jolt of reality. Jase had indeed succeeded in distracting her from her troubles, but now that dinner was over, she had things to do. She stopped and turned to him with a rueful smile. "I don't have anyplace to go, remember?" She reached for her cell phone. "Let me call some hotels—"

Jase placed a hand on her arm and she froze. "Come on, Carrie. Why don't you just stay with me?"

Why? There were so many reasons, and she struggled to remember every last one. "I already told you why."

"I won't push you into anything. I'm not going to touch you unless you damn well ask me to."

She believed him. Jase would never force himself on her. But that wasn't what she was afraid of. Despite her best intentions, she'd enjoyed the past hour. She wanted more. More distraction. More time with him. What she wanted would continue to grow if she let it.

And since she couldn't let it, she forced herself to say, "That's not going to happen."

"Then what's the problem?" he challenged her.

She cursed her pride. It was going to make things extremely uncomfortable for her. But she simply nodded. "Fine. I could stop by my place, but it'd be easier just to go to the store for a few things. A toothbrush.

Toiletries. That kind of thing. Unless, of course, you have a supply at your house for your women?"

She sounded snotty and she knew it. She also knew why—it was a last ditch effort to protect herself. By reminding herself of Jase's history with women, maybe she'd be able to prevent anything from happening between them. If nothing else, it would annoy him, right?

But instead of calling her on her obvious tactics, Jase simply said, "We'll stop by the store."

JASE'S HOUSE LOOKED exactly as she imagined it would.

Stylish. Orderly. Sleek modern lines. Superb taste yet utterly masculine. Comfortable.

When he tried to guide her toward the bedroom, she balked. "If you can just give me some sheets, I'll set up on the sofa," she said.

"I'm more of a gentleman than that. You'll take my bed."

She almost physically recoiled. She imagined all the women who'd been in this house before her. All the time they'd spent in Jase's arms. "I don't think so."

He crossed his arms over his chest and leaned against the door frame of his bedroom. "Is there a problem?"

"No problem," she lied. Then, egged on by the knowing look in his eyes, she said, "I'm not going to sleep in the same bed you've had sex in with countless women, Jase."

"No, you aren't," he readily agreed. "I've never had sex with a woman in this bed."

"Right." She drew out the word in patent disbelief.

"I'm serious. I moved into this place four months after I started at SIG. The job's been a priority for me, and as far as sleepovers go, I don't do them. Not here. I've always gone to the woman's place. Makes it easier if I get a call and need to leave. And by the way, since we're on the subject, I may be a serial dater, as you called me, but it doesn't mean I screw every woman I date. I'm a lot more discriminating than you seem to think."

It wasn't that she didn't think he was discriminating, but there were so many women who'd be attracted to him. Women who wouldn't be shy about making their interest known. What man would be able to resist that kind of attention? Especially a man who worked as hard as Jase did. He deserved his playtime without having to be judged for it. Even so, despite his reassurances, she knew sleeping in his bed, against the same sheets his body intimately touched night after night, would be dangerous to her peace of mind. "Still...I'm taking the sofa or I'm not staying."

Straightening, he shook his head. "Fine." He disappeared, then returned less than a minute later with folded sheets and a blanket, which he handed her. "You know, it wouldn't make you any less of a cop to acknowledge you're a woman sometimes."

"Meaning you only offered me your bed because I am one, right?" She covered the sofa with the linens.

"No. I offered because you're you, Carrie. And having you in my bed has been a fantasy for a long time.

I figured even if you were in it alone, it would be better than nothing."

She threw her hands up in exasperation before sitting down on her makeshift bed. "Jase, you have to stop. Please. I have so much to deal with right now. This case. My house being burned down. The lawsuit. I can't deal with you, too."

Quietly, he sat beside her. "The woman outside McGill's that night. She's the one who filed an unlawful death case against the department."

"Yes. But what does that—"

"You were upset that night. I mean, that's understandable, but why the panic attack? Can you tell me that?"

"Why? So you can report to Stevens again?"

"I won't repeat what you tell me."

"I'm just trying to deal with everything that's happened. It was bad enough before, but now, to have lost my house, my things…"

"You lost your photo albums," he acknowledged.

The photo albums he'd looked through. The ones that had informed him of her ridiculous middle name. They'd been important to her, but not as important as the knowledge that he'd been curious enough about her to look through them. Still, there had been other things she'd lost. Cards her mother and father had written to her. Small things. Personal things that proved she had a life outside her work.

"It's just stuff," Jase continued. "You're okay. That's

all that matters. God, when I think about what could have happened if you were at home…"

She wasn't surprised by his relief. If nothing else, they were friends. She knew that. It was only when she imagined herself meaning more to him that she doubted her own appeal. "Hey, it wouldn't have been all bad," she joked, instinctively pushing away the notion that they could be more than friends. She tried a smile. "You'd have gotten the lead on this case, after all."

"Don't! Don't even joke about something like that, Carrie. I was a big enough wreck when you'd been shot in the leg, even after I found out you were going to be okay. If anything worse happened to you…"

"Given our jobs, there's always the chance something worse is going to happen to me. To both of us."

"I know. And that's why I wish I didn't care so damn much about you, Carrie."

He kept saying that. Kept wanting to pull her closer to him. Why? What did he think it would accomplish? They didn't have a future together. His future was with the feminine, gorgeous women he dated, not a woman who wanted so badly to fit into a man's world. "You can't care about me, Jase. You don't really know me."

"I know enough. You fascinate me more than any woman I've ever known."

"That's because I'm different. I don't dress like your women. I don't talk like them. I probably don't even have sex like them. I'm a cop, Jase, that's what I am." Someday, that's how he'd see her again, and then he'd realize he wanted more.

He grabbed her arms. "Is that what you really think? That you're just a cop? Because you're so much more than that, Carrie. You look better than other women. You talk better than them. And I know damn well that if we ever got around to having sex, you'd—" Closing his eyes, he cursed softly. With what was obviously extreme effort, he released her and stepped back. "Look, you've had a hard day. I don't want to make it any harder for you. I need to let you go to sleep. Unless you need anything?"

I need so much, she thought. *I need you. But I can't have you.*

I can't. "No," she whispered. "I'm good. Thanks for letting me crash here."

"Anytime. Remember that. And remember this conversation is far from over. Good night, Carrie." He went back into his bedroom and lightly shut the door.

Carrie sighed and got ready for bed. Finally, she settled into the sofa. She thought about what he'd said about their conversation not being over. And she wondered why that statement made her feel just as happy as it did afraid. Within minutes, she dozed off.

Eventually, the nightmare came.

IN HER DREAM, CARRIE, dressed in dark clothes and camouflage, crept silently up to a house with the rest of her team. At her signal, DeMarco fired four tear-gas shells through the window, and Simon kicked in the door. Carrie and Jase followed close behind him, the light on their rifles penetrating the darkness, revealing plumes of smoke and shadows.

Her eyes strained to identify movement. Suddenly, she saw them. The Embalmer's first three victims covered in garish makeup. Then another stepped out of the shadows. Kelly Sorenson. Her body whole but weeping blood.

As Sorenson approached her, the shadows behind her moved. It was Sorenson's killer. The Embalmer. Or someone different? She didn't know, but she could see the whites of his eyes, his irises colorless in the dark. She tried to aim. Couldn't move. Why couldn't she fire? She watched the killer lift his gun. Saw the flash of his white teeth as he grinned. Tried to call out but couldn't.

She didn't hear the pop of the gun, but she saw the sudden flash from the muzzle as the killer shot each of the victims in the head. One by one, they dropped to the floor in front of her. She registered another flash in the dark and heard Jase scream behind her.

Before the shock could register, she felt heat explode in her chest, flinging her back and down so that she lay on her stomach, her face turned to the side.

Blood drained out of her, and she was paralyzed. Unable to look away from the carnage in front of her. Jase's body was in the distance, and she struggled to get to it. Kelly Sorenson was closer, her face tilted toward her.

Carrie could see her eyes. Lifeless, yet staring back at her.

She tried to scream, but her mouth was frozen in a wide yawning hole of silent despair. She heard the pounding of her heart slow. Slow. Slower still. Until there was no sound. No sight. Nothing.

Nothing but darkness.

And the inescapable knowledge that she'd failed.

Again.

CARRIE BOLTED UP, shaking and sweaty. Her breath came in such rapid pants that for a moment she felt close to hyperventilating. The scene, the emotions, had been so clear, so vivid in her mind, it took her a moment to realize where she was and that she'd been dreaming. The unfamiliar surroundings made her panic spiral out of control.

She scrambled for her gun, which she'd placed next to the sofa, and disengaged the safety. She swept it in an arc in front of her, scanning the room for movement. Nothing.

But then Jase barreled into the room, bare-chested and pajama bottoms hanging low on his hips, his own gun in his hands.

They stared at one another.

She forced herself to loosen her shaking grip on her gun and to take slow calming breaths. After a while, her breathing returned to normal and she engaged the safety on the gun before laying it back down. "Sorry. Bad dream." She covered her face in her hands, trying not to cry.

The nightmare had been different, but worse. It had magnified her failure to shoot Kevin Porter, but this time, instead of resulting in her own death, Jase and others had died. Was it prophetic? No. No way was she going to let anything happen to anyone else. Especially Jase.

"Carrie."

"I really need to be alone, Jase."

"I think that's the last thing you need right now." He sat beside her and lifted her chin. "Talk to me. Tell me what your dream was about."

"Death," she said tiredly. "My dreams are almost always about death."

"Whose death? Yours?"

She shook her head. "That's the worst part. It's never about *me* dying. It's about all the people I fail to save. Even—even the ones I've killed."

"You mean Kevin Porter, don't you? Damn it, Carrie, you know it was him or you. He didn't give you any choice."

"Logically, I know that. Logically, I know that I'm not responsible for Kelly Sorenson's death, either. But my dreams aren't about logic. They're about what I *feel*. I'll always feel like I should have done something different. Something more." She looked at him now. "Don't you ever feel that way?"

"Sometimes. Sometimes it's hard not to think that. But no one can beat death. All we can do is delay it, and we can't do it alone, not when others are working against us. So when logic eludes me and I start to feel hopeless or helpless, I focus on other things."

"Like what? Your women? Pleasure?" Far from sounding critical, she merely sounded skeptical. As much as it hurt her to think of him with other women, she couldn't begrudge him whatever solace and pleasure he could manage to attain in life. But neither could she quite understand how it actually worked for him.

"Sometimes grabbing pleasure when we can is the only way to survive the other stuff. What we do, it's so dark. You tease me about my women, but, yes, they're my way of trying to balance things out. To remember that there is beauty and pleasure in life, too."

"I don't believe there's as much beauty and pleasure in the world as you do, Jase."

"That can't be true. I've seen your house. You like to surround yourself with pretty things. You just need to accept that one of the beautiful things in the world is you."

"Don't," she said, voice clipped.

"Don't what? Don't call you beautiful?"

"I've seen the women you date. I can't compete."

"You're wrong. They're the ones that can't compete with you. But it's not a competition. It's just life. Trying to do as much good as you can but also not forgetting to take the pleasure you can, too."

"Pursuing pleasure is a luxury I can't afford right now."

"I have a feeling you've been telling yourself that for a while, haven't you?" He sighed and stood. "I'm sorry. We're talking in circles and you must be tired. Let me know if you need anything."

He smiled gently and turned to walk back into the bedroom. Panic wound through her. Suddenly, all her logic and arguments and defenses dropped away. All she knew was she couldn't stand for him to leave her. "I need *you*," she blurted out. "I want pleasure, Jase. I just—I just don't know how I can have it and do what I'm supposed to do, too."

He froze. When he turned back, he looked as stunned as she felt.

The longer he stared at her, the more she regretted her foolish words. "Never mind. I don't know why I said that. You're right. I *am* tired. I—"

He knelt down next to her and cradled her face in his hands. "You're a good cop, Carrie, but you're more than that. You have to *let* yourself be more than that. If you need me, you have me. I'm right here. If you want pleasure, I can give it to you. I *want* to give it to you."

"But it's not that easy," she said, her eyes growing moist. She blinked rapidly, commanding her tears away.

"How long has it been since you've allowed yourself to be pleased, Carrie?"

She averted her eyes. "I do things for myself all the time."

"Let's start with the most obvious answer. Sex."

Her breaths were escalated now, but hearing Jase mention sex made the air rush completely out of her lungs. "I'm not sure we should be discussing this—"

"How long?"

"Six years."

He didn't appear shocked by her answer, which irked her a little. Her first instinct was to ask how long it had been since he'd had sex, but she was afraid the answer would simply make her feel worse.

"Why so long?" he asked without a hint of judgment. "If nothing else, sex is usually a great stress reducer. It should be enjoyed. Freely given and freely accepted."

She pulled away and his hands dropped. "Nothing's free. Everything comes with strings attached."

"Sex shouldn't. And it wouldn't. Not between the two of us."

She stood. "Right. So you'd still respect me as a cop once you'd had me naked and under you? Once you'd been inside me? You wouldn't think maybe it gave you rights? To protect me? To tell me what to do, on the job and in the bedroom?"

Jase rose slowly. "Is that what other men you've been with have done? Slept with you and then started bossing you around?"

"With me and men? It always becomes a power play, with them needing to prove they know best and can teach me a thing or two whether I want to be taught or not."

"Slow down. Are we talking about a man trying to dominate you in bed or out?"

"There never seemed to be a difference, in my experience."

"Then you need more experience."

"Says the voice of experience," she said drily.

Jase shrugged. "Like I said before, I'm more discriminating than you give me credit for, but I certainly haven't been abstaining for six years. One thing's for sure, who we are at work won't have anything to do with who we are in bed together."

"That's certainly true given we're not going to be in bed together. I'm comfortable right here on this sofa."

"You sleeping on my sofa is the safe thing, but it's not what either of us really wants, is it? But I have to admit, this whole conversation has me a little confused about what you'd really want in bed. I don't mind a woman who's assertive in bed and takes what she wants. It doesn't threaten me to be with a strong woman. Does it threaten you to be with a strong man?"

He was watching her carefully. So she chose her words just as carefully. "This conversation is going in circles. Men who use their strength, whether in bed or out, tend to use it to get what they want, not to give others what they want."

Fury, then something that looked perilously close to pity flashed across Jase's face. "I think I'm beginning to understand. And I'm not liking what you're implying. Have men hurt you in bed, Carrie? Have they used their strength to take what they want whether it was something you wanted or not? Have you been raped?"

Carrie's head was spinning. She couldn't actually recall how they'd gotten on this topic. One minute they'd been talking about pleasure coming with strings, and the next...

She crossed her arms over her chest and looked around, but there didn't appear to be a handy escape route in sight. Besides, where would she go? She didn't have a home to go to right now, and Jase's bedroom certainly wouldn't be a good idea. "I'm not having this conversation, Jase."

His jaw tightened. "And that's quite an answer. Who was it?"

"Let's not go there." *Please,* she thought. *Not there. I don't want you to pity me. I don't want you to see me that way. A woman pretending to be strong because all she's ever been is weak.*

"Go where? Into the personal? The uncomfortable? Fuck that. I want you to answer my question. Have you been raped?"

It was the second word he'd uttered that night that shocked her. The first, because it had made her picture the two of them together. Naked and intimate. This one because it made her picture herself naked. Vulnerable. Unworthy. Indeed, she was nothing like the women Jase normally dated. It was best that he accepted that once and for all. She faced him head-on. "Yes. I have. Are you satisfied now?"

He didn't dignify her question with an answer. Instead, he turned away from her and strode to the window where he clasped the frame so hard his knuckles turned white.

Warily, she watched him. Watched his back heave as he struggled for control. Watched as he wrestled with what she knew would be feelings of anger and helplessness. Yes, Jase was a good cop. He'd be outraged by the idea of any woman being assaulted. But as he'd been telling her, as she now accepted on every level, he did care for her. She wasn't sure why and she wasn't sure how deep those feelings ran, but she knew he was hurting for her. And that made her hurt for him.

"Jase, it's okay—"

He whirled around and pointed his finger at her. "It is not okay. Don't ever try to pretend what happened to you was okay."

"I didn't mean that. I just meant... It was a long time ago," she said. "But it taught me an important lesson. Men might like strong women, but not when they're afraid the woman is stronger. Not when they feel threatened. When most men are threatened, they think they have something to prove, however they can prove it."

"Who was he?" He didn't move any closer. Did he doubt his ability to remain distant? Was he afraid to reach out to her now that he knew what had happened to her?

"Why does it matter?"

"It just does."

She hesitated. Giving Jase too much information was a bad idea. They were working a difficult case right now. The last thing she wanted was for him to get distracted by thoughts of avenging her, but she also knew he wouldn't let things go until she gave him some kind of answer. "A college boyfriend. But there've been men since him who've walked the line. And I've decided I'm sick of walking that line. I'd just as soon pleasure myself, if you get what I mean."

"Oh, I get what you mean in spades. And I understand why you would think that way. But do you really think I'd ever use my strength to hurt you? To do anything that you don't want, in bed or out?"

"No. I don't think that, Jase."

He closed his eyes in relief. "Thank God."

She couldn't stand the distance between them anymore. She moved closer. Closer. Until she was right in front him. Until she could place her hand on his shoulder.

That's when she noticed he was shaking. "Jase?"

He pulled her toward him and buried his face in her neck. The arms he wrapped around her felt desperate, but they made her feel safe. Loved.

This strong man cared so much about her that he was shaking over something that had happened to her years ago. She stroked his hair. "Shh. I'm okay, Jase."

He was quiet for a long time. So quiet that she pulled back and cupped his face, making him look into her eyes. "I'm okay, Jase," she whispered. "You—you make me feel okay. You make me feel like I can be strong and less than strong, too." It was true, she thought. She'd exposed her weakest self to this man yet he made her feel far from weak. She felt worthy. Worthy because he cared for her. Wanted to protect and pleasure her.

And she wanted him to, she realized.

Now. This very moment.

Tentatively, she touched her finger to his mouth. Instantly his eyes flared with desire. "We got off track here, Jase. I—I said I need you, remember? And you said you were here for me. Has what I told you changed that?"

He frowned. "Of course not, but what you've told me—"

"What I told you is my past, Jase. The future can bring something else. Pleasure. No strings attached. If it's what you want, too."

Staring at her, he didn't smile. He didn't joke. He didn't reassure her. Not with words. Instead, he studied her expression, looking for any sign of hesitation or fear on her part. Finding none, he reached down, took her hand and led her into his bedroom.

CHAPTER THIRTEEN

JASE HAD NEVER BEEN so conflicted about bedding a woman before. Conflicted, hell. He was scared out of his mind right now.

What she'd told him hadn't changed his feelings for her—he still wanted her more than he'd ever wanted a woman—but it did make him uncertain about how to proceed. The last thing he wanted was to scare her or bring back bad memories.

He wasn't surprised to learn what she'd gone through. With her military and police background, Carrie would have met and attracted a lot of men who would have been equally drawn to and repulsed by her strength. That a man had crossed the line to prove his power to her didn't surprise him, especially because it had happened when she was in college. She would have been young and still trying to figure out her place in the world.

She couldn't have known that her place in the world was right here with him.

God, she'd been raped. Carrie. His strong, tough, passionate Carrie had been violated in a way that made him want to kill someone. At the same time, it made him want to sweep her into his arms and carry her away someplace safe, where danger and pain could never touch her.

But that could never happen. Darkness and pain were parts of Carrie's life the same way they were his. Plus, she'd hate him for trying to protect her. For seeing her as less than capable of protecting herself.

So he'd take what she'd offered. The chance to show her that while she was strong, she could be more—and less—than that, too. He could admire her for being the cop, but he could offer the woman something, as well. Pleasure. With no strings attached. Just as he'd told her.

As they stopped in front of his bed, Jase thanked God that he didn't fold easily under pressure. As much as he wanted to savor the pleasure of being with Carrie, he knew something momentous was on the line here. He wasn't just about to please a woman sexually, he was going to solidify or destroy her preconceived notions about men and their inability to handle a woman that was strong yet vulnerable, feminine yet tough.

Jase wouldn't have a problem with her strength in bed. He wanted her to take what she wanted, especially if what she wanted was him. The question was, how was *he* going to proceed tonight?

The only answer he could think of? He'd proceed exactly how Carrie wanted to proceed. Whatever she needed from him, he would give her. But she'd have to be the one to decide exactly what it was she wanted from him. All he knew was that he wanted her.

He'd take her however he could get her.

CARRIE WASN'T SURE if she was about to make the biggest mistake of her life or if she was finally being brave enough to reach out for what she'd wanted for so long but had been too afraid to take. To distract herself, she looked around Jase's bedroom, liking the clean lines and simplicity of it. It was like him—attractive and compelling without too much effort, yet the effort was there. Things matched. Reflected care and good taste. But nothing was overblown or garish. His private space showed he took care of himself and enjoyed the finer things in life but that he was a man of substance, too.

Once again, she wondered what she was doing here. Why he even wanted her. She wasn't like the fine things he filled his life with. The expensive tailored suits. The hundred-dollar haircuts. The expensive bottle of wine he'd ordered at dinner. She was more common. Simpler. Plainer. She was vanilla ice cream to his dulce de leche gelato. She was steak and potatoes to his filet mignon and lobster bisque. She was ugly and unfeminine compared to the beautiful women he dated. Beautiful women like Kelly Sorenson. At least, she'd been beautiful, before a killer had gotten to her.

The reminder of the job they had waiting for them in the morning had her frowning. He'd said it was important to look for beauty and pleasure when they could, not in spite of the job they did but because of it even, but it didn't seem right, reaching out for pleasure when there was such dark, horrible stuff happening in the world. When there were boys like Kevin Porter that were being shot by cops like her and leaving their grandmothers to grieve and—

"Shh," Jase whispered as he framed her face in his big hands again. "I can tell your mind's going a million miles per minute. Come back to me, Carrie. Stay with me."

She shook her head. "We have to work tomorrow, Jase. Kelly Sorenson—"

"Kelly Sorenson is dead. We're going to do everything we can to find her killer, but the fact remains, we're alive, Carrie. Here. Now. Whatever we do, no matter how thoroughly we dedicate ourselves to helping victims of crime, we can't lose ourselves in the process. We have to live our lives, too. So let me help you live. Let me help you feel alive. Let me give you pleasure with no strings attached."

She stared at him, wondering if this was really happening. Could he be the man to finally give her pleasure and really not expect anything from her in return? Not expect her to bow down to his masculinity afterward? Not expect her to diminish her strength in order to pave the way for his own ego?

Yes, she realized. Jase could be that man. He was good. A good cop. From everything she'd heard and witnessed, he was popular with the ladies and obviously a good lover. He didn't have anything to prove. Not through her. He was already secure in his life. In who he was. Maybe that's what had drawn her to him all along.

"Do you have protection?"

"Nightstand."

With a sigh, she put her arms around his neck. He wore nothing but the baggy pair of pajama pants, and through the thin material of her T-shirt, she felt her hardened nipples drilling into the hard muscles of his chest. She rubbed herself against him, trying to ease the ache that had insinuated itself into all her nooks and crannies, but she couldn't seem to get close enough. Even with his hard shaft pushing against her through the thin material of their pajama bottoms, it wasn't enough. She needed all the barriers between them to be gone. Now.

Wrenching away, she swiftly pulled her T-shirt off her head then pushed down her pants and panties in one fell swoop. His eyes devoured her, traveling over her breasts and lower body with a searing gaze that lasered into her and made her feel all warm and gooey inside, like honey simmering over an open flame.

Holding his gaze with her own, she reached out and pushed down his pants and boxers, as well. As soon as his shaft sprang free, she encircled it with her fingers. He groaned but kept his hands loose and at his sides, as if he was at her command, willing for her to do with him what she wanted.

But his eyes, heavy-lidded and drowsy, burning with the fire of a thousand suns, blazed into hers and made her feel as if she was the helpless one. The one under his command.

"You said you wouldn't have a problem with me... taking over. That still the case?"

He smirked and finally lifted his hand to caress her cheek. "Take all you want," he said hoarsely.

She laughed and pushed him so that he sprawled back onto the bed. Swiftly, she retrieved the box of condoms from the nightstand. Then she climbed on top of him, took what she wanted and relished the knowledge that it was exactly what he wanted, too.

SHE MIGHT NOT HAVE had sex for six years, but Carrie was far from out of practice. At least, that's how it seemed to him. Lying flat on his back, he marveled at her graceful movements as she kissed his throat and chest, working her way down his body with flattering enthusiasm. She hadn't kissed him on the lips yet, something he hadn't missed and wasn't about to let her get away with, but for now...

He hissed when she enveloped him. His flesh felt scalded by the wet heat of her mouth and for a moment he closed his eyes to savor it. But he didn't keep his eyes closed for long. He couldn't. He wanted to imprint the image of his fingers tangled in Carrie's glorious red hair on his mind forever. Her body was pale but sleekly muscled, with a solidness that was absent from most fashionably thin women today, but he liked the differences he saw in her. It made her seem more real somehow. Made him feel confident that she could take anything that he dished out and still have enough left over to dish some out, as well. Even though right now he was having doubts about how much more he could handle.

Jase wasn't ashamed to admit he loved being the focus of a woman's intimate attention, probably more so than even the average guy, who he was sure loved it plenty. And Carrie seemed to be born for this particular task. She moaned as if the taste and feel of him in her mouth gave her just as much pleasure as it gave him, and if that was anywhere close to being true, he was glad.

Obviously, she'd made her choice. Playing the submissive wasn't in the cards for her today. So Jase tamped down on his very strong desire to flip her on her back and show her exactly what he could do with his mouth, too. It had nothing to do with competition but rather with wanting to give her so much pleasure that she couldn't help coming back for more. And more and more. Until not a day went past that they didn't touch each other and pleasure each other with a mind-blowing intensity despite the darkness of their jobs.

She increased the suction, and her tongue lingered against a particularly sensitive spot on the bottom of his shaft, causing him to hiss and punch his hips upward. She peered up at him, her gaze hot and intense, filled with satisfaction at the pleasure she was giving him.

"I'm supposed to be pleasing you," he gritted out, not exactly in protest but to communicate he hadn't forgotten.

She swirled her tongue around the head of him, then straightened and moved over his thighs, straddling him and rubbing her wet core against him. "You are. This is pleasing me. This is what I want. No strings attached, right?"

He folded his hands behind his head in order to stop himself from reaching out to her, then thought, what the hell. Just because she was on top didn't mean that he had to be completely passive. While she slid a condom on him, he cupped her breasts then circled his palms against her pointed nipples. She moaned and closed her eyes, arching forward for more of his touch. Unable to resist, he craned his neck up and sucked a nipple into his mouth. She tasted damn delicious, so he stayed there for some time. Sucking. Licking. Nibbling. Then moved on to the other nipple as she cradled his head in her hands. He was so immersed in what he was doing that he barely noticed that she'd shifted.

He shouted and fell back as she took him to the hilt. His fingers clasped her hips and flexed, struggling not to immediately lift her up and slam her back down. This was her ride, he reminded himself. Her show. Whatever she wanted for her own pleasure, not for his. But he knew they were one and the same. Anything that pleased her would inevitably please him, as well.

She stayed still for several minutes while he throbbed inside her. Her eyes were closed, her brow furrowed in concentration, as if she was trying to absorb every flutter of sensation she was feeling. Finally, without opening her eyes, she began to move. She lifted herself up, slowly, until he almost slipped out of her altogether. Then, with a desperate whimper and a bite of her lip, she sank down on him again, slowly again, so slowly.

She repeated the torturous, motions several times, until Jase was clawing at the bedsheets and grinding his teeth to keep from begging her to take him harder. Faster.

She was so glorious. Beautiful. Powerful.

And he happily relinquished himself to that power. His time would come later. At least, he hoped and prayed she'd trust him enough to give him that.

For a second, the memory of their conversation came to him, including her confession that she'd been raped. He felt the punch of anger again. Regret. He wished he could take every ounce of pain she'd suffered and make it disappear as if it had never happened, yet he knew her past had formed who she was today.

A sexy, amazing woman who didn't realize the joy she brought others.

The joy she brought him.

As if she read his mind, her eyes flew open and locked with his. Jase sucked in a breath at all the pleasure and delight he saw reflected in their blue depths. Her hips began to retreat and return with more speed and more force than before, shooting sensation up his legs and down his spine to gather inside the flesh that was so happily buried inside her. Even as she embraced the pleasure, Jase felt a moment's hesitation.

Hell, what was he thinking? Sex with Carrie was something he'd wanted for a long time, but did he honestly think her place was with him? Not just here in bed, for the here and now, but forever? Hadn't he always told himself that he couldn't handle that, being with a woman as strong-willed and passionate as Carrie, one who would constantly challenge him?

That's what he told himself, he acknowledged, but with her on top of him, with him inside her, with the memory of how well they'd worked together and fought together these past few days, he couldn't remember why he'd ever considered Carrie challenging him for the rest of his life a bad thing.

It could only give him pleasure. As much pleasure as she was giving him now. Even more, so long as he knew she was truly his for the rest of their lives.

Her thrusting hips picked up speed right along with their breaths. Her palms were flattened on his chest, her fingers brushing his nipples as her hips shuttled back and forth over him. In and out. Hot and hotter. Wet and wetter. Everything taking on more intensity and more vibrancy the longer she moved. Until each individual sensation began to tangle with the other, winding itself into a bigger and bigger mass that soon became too huge for their bodies to contain.

Jase doubted he'd ever felt this much pleasure before. And as Carrie began to moan and shudder with the strength of her climax, he knew the same was true for her.

ALL CARRIE'S FOCUS had been on the feel of Jase's body inside hers and the ecstatic expression on his face as she'd ridden him. From those things alone, she'd derived more pleasure than she ever had. That's why, when her body suddenly exploded with pulses of intense pleasure that just kept building and building, it took her a second to realize she was actually having an orgasm.

And Jase had hardly done a thing. He'd held himself beneath her, allowed her to take the lead and except for when he'd suckled her breasts, he hadn't even touched her. And yet here she was having the most intense climax of her life.

And the longest.

It kept going and going, giving no signs of waning. His hips pulsed against hers, and she realized he was somehow keeping the sensations going, proving to her that he wasn't passive at all but guiding her toward the ultimate pleasure with ease.

"Jase. No more," she finally gasped when the feelings became too intense. He immediately stilled and caressed her back while she came down from the heights to which he'd flung her. As she did, however, she realized that while she'd climaxed, he hadn't. He was still thick and hard inside her, and holding himself ruthlessly still.

Did he think he was going to give her amazing pleasure and take none for himself?

She wasn't about to let that happen.

She clenched her internal muscles around him. Surprise flickered across his face an instant before he groaned. Planting her palms on his chest to steady herself, she began to move. Slowly but surely. Easing him out of her body a fraction of a time before pushing him back inside. His hands found her hips, guiding her, increasing her speed until the sound of their flesh meeting echoed like a drum. Jase kept his gaze on hers, refusing to look away, letting her see every second of pleasure she was giving him. When those beautiful eyes of his finally shut, she knew he was close. She dragged his hands to her breasts and whispered, "Now, Jase. Come for me."

The hands that gently cupped her were a sharp contrast to the frantic movements of their hips and the grimace of pleasure-pain on his face. With a final, urgent thrust of his hips, Jase exploded. He shouted out his release, gloriously uninhibited and so sexy she couldn't take her eyes off him.

It took him a few seconds to open his eyes. When he did, he pushed back her damp hair and smiled. His satisfied expression sent a sharp echo of the joy she'd experienced zinging through her.

"Kiss me," he said.

Instinctively, she wasn't even sure why, she shook her head. She'd kissed him before. Had enjoyed it. Why wouldn't she kiss him now? But something about the painfully full feeling in her chest told her that if she kissed him, it would be too strong an intimacy and would cause her protective shell to explode, leaving every part of her vulnerable and bare. She trusted him, but that didn't matter. She'd never shown anyone all of herself. She never would.

But apparently Jase wasn't happy with that plan.

With his eyes narrowing, he suddenly flipped her over. The next thing she knew, she was pinned underneath him, with her wrists bracketed in one of his hands and held over her head. He was still inside her, his hips resting heavily within the cradle of her splayed thighs.

"Kiss me," he ordered again. "Now."

She trembled at the dominance in his voice and was certain he didn't miss her reaction. She forced herself to lift a brow. "Or?"

He leaned down until his nose touched hers. "Or I'll make you come again, and I won't ease off this time no matter how much you beg."

She couldn't help herself. She smiled tauntingly at him. "Really? Considering I already came and that was a major feat in and of itself, I'd say you have a pretty tough job in front of you."

He smiled a fierce smile that had her shivering with nerves. "That's what I was hoping you would say."

CHAPTER FOURTEEN

BRAD STARED AT THE BOXES littering the small apartment he rented. It was a ridiculous way to live, and the twin mattress on the floor wasn't exactly luxury accommodations. But it wasn't as if he'd had a lot of options in the matter.

It had taken all the money he'd been able to scrape together to move to San Francisco, but he'd truly believed it would be worth it. After all, he had *family* here. Plus, he'd been picked on his whole life. He wasn't going to let Dr. Odell Bowers get away with what he'd done.

Deceiving Brad. Lying to him. Bilking him of all his money.

And that didn't even take into account all the physical pain Brad had suffered over the years. Because of *him*.

That, more than anything, required payback.

The question was, knowing what he now knew, what type of payment was Brad going to extract?

Money was always good, and the good doctor had more than enough of that to go around.

A little suffering would be nice, too, of course. Very

nice. For once, Brad wouldn't be the worm writhing on the hook, someone else would.

And then there was always good old-fashioned gloating. If there was one thing Dr. Bowers had more than his fair share of, it was pride. He thought he was so damn superior. So smart.

Yet Brad had put all the pieces of the puzzle together within minutes.

Bowers had been his doctor for years. His sole task: to rid Brad of the port-wine stain that had plagued him his entire life. The damn doctor actually thought he'd been successful, when Brad knew the difference. At first, Brad had thought he'd been the crazy one, seeing a deformity when it was no longer there. But then he'd heard someone talking in McGill's Bar. Someone talking about the serial killer who cut the eyelids from his victims.

Brad had immediately thought of Dr. Odell Bowers and the various horror movies they'd discussed over the years. Bowers's favorite had been a movie about a killer who cut the eyelids off his victims. It had been a detail too unique to ignore.

Of course, he'd figured it was a weird coincidence. It certainly didn't prove Bowers was a killer. Not by itself. Then Brad had overheard two other details. That the killer performed some type of "beautifying" procedure on his victims afterward. And that the killer had started his work in Fresno before moving on to San Francisco.

Bowers had moved his practice from Fresno to San Francisco.

And Bowers was a doctor who helped improve the looks of his clients. At least, that's what he was *supposed* to do.

Brad might be hideously ugly, but he wasn't stupid. He knew how to put two and two together, and this case, two and two equaled Bowers.

It was Bowers who was crazy, not him.

Bowers who saw a scar that was gone, when it really wasn't.

And in the end, although he hadn't done the job the way he was supposed to, Bowers would still be the one to help Brad rid himself of his deformity. Because it had been Bowers who'd motivated Brad to approach Kelly Sorenson. And then to kill her.

Now Brad had all the information and the power he needed. With it, he would not only get everything he'd ever wanted, he'd get more than he'd ever imagined was possible.

And whatever form of payment Brad extracted from Odell Bowers, one thing was certain.

Brad was going to make sure he witnessed, acknowledged and spread the news that it was Brad who had the power now. Then Brad would find his next victim.

No, not his next victim, he thought. His next donor.

The word victim implied Brad was taking something he had no right to. That wasn't the case. Did the lion victimize the gazelle?

No, the gazelle had its place in the world. Its place was to feed the lion.

Just as Brad's donors had their place.

To give Brad the power and beauty they were too weak to keep for themselves.

To give him the means to have Nora.

CHAPTER FIFTEEN

WHEN JASE WOKE IN the morning, he wasn't surprised to find himself alone in his big bed. He didn't bother calling out Carrie's name, either. She wasn't in the house. He suspected she'd hightailed it out a while ago and was now in full-on denial mode.

The question was whether he was going to let her stay in it.

Truth be told, after their explosive night together, he was feeling shell-shocked enough to think that some denial could be a very good thing. He'd known bedding Carrie would be a momentous experience, but he couldn't have known just how earth-shattering it would be. Once again, thoughts of a future with her kept intruding, and it was enough to scare the shit out of him.

Though he wasn't the player everyone, including Carrie, thought he was, he definitely valued his freedom and had always savored the variety of women he dated and bedded. In addition, he truly appreciated the benefits of simplicity when he was off the job. Sure, he'd enjoyed the past few days he'd spent with Carrie, and that included their circling and sparring, but he couldn't be sure it wasn't just a fluke and that Carrie's combative nature wouldn't grow tiresome as more and more time passed.

He had to tread very carefully here, not just for himself, but for Carrie, too.

Though Carrie hadn't let him completely inside her emotional walls, and certainly hadn't declared her undying love for him or demanded any kind of commitment, the fact that she'd slept with him wasn't something that he could take lightly, either. Hell, the fact that he was her first lover in six years was meaningful enough, but given what he knew about her, that she'd been raped, that she had major trust issues when it came to men finding her attractive in spite of her strength, he knew the chances that she felt something for him besides just sexual attraction were high. What bothered him most, however, was how pleased he was by the thought. And how much he wanted her to ask for a commitment from him.

Thoughtfully, he rubbed his jaw, then got up and got ready for work. When he went out to the living room, he found a note on the kitchen counter. *Gone shopping and have several appointments this morning but I'll catch up with you afterward. Carrie.*

Well, that was right to the point, wasn't it? No smiley faces, hearts or even a "love" in the signature line to make him believe she viewed last night as anything more than having scratched a much-needed itch. So he'd play along for now. At least until he got things straightened out in his own head.

He called her cell phone.

"Hi, Jase. What's up?" she asked softly.

Hearing her voice immediately had him recalling how she'd sounded when he'd been on top of her and making her beg, just as he'd promised she would.

Jase, please. Stop. Don't stop. That feels so good. That feels amazing.

He closed his eyes and replayed the moment he'd finally relented and let her come down from her release, but only because he'd been about to explode himself and he'd wanted her to be looking at him when he did. Despite his heated thoughts, his voice was measured and calm when he spoke.

"Have you heard anything about the firebombing on your house?"

"SFPD picked up some suspects. They claim they've never met Kevin Porter. But they're verified as being with the same gang, so that's not likely."

"You said you need to go shopping? Anything I can get you?"

"Thanks, but I just need some clothes to get me through the next couple of weeks. I've contacted my insurance company, but I'm not going to worry about anything but the case for right now. I can't."

Message received, Jase thought. Loud and clear. "Speaking of the case," he said. "Have you gotten any results on the legwork we've done so far?"

"As far as tracking down embalming supply purchases, nothing. As far as tracking down a privately operated kiln or unlawful access to a crematorium, also nothing," Carrie said. "But I did discover that having a body cremated is no easy task. Although it would take only a few hours for the actual process to be completed, we're talking something whose temperature can get as high as 1100 to 1800 degrees. That would require a massive amount of gas that would be trackable through the energy companies, but that's turned up no clues, as well. In addition, having a body cremated by a licensed professional requires the submission of a variety of forms, some signed by various doctors confirming the victim's cause of the death and providing authorization for the cremation."

"So if it's so hard to actually cremate a body, maybe he's lying about that," Jase said.

"I had the same thought. He might be lying about the embalming process, too. All we have are some photographs and The Embalmer's word." She hesitated and he knew immediately what she was thinking.

"You think the photos were doctored?" he asked. It was a definite possibility, but they couldn't make any assumptions.

"For all we know, the ashes that had been found with the testable items of victim DNA weren't actually the victim's ashes. We can't know for sure because it's impossible to run DNA tests on ashes. Given all that, I think our best bet for now is focusing on the college connection between Cheryl Anderson and Kelly Sorenson."

She was right. They'd still have to explore the cremation angle, but the common connection between the victims was their strongest chance of finding their killer.

"I'll work on contacting witnesses from McGill's. I haven't reached DeMarco yet…."

"The commander said he had a family emergency, but it's weird we can't reach him on his cell."

It *was* weird and some of the concern he heard in her voice poked at him. Still, DeMarco could handle himself and there was no point in worrying. "I'm sure it's nothing. We should also start questioning witnesses at the college. See if we can find another connection between our vics that maybe Susan Ingram doesn't know about or maybe wasn't copping to. What are you doing after your appointment? Should I meet you at SIG?"

"Why don't you get started with interviews on campus, focusing on anyone who knew Kelly Sorenson, and I'll meet you there as soon as I can. I'll focus on questioning witnesses who knew Cheryl Anderson."

"Okay." He almost hung up, but with the vibrant images of their lovemaking still in his head, he impulsively said, "Carrie, last night—"

"Was a mistake, Jase," she said in a rush. "A big one. I mean, it was fun, getting to experience your brand of magic firsthand, but we work together. It can't happen again."

He wasn't in the least surprised by her words. By the fact she was not only in denial, but in retreat mode. She had to be feeling as shaken up as he was, wanting to put things back the way they were, with each of them in their respective corners and a safe, respectable distance away. He'd let her get away with it for now, but he wasn't going to lie to her, either. "I disagree with you, but it's obviously your call."

"That's it?" she asked suspiciously. "No trying to change my mind? It must not have been that great for you, after all."

He looked at the phone chidingly, as if she could really see his expression. "Oh, it was damn good for me and you know it. The best. I just know better than to try and argue with you."

"That's never stopped you before."

"True." He leaned back against the counter and took a sip of his freshly poured coffee. "But I said it's your call. I never said I wouldn't do all I could to change your mind."

She didn't seem to have a comeback for that, so he said a quiet goodbye and hung up.

DESPITE HER BEST intentions, when Carrie disconnected the call with Jase, she was smiling.

I said it's your call. I never said I wouldn't do all I could to change your mind.

That was the Jase she knew and loved.

She stumbled at her unfortunate choice in words. She loved what she'd done to him last night. She'd loved what he'd done to her. But she didn't love Jase. She couldn't.

So why did it feel as if she did?

Thirty minutes later, she walked into Dr. Lana Hudson's office at the SFPD. She'd thought she'd had her last appointment with Lana before she'd returned to

SIG, but Lana had left a voice mail for her yesterday asking to see her again. Carrie assumed it was just a follow-up to check in with her now that she'd returned to work, and that's exactly what it was. Of course, Lana also knew other things were adding to Carrie's stress since she'd returned to work, and Lana had homed in on those like a vulture tearing into fresh meat. Well, with a little more class than that, Carrie thought wryly. Lana was so pretty that the vulture analogy wasn't all that appropriate.

They spent most of their time talking about Martha Porter's lawsuit, in which she claimed Carrie had unjustifiably killed her grandson, but then Lana got down to the heart of the matter.

"You've got a lot going on, Carrie. More so than you did before with this lawsuit and your house burning down. I'm afraid it's too much. I'm glad Stevens has you working with Jase, but you've always had a bit of a contentious relationship with him."

Carrie thought about all that had transpired between them. In bed and out. They actually worked fabulously together, and she wasn't just talking about the sex. She was learning a lot from Jase and couldn't deny it had been a good move on Stevens's part to team them up.

"Don't worry, Lana. Nothing will get in the way of the job, I promise. I feel confident. Strong. Jase and I are making inroads with a difficult case. We'll get this guy."

"Sure. Getting the bad guy. That always comes first, right?" Her last words were almost bitter, and Carrie wondered why. For a brief moment, she thought of Simon Granger, fellow SIG agent and now acting supervisor while Mac was on vacation. Simon and Lana had dated for a while, just before Simon had taken a desk job at SFPD, but the day Simon had unexpectedly returned to SIG appeared to be the day their developing relationship had ended. Was it Simon's inability to let go of his job as a special agent that was the cause of their split? The cause of the bitterness in Lana's tone?

Carrie suspected it was. She didn't know much about Lana, but she did know the doctor was a widow and that her husband had served in the military. Two years after his death, Lana still wore her wedding ring. It would be perfectly understandable for her to resist dating yet another man who had a better than average chance of getting killed on the job.

Was Lana right? Did the job always come first? For Carrie, it had always seemed to. She had never thought there'd come a time when it didn't. But now? Now she wasn't so sure.

She knew she had no business asking, but she did anyway. "Would you change that? If you could? If you had the power to make Simon leave the job, would you?"

Lana inhaled sharply. No surprise given how Carrie had turned the tables, but the other woman didn't try to deny anything. "Honestly? I don't know. I know why he's a cop. It's who he is. Who he has to be. I can't ask him to give it up. But does a small part of me wish he loved me enough to do so? Of course. And that's the rub. It is what it is."

Acceptance radiated from her, making Carrie's heart ache. Love never seemed to work out the way it should. Especially not for cops. And it seemed to be true whether that cop was a man or a woman, which actually didn't make her feel any better about it.

"What about you, Carrie? Would you give up the job? If it meant you could be with the person you loved most?"

It was Carrie's turn to be stunned as her thoughts automatically turned to Jase. Once again, she asked herself the question: Did she love Jase? More to the point, would she give up her job for him? She'd have expected her answer to be a resounding no. Was slightly appalled that it wasn't. It was more like a soft no, but a reluctant one. A tenuous one. But like Lana had said, it wasn't that simple. "You're right. It's not an easy answer," she said. "I shouldn't have pried." She stood again. "Thank you for being concerned about me, Lana, but I need to go."

"Carrie—" Lana began.

But Carrie didn't wait to hear more. She walked from Lana's office, but inside she was running. She wasn't exactly sure why. Her conversation with Lana had merely confirmed what she'd already known. What she'd reminded herself time and again. When you were a cop, there wasn't room for softer emotions like love. There wasn't much room for anything. Not if you wanted to truly be good at your job. Not if bringing justice to victims and catching the bad guys was to be your number one priority.

CHAPTER SIXTEEN

BRAD WATCHED AS Tony Higgs and Nora Lopez exited the café and walked to her car. He'd been watching the two of them for weeks. He'd seen the way Tony toyed with the girl who clearly adored him and then mocked her when his friends showed up. Brad was quite familiar with those mocking glances himself. Had been privy to them all his life. Tony and his friends hadn't tried to hide their disdain for him. As if he was some freak who didn't deserve to breathe the same air as they did.

He wished he could take care of all of them. Line them up execution style and watch the horror on their faces when he pulled out his knife and began slicing their perfect faces to pieces. First his slutty girlfriend who liked to parade around in short outfits. Then his friend who looked like he feasted on steroids for breakfast. And then the cocky asshole who got off on using and abusing poor little girls who didn't know better.

But of course he wouldn't. That would ruin his plan. He needed to be smart.

As smart as he had been. As ruthless as he had been.

Things were finally making sense, going his way, turning out the way they should.

He could feel the difference in himself. The inner transformation that was taking place along with the physical one.

He wasn't going to let anything, not pride, not impatience, not jealousy or fear, get in his way.

He wiped down the table that Tony and Nora had vacated. The glass of chai tea Nora had been drinking was half empty. Brad picked it up and pressed his lips against the rim, imagining that he touched the exact spot she'd drunk from.

He'd always felt comfortable talking to Nora. But in the past few days, he'd started talking to his other customers, too. And they'd been responding well. As if he were one of them. As if he were normal. He liked it. Deserved it. Wanted more of it.

Soon, he'd have the nerve to ask Nora out. She'd look at him with the same adoring eyes she normally reserved for Tony, but unlike him, he'd return that affection. He wouldn't hurt her or laugh at her the way Tony did. And he'd make her see what she'd been too blind to see before.

That they were destined to be together.

BY THE TIME CARRIE MET up with Jase at Sequoia College, he'd interviewed almost twenty people in his hunt to find a link between Cheryl Anderson and Kelly Sorenson. Hours later, neither one of them had come up with any leads. No one had ever seen the two women together. And no one had recalled seeing anything strange or suspicious where either woman was concerned, either.

"So maybe they really didn't know each other. He picked them out simply because they went to the same college. But how can we narrow it down from there?" Carrie muttered, more because she was thinking out loud than because she was really asking Jase for an answer.

She'd avoided talking to him directly ever since they'd met up. Had only communicated with him to share the facts and nothing but the facts so they could avoid duplicating each other's work. Yet she couldn't deny the intense pleasure she'd felt at seeing him again. Her body and heart always responded to Jase's proximity, but now that they'd been intimate, it was difficult to keep memories of their night together at bay. Even worse, she found herself getting alternately angry and sad at the thought of never experiencing his touch again. If Jase felt the same conflicting emotions, he was doing a good job of hiding it.

"We need to look into other ways to link them," Jase replied. "If we don't come up with something soon, we have to seriously consider the possibility of a copycat. There are more differences between the murders of Cheryl Anderson and Kelly Sorenson than there are similarities."

"But the similarity that is there, the cutting off of the eyelids? It's such a distinctive detail. I've never heard of that happening before, have you?"

"Just because we're trying to keep The Embalmer's

M.O. a secret doesn't mean some facts haven't spread to the general public. Cops can get sloppy, too. Talk to people they shouldn't. Hell, The Embalmer might have bragged about his crimes and gotten someone else interested."

"That's true," Carrie conceded. "I can't imagine he'd like that very much, but it's a possibility."

"It actually makes the most sense," Jase insisted. "The first three victims all had light brown hair. They were all teachers of some sort. Kelly Sorenson had darker hair and wasn't a teacher."

"There's still the connection of Susan Ingram having Cheryl Anderson as a professor," Carrie reminded him.

"Yeah, but without anything else, that means nothing. So let's see what else we can dig up. Let's look into where they've been. Things they've bought. Movies they've seen. We need to request copies of their canceled checks and look at their credit-card charges. Find out if there's a link that way."

"Okay," Carrie said. "I'll do that as soon as I get back to the office. I'll meet you there?"

He remained silent and for the first time, Carrie looked at him directly. He studied her with an intense expression, as if he wanted to say something. As if he wanted to push things. Not things having to do with the case, but things having to do with them. She held her breath, not sure what she'd do if he brought up the previous night and what they'd done, but luckily he just nodded. "Yeah. I'll see you at the office."

CHAPTER SEVENTEEN

"I'M TELLING YOU, I don't think she's ready for this."

Leaning back in his desk chair—which was actually Mac's desk chair—Special Agent Simon Granger focused on keeping his face impassive as he listened to Doctor Lana Hudson. It wasn't the first time she'd advised someone to go slowly with Carrie. Apparently, she'd made the same recommendation to both Mac and Commander Stevens before they'd decided to give Carrie the lead on The Embalmer case. "I know what you told me," he said. "But Carrie assures us she's fine and there's been nothing to indicate otherwise. She's an experienced agent. There's no reason to think she can't handle a serial case."

Lana leaned aggressively over Simon's desk, her palms planted firmly on the smooth wood surface. His muscles tensed at her proximity, and his nostrils flared at her familiar scent. He struggled to concentrate on what she was saying. He focused on her left hand, the one that still bore her wedding ring.

"But none of her cases have been like this. The homicides she handled were all cold cases. The rest, a domestic violence case or two. A family abduction.

Nothing so dangerous, so twisted, as a serial killer. I think it was a mistake to give her such a big case so soon after the Porter incident."

"She needs to move on and she's earned this chance. Mac thinks so and so does the commander. I'm not going to stand in her way."

Lana straightened and shook her head in disbelief. "Fine, Captain Granger."

Captain Granger, my ass, he thought, frowning. *I've seen you naked, lady.* He clenched his fists and ruthlessly pushed away the thought that he'd probably never see her naked again. "I'm not a captain anymore, Lana. I'm just a special agent again, remember?"

Lana paused for a moment, then opened her mouth to continue. He interrupted her.

"I've kept tabs on her. Before she came back, she went to the range twice a week. Her shooting is as accurate as ever."

She still didn't look convinced. "That's true, but you know as well as I do it's not the same as pulling your weapon on the street. Lots of officers draw their weapons. Few shoot it. We can't be sure what happened at the Porter scene, but bottom line, he got a drop on her. And then she killed him. It's too soon to know how that's going to affect her."

"Are you telling me you think she's unfit for duty?" God, he hoped not. For the case's sake. And for Carrie's. He didn't know her that well. Hadn't allowed himself to.

Lana hesitated for several seconds. Then she shook her head. "No. No, I'm not saying that. But she hasn't forgiven herself for failing to subdue Kevin Porter without killing him. Yes, she's been healing. Getting stronger. Still, I can't help wondering if this case may be too much pressure. Maybe you can give her more time…."

Granger. Only slightly more personal. She hadn't called him Simon since she'd broken things off with him.

"Well, unfortunately, time is something we don't have." Simon stood up, noting that Lana immediately took several steps back. He towered over her, but he knew she wasn't afraid of him. At least not physically. He took some satisfaction knowing he could still rattle her emotionally. In fact, he wanted to do more than just rattle her. He wanted to crowd her. To make her admit that she was still feeling the same attraction he was. But he didn't. Couldn't. He needed her to come to him on her own. Still, he kept the desk between them. Just in case he was tempted to reach out to her. "The only way she's going to truly get past the shooting is to get back to the job. To the team. She worked her ass off to get where she has, and there's no way we're not going to support her."

It was a little strange thinking of himself as a SIG member again, but he hadn't been able to handle the change. He'd needed the action of the streets. The challenge. So he'd given up his appointment to captain and returned to SIG. And that had been the day Lana had broken up with him.

She stood her ground, but her features softened slightly.

"She needs time to deal with what happened, Granger. Whether we like it or not, women are raised differently in society, and that influences our response to certain situations. It's a known fact that women are far more likely to be affected by having to kill someone than their male counterparts...."

Simon didn't buy it. Carrie needed to face her fears and move on with her life. Just like Lana. "She's strong. Stronger than most men."

"Yes, she is. But people who reach that level, your level, of discipline are generally obsessive. Big thinkers who need to control most aspects of their lives. That makes them more predisposed to develop post-traumatic stress disorder, which is exactly what she has."

Simon let out a frustrated sigh. Returned to his seat. "Look, we're never going to agree on this. I know she's blaming herself. Shit, we've all had to deal with guilt at one time or another. But we're more experienced. We've had years on the job to deal with this kind of thing, to balance the bad with the good. Shit, it was her first op."

Uh-oh. Lana's eyes lit up, and Simon knew immediately he'd made a mistake. By acknowledging Carrie's vulnerability, he'd only reinforced Lana's argument that she shouldn't be working on a case like The Embalmer. Hell, he'd had the same doubts initially. But it hadn't been his call. He trusted Mac and Stevens's decision and he'd stand by them. He'd stand by Carrie, too. She deserved this chance.

But just as he knew she would, Lana continued to

argue with him. "You're right. She was already at a heightened level of anxiety because of the newness of the situation. Having to shoot someone on the job is always a risk. Whether it's the bad guy or an innocent that dies, chances are good that someone's going to. She couldn't do it then, yet you've assigned her to a serial case that's bound to end up in more deaths. I just don't think she's ready to deal with that."

Simon immediately recognized the unspoken message behind her words and wanted to howl with frustration. Lana hadn't been able to deal with it, hadn't been able to live with the implications of Simon's job, especially once he'd chosen to go back on the streets. And he wasn't willing to give it up.

Rationally, he understood she was just protecting herself. But, God, he missed her. It had been weeks since they'd been together. Weeks of trying to forget her. And finally realizing that no matter how many women he slept with, she would always be the one he thought of when he went to bed at night and when he woke in the morning. "Lana…"

She cleared her throat. "So please tell the commander that my recommendation remains the same. I'd be happy to talk to him further if he likes."

He stared at her. Her body language gave nothing away. Usually, people saw only what she wanted them to see. But he knew there was more. He saw the regret in her beautiful blue eyes. Echoing his own.

"All right. Thank you."

She nodded. Looked at a point somewhere over his right shoulder. "Goodbye."

Refusing to respond, Simon watched her walk away. Again.

CHAPTER EIGHTEEN

CARRIE HUNG UP THE PHONE and turned to Jase, who was sitting at this own desk at SIG headquarters. "Well, looks like you'll have me out of your hair soon," she said brightly, hoping to mask the disappointment she was feeling. "My place is finally ready. I'll have to shop for a new sofa and stuff, but other than that..."

He nodded. "That's great, Carrie. And they even caught the guys who did it. Looks like you're in luck."

"Right. Luck." The cops had gotten a positive ID on two known gangbangers who used to run with Kevin Porter. That his gang had taken revenge on her didn't surprise her, but the fact they'd chosen to do it on her own personal turf did. They had to have followed her to her house without her knowing, and that reminded her of how vigilant she had to be given the kind of work she did. It was too easy to let down her guard and pretend she was safe.

Even though it wasn't fair, her thoughts about the gang members led her to another: Jase, and the way she'd let her guard down around him. Granted, they'd only made love the one night, but each day they were together, she could feel her defenses deteriorating more and more where he was concerned. Talk about dangerous. Shaking her head, she stood and stretched her arms over her head, trying to work out the kinks that had settled into her back. "If I was lucky, we'd get a damn break on this case."

"We'll get there." With that and one last enigmatic look, he returned his attention to his file.

Days had passed since they'd made love and, amazingly, the mutual desire between them had ceased to be a source of tension as they worked on the more pressing matter of finding a killer. In truth, they didn't have time for anything else. All their energy went to tracking down leads on the case, and when they had a spare moment, it was to eat or sleep. Though the thought had occurred to her more than once that she should leave Jase's house and check into a hotel, it hardly seemed worth the effort, given all the time they had to spend together. In a sense, they became the same person, the same cop.

That meant they shared the same frustration, too. It was only a matter of time until the killer struck again. They were hoping that Kelly Sorenson had been a fluke, that the killer would return to his more predictable, slow-moving ways, but they didn't really believe it. Something had set The Embalmer off course, prompting him to deviate from his routine. Once that happened in these types of cases, it was almost always the beginning of the end.

"Let me know if you need help moving in that new sofa, Ward," DeMarco said.

She glanced at him. He was walking toward the doorway, jacket in hand. "I will. Thanks."

DeMarco had returned to SIG two days after they'd discovered Kelly Sorenson's body. When he did, it was clear something devastating had occurred. He walked around with a dark cloud over him, blowing off any attempt they made to make him feel better. When they finally asked him about Sorenson, he'd stared at them with obvious shock in his eyes. "The brunette who gave Jase her number? She was a hooker? And picked off by your serial killer?"

"A high-class escort," Carrie clarified. "A picky one normally. But her roommate said she left McGill's around nine that night with a 'charity case' of a client. Those were her words, not mine."

"Shit." DeMarco looked at Jase. "Did you keep her card?"

"No. I didn't. But we got copies. She had two kinds. Purple for social situations, green for business calls."

DeMarco shook his head. "Figures."

Carrie and Jase shared a confused glance. "What do you mean?'

"I mean, despite the fact she clearly favored Tyler here, there was something about her I liked." DeMarco pulled out his wallet and took out a small green card. Carrie immediately recognized the distinctive color and cursed.

"Kelly Sorenson's business card," Jase said. "She gave it to you after I left?"

"No. Worse. She disappeared after talking to us, so I snagged it from the bar."

"She left her calling cards at the bar?"

DeMarco shrugged. "I was talking to the bartender about her. He said they were friends. That I should call her sometime. And he gave me her card. Have you talked to him?"

Carrie shook her head. "Not yet. We've been working our way down the list of witnesses from McGill's. He hasn't called us back yet."

"You got his name?" DeMarco asked.

"Lance Reynolds."

Now, Carrie watched DeMarco leave with a frown on her face.

"What's wrong?" Jase asked.

Carrie shook her head. "Nothing. But DeMarco doesn't seem like himself. And he seemed pretty upset about Kelly Sorenson. Like he really liked her or something."

"He did like her. So did I. She was a likable person. And beautiful." Jase shrugged. "If he took her card, he was obviously attracted to her. Maybe he actually planned on calling her. It would be a shock, that's all."

"Right," Carrie said. "That's all. I finally tracked down Lance Reynolds. I'm going to talk to him. You want to come along?"

"You bet," Jase said.

Once again, they found themselves back at McGill's. Lance Reynolds denied knowing what Sorenson did for a living. According to him, he'd simply given her card to men he thought his friend would take a liking to.

"Had you ever slept with her?"

"Yes," Lance said.

"But you didn't mind finding her other lovers?"

"I wasn't in love with Kelly, if that's what you mean. We were together one night. It didn't mean anything, but we were friends, and I know she liked to have fun. Who she liked to have fun with."

"Did you see her leave that night?"

"I saw her talking to him and the other one," Lance said, referring to Jase. "She left soon after that."

Carrie frowned. "What time?"

"I don't know. Early. Maybe eight?"

"Susan Ingram says Kelly called her from McGill's at nine."

"I saw her leave at eight. I remember because I gave your friend her card a few minutes later, then went on break. Maybe she came back, but I didn't see her. I worked my shift until the bar closed that night."

That was something they'd already confirmed. And since the coroner had estimated Kelly's time of death as approximately 11:00 p.m., that pretty much put Lance Reynolds in the clear. It also meant DeMarco had the card with her phone number before she'd died.

Jase had wondered if DeMarco had planned to call her. But maybe someone had called her. If they couldn't find a witness who'd seen her leave with someone, she'd probably have to check Sorenson's call log to her cell-phone number. That would involve filling out the appropriate paperwork and waiting on the phone company to do their thing. Nonetheless, she added the task to her already extensive list.

That was how things pretty much progressed, with them chasing one lead after another but coming up with absolutely nothing.

One afternoon, in the midst of yet another review of the file, Jase threw his pencil on his desk. He stood, stretching muscles weary from lack of use. Both of them were very active. Used to physical exertion, whether it was on the streets or in a gym. The back-to-back shifts of investigative work were beginning to take their toll.

She was about to suggest he go to the gym when Jase turned to look at her.

"Let's get out of here."

Her head throbbing with a persistent headache, one likely spurred on by all the time she'd been spending looking at a computer screen, Carrie leaned back in her chair and frowned. "Where do you want to go?"

"I just need some air. Let's take a ride. I'll meet you outside."

He walked out, not giving her a chance to argue with him. She took her time, needing to remind him and herself that she wasn't going to jump simply because he snapped his fingers. But she had to admit, she was curious. And excited to be going somewhere with him. Ten minutes later, she couldn't take it any longer and she met him outside. Silently, he led her to his car, a gorgeous little Mustang that she'd always secretly coveted. At first, he simply drove, luring her out of her dark thoughts with a little fresh air and scenery. About an hour later, he pulled up near the San Francisco Zoo.

"What are we doing here?"

"Come on. Let's go for a walk."

There were myriad trails near the zoo that she'd run before. She'd always enjoyed the scenery, and after walking several minutes, she felt some of the tension leave her body. When they worked their way back to the zoo, he grabbed her arm and dragged her toward the front entrance where he bought two tickets.

Knowing how restless he'd started to become, she decided to indulge him. They made their way past the flamingos and toward the red panda habitat. At some point, he bought her an ice-cream cone and grabbed her other hand while they walked. The casual gesture of affection felt foreign to her, and she tried to recall the last time she'd held a man's hand.

To her surprise, she wasn't sure she ever had.

Such a simple gesture between two people, yet she'd never done it? What a sad commentary on her life. What a sad commentary on who she was, Carrie thought.

She held her arm stiffly for several moments, but by the time they reached the chimpanzee exhibit, she'd finished her cone and had gotten used to the feel of her hand in his. It didn't take them long to navigate the small zoo, and she felt the sharp pang of disappointment when they reached the exit. She smiled at him.

"Thanks, Jase. That was fun."

He shook his head. "We're not done yet. Let's get some popcorn and do one more lap. I'm not ready to dive back into the case. Not yet. Are you?"

She raised her eyebrows and said nothing. He was in an odd mood. Playful and intense at the same time. She wasn't sure how to deal with him. But she nodded. Because, no, she wasn't quite ready to get back to work. Frankly, she was enjoying this time with him too much.

They viewed the animal exhibits a second time. Ate popcorn. Even held hands again, like teenagers at the county fair.

"So about this new sofa you're going to get? You have anything in mind?"

Startled, she looked at him, unable to believe he actually cared about something like her choice of furniture. "Um—I figured something floral, like the other one I had, would be good."

He smiled slightly. "Yeah, I noticed you go for the flowery stuff."

"Surprised you, huh?"

"Yes. And, no," he said.

"What do you mean?"

"It surprised me that you'd like a flowery sofa. It didn't surprise me that you'd keep something like that a secret."

She stopped in her tracks. "A secret? Because I didn't advertise it? Listen, Jase—"

He tsked and, making her heart thud against his chest, raised their clasped hands to his mouth and kissed her fingers. "I'm going to miss you," he said quietly.

She stared at him blankly, struggling over what to say, but the words didn't come easily. Finally, she managed, "Don't be silly. You'll see me all the time. We have this case to finish."

He shrugged. "It won't be the same. But tell you what, if you need help moving your sofa and DeMarco's not available, feel free to call me, too. That goes double if you want to talk about the punks the police caught. If you want to talk about *anything*. Okay?"

With that, he started walking again.

"Yeah, sure," she responded softly. They took a few steps before she did something completely out of character for her. She raised their still-joined hands in turn and, just as he'd done, kissed his fingers. "Thanks, Jase. You've been a good friend through all this."

"We'll work on your definition of friendship later, Carrie. Now, let's head to the parrot cage. I wanna see if I can get 'em to talk again."

It was an amazing couple of hours that managed to push darker thoughts out of their heads. At least for a brief moment in time.

On the drive back to work, however, the pleasant haze that had surrounded her began to fade. Inevitably, her thoughts returned to work and all the dead ends they'd encountered. She'd heard back from all the local hospitals and funeral homes she'd contacted and none of them had reported thefts of supplies or unauthorized usage of their facilities. It was becoming more and

more likely that if The Embalmer was indeed perform-
ing gruesome procedures on his victims, he was doing
so in a private space, someplace he'd likely retrofitted
and stocked between the time he'd moved from Fresno
to San Francisco....

"He moved!" Carrie exclaimed.

"What?" Jase asked even as he kept his attention
on the road.

"The Embalmer. His first two victims were in
Fresno, his next two in San Francisco, with a year in
between. I was thinking that the move explained the
year lapse, and that he would have used that time to
set up shop. Maybe he found a private place to do his
work or maybe he renovated his house so it could ac-
commodate his needs."

"Right. And that makes total sense," Jase agreed.
"Only he's done his job too well, and we can't find
where he's holed up."

"Even so, maybe what we need to be searching for
isn't his location, but his identity."

Jase frowned then slowed the car. He pulled to the
curb and shifted in his seat to face her. "Explain."

"We know The Embalmer is organized and methodical. What he's choosing to do to the victims, embalming them and cutting off their eyelids, presenting them
in such a meticulous way in the photographs, it hints at
someone who knows what he's doing. Someone who's
been trained for that kind of thing. That's why we've
been focusing our efforts, in addition to anyone associ-

ated with the college, on finding someone who's been medically trained, like a doctor or a mortician."

"I'm still not getting where you're going with this."

"Medically trained, Jase," Carrie said. "As in licensed to practice within a particular state or county. When someone in a licensed profession moves, even within the same state, don't they have to let the appropriate governing authority know? Wouldn't that governing authority then keep track of where they've set up practice again?"

"Damn, you're right. Funeral directors and morticians need a license to practice. So do doctors. Lawyers."

"Since we know he was in Fresno and is now in San Francisco, we can focus our inquiries on professionals who've moved their practice in the past year. Check with whatever licensing agencies might be appropriate, as well as places like the Chamber of Commerce."

He pulled his car back on the road. "Let's talk to Stevens. See how many hands we can put to work on this. It's a good lead, Carrie. A damn good one."

She settled back into her seat, excited by the prospect of exploring another lead when before there'd been so pitifully few. From the corner of her eye, she saw Jase smiling, as well. When he caught her looking at him, he said, "I told you so, Ward."

Her eyes rounded with surprise before she laughed in disbelief. "And what, exactly, was it that you told me?"

His eyes widened in mock innocence. "Just that a drive and a breath of fresh air would do you some good.

Maybe the next time I make a suggestion, you'll be more amenable to going with the flow rather than questioning me like you always do."

He placed a friendly hand on her knee and patted it.

Carrie laughed. Reaching out, she took his hand in hers again. "Maybe I will, Jase."

ONCE THEY KNEW WHAT THEY were looking for, it didn't take them long to come up with a list of names. That was especially true given the manpower Stevens had gathered to help them with their quest. By the next day, after checking with a variety of state agencies, they knew that six doctors had started practices in the San Francisco area in the past year, and two funeral homes had changed ownership. Jase and Carrie were going to spend several hours meeting with the individuals on their list.

The first doctor they visited was a cheery pediatrician who wore brightly colored Adidas. He'd been a keynote speaker at a conference at the time Kelly Sorenson was killed. The second doctor was female, a slight Asian woman with a serious demeanor and a clipped way of speaking. She'd moved from Fresno because her husband had been transferred to the bay area. They'd just returned from a monthlong vacation overseas.

"Who's next?" Jase asked.

"Dr. Odell Bowers, a reconstructive surgeon. He's practicing near Coit Tower." He followed the directions Carrie gave him. "Weird," she said. "This is the same building I used to visit for my physical-therapy appointments."

"You haven't had one in a while."

"No. I've been a little busy."

He shot her a chiding look, but before he could speak, she interrupted, "I know. I'll make an appointment soon. I'm not going to ruin all the progress I've made by being careless now."

"Good," he said.

Still, as she followed Jase up the stairs of the building, she was conscious of how her leg was dragging slightly behind her. When she reached the top, she was even breathing a little harder, and the evidence of her weakened stamina nearly made her cringe.

Though she tried to be discreet about it, Jase caught her rubbing the side of her leg.

"Need another massage?" he asked mildly as they maneuvered their way to Dr. Bowers's second-floor office.

"Nope. I'm good."

"I guess instead of asking the question, I should have just said I'd give you a massage. After all, you said you were going to be more amenable to my suggestions from here on out."

He held the door of Bowers's office open for her. As she walked through, she reminded him, "I said *maybe* I would. Convenient of you to forget that small detail."

Laughing, he shrugged. "Convenience has nothing to do with it."

They stepped up to the reception desk where a

harried-looking young woman was talking on the phone. "I'm sorry, ma'am, but I already told you I don't know when Dr. Bowers will be back in the office. I'll call you back as soon as I—" She gritted her teeth when the other person on the line hung up on her.

She hung up the receiver and started jotting down some notes but didn't acknowledge them in any way.

Jase cleared his throat. "Excuse me," he said.

The woman didn't even look up. "Can I help you?"

"We're with the Department of Justice and we need to speak with Dr. Odell Bowers right away."

The minute he mentioned they were from the DOJ, the woman's head snapped up. "Are you cops?" she asked. "Finally. You'd think with the number of times I've called you guys that you would have arrived before now."

Carrie stepped forward. "We're special agents with the Department of Justice, not patrol officers. But you've asked for help from the police. Why?"

"Because my boss hasn't shown up to work for the past couple of days, and I can't get ahold of him. I've been fielding phone calls and visits from angry patients and I'm sick of it, but I need the job. I don't want to leave things completely hanging and then have Dr. Bowers fire me when he gets back from whatever he's been doing."

Carrie looked at Jase, who said, "We need to know everything you've told the police. You can tell me that while Special Agent Ward looks around Dr. Bowers's office. We'll also need his home address."

THIRTY MINUTES LATER, Carrie and Jase were racing to
Dr. Bowers's home in the Presidio. According to the
receptionist, Marlene Harrison, Dr. Bowers was ruthlessly efficient when it came to keeping to his office
hours and scheduled appointments. In the six months
that she'd been working for him, he'd never called in
sick. Yet he wasn't answering his home phone or his cell
phone, and he hadn't answered his door when Marlene
had stopped by his house the night before.

She should count herself lucky that she hadn't.
After all, there was little doubt in Carrie's mind that
Dr. Odell Bowers was in fact The Embalmer. A quick
search of his medical records had revealed a link between the first three victims—they'd all been prospec-
tive patients. Each of them had come in for an elective
cosmetic-surgery consultation and had disappeared
within a few weeks of their appointment.

There'd been no credit-card bills or cancelled checks
evidencing payments to the same doctor because the
initial consultation with Bowers had been free; up to
that point, there'd been nothing to charge them for. But
that visit had been enough for Bowers to set his sights
on them and get their personal information. Address.
Phone number. Maybe he'd even arranged to meet them
for coffee to talk over their options. Granted, the phone
records of the victims should have resulted in a match
if they'd each called Bowers's office number at some
point, but it was entirely possible they'd called from a
third-party line or walked in to make an appointment.

"He knew what he was going to do to them the moment he met them," she said. "Those damn movies..."

They'd found no evidence of how Bowers had first seen Kelly Sorenson, but they'd found a collection of DVDs in one of Bowers's office cabinets that hinted at why he'd done what he had to her and the others.

Odell Bowers had been a huge horror-movie buff. Marlene said he often spent his lunch break watching a movie and had even invited his staff to sit in with him a few times.

"We thought it was weird and he stopped asking after the first few times," Marlene had said.

Halfway joking, Jase had asked, "Did any of the movies happen to involve slicing someone's eyelids off?"

"Are you kidding?" Marlene had retorted, rolling her eyes. "That one was his favorite."

The movie was about a family who moved into a new house that, unknown to them, had been a mortuary. As soon as the family moved in, the young son had started to act strangely. Somehow, a former serial killer was involved, and the family discovered his collection of dried-out eyelids under a floorboard of the boy's room.

"I've always hated horror movies," Carrie said as they pulled up to Bowers's residence.

"Me, too," Jase responded.

They waited for their backup team from the SFPD to arrive. With several officers covering other access points, Jase and Carrie made their way to the grand front entrance flanked on either side by fancily trimmed topiary trees.

"The guy likes his creature comforts," Jase remarked.

"Yes," Carrie said. "I bet he has a fancy home theater room with a huge flat-screen TV to watch his movies."

"Don't malign the benefits of home theater technology simply because of one sicko, Ward," Jase chided back. Their teasing banter was meant to relieve some of their tension, the same way cops often used black humor at crime scenes to deal with the horrific things they encountered day in and day out. It was yet more proof of how comfortable they'd become working together. It was hard to believe that the case they'd been so vigorously pursuing could very well be solved in a matter of minutes.

"We're going to get him," Jase said. "And it's going to be because of you, Carrie. I'm damn proud of you."

She felt more than a small amount of pride at his words. Carrie mirrored Jase's stance, bracing her back against the wall and holding her weapon at the ready. "I couldn't have done it without you, Jase. I mean that. Now let's get this guy."

BOWERS INDEED HAD a first-class theater room, with a giant screen, blackout drapes and cushy recliner chairs. Despite the ample seating, Jase suspected Bowers didn't socialize much. There was a clinical sterility to his home. Finely furnished, yes, but everything ruthlessly in its place. He got the distinct impression that visitors would be unwelcome simply because they might mess things up. Track dirt in. Muddy up the shiny surfaces of his tables with fingerprints. Bowers would abhor the unpredictability of it.

They'd announced their presence but Bowers didn't appear to be home. Still, to insure he wasn't hiding inside, they cleared each room, one by one.

"Garage?" Carrie asked.

Jase spotted the most likely door, and nodded toward it. They motioned one of the SFPD police officers over. Together, they opened the door, unsurprised by the steep flight of stairs that led down to the garage. From the doorway, Jase saw the back end of a polished black vehicle. On the other side of the stairs, however, was another door. He pointed to it.

"We'll go down together," Carrie said. She turned to the officer beside them. "You make sure to cover us from up here."

"Yes, ma'am."

Normally, Jase would have teased her about being called "ma'am" by a fellow cop, but his nerves were too intense for that. They took the narrow stairs slowly, pacing each other back-to-back. "Check the car first," Jase said.

"Right."

As he kept his gun pointed toward the closed door, Carrie checked the vehicle.

"Nothing. You're clear on this side."

"Okay." He tried the door handle. It was locked. "Dr. Bowers," he called. "This is Special Agent Jase Tyler with the California Department of Justice. I'm here with backup. Open the door."

Nothing. No sounds. No attempt to open the door.

"I'm coming in," he yelled. Raising his foot, he kicked in the door. They went through together, weapons drawn.

They entered a huge finished basement that appeared to have been converted into a makeshift operating room. It was loaded with steel tables and drawers of tools and shelves of bottles. Immediately in front of them lay a body.

Carrie caught sight of the feminine kimono and gasped. "He killed another woman."

"No," Jase said. "It's a man. Look at the face. The hair."

It was Bowers. Dressed in feminine clothes with makeup on his face. Makeup that had been applied with the same heavy hand as the rest of The Embalmer's victims. There was one big difference, however. In Bowers's case, the makeup was marred by the blood running down his temple. He'd sustained a major head wound.

Everything they'd discovered—the weirdly renovated garage, Bowers's makeup, what his secretary had told them about his favorite movie—it all pointed to Bowers being The Embalmer. The man who'd murdered four women. The man who'd taunted and eluded the cops for so long. Yet now...

Cautiously, Jase checked for a pulse, confirming what he already knew.

Bowers was dead.

CHAPTER NINETEEN

WASN'T IT WRONG to celebrate someone's death, even if the death you were celebrating was a serial killer's? The question nagged at Carrie the entire next day.

She had a friend who was a deputy attorney general for the DOJ. Renee responded to death-penalty appeals, and sometimes those appeals raged on for decades. One time, her friend had called to tell her a death-row inmate had died in prison. Carrie couldn't even remember how he'd died. The thing that had stuck with her the most was her friend's relief.

Wasn't it wrong to celebrate someone's death, even if the death you were celebrating was a serial killer's?

Carrie wasn't celebrating, exactly. It didn't matter that Bowers had been a killer. He'd obviously been a man driven by some pretty powerful ghosts. They hadn't found a kiln in his basement. What it did have, though, was a half-dozen deep drawers, the kind often seen in the movies when someone visited a morgue to identify a body.

To their profound relief, there weren't any bodies inside. They did, however, find pictures. Copies of the same pictures Bowers had sent to the police. Pictures of three women.

Mary Johnson.

Theresa Steward.

And Cheryl Anderson.

He'd been a killer, a smart one, a vicious one, yet now he was dead.

The cause of death? That was a question for the coroner to explore. Bowers had suffered blunt force trauma to the head, but the wound had been generic enough that, for all they knew, he'd slipped and hit his head on the basement's tile floor. Unlikely, but it seemed just as unlikely that someone had caught Bowers by complete and utter surprise, especially given the way he'd been dressed, and killed him. Unless, of course, he'd had a partner... But that didn't seem likely, either. Not only was there no evidence of a partner being involved, but Bowers's crimes had had a distinctly personal quality to them.

Speculation about Bowers's motives would rage on, but Carrie was betting it had to do with the death of his sister, Laura, who'd died several years ago in a car accident. Laura, with the light brown hair. Laura, who'd been a teacher. Laura, who'd been so badly injured in the car wreck that she hadn't been able to have a normal funeral service. No viewing. No burial. Could it be that Odell was using his victims, preparing their bodies for burial in a way he hadn't been able to prepare Laura?

Of course, that didn't explain why, if he loved his sister, he'd actually hurt his victims by keeping them alive during the embalming process, but that was an explanation they were obviously never going to get.

She was just glad Odell Bowers couldn't hurt anyone again. That gladness wasn't completely free of regret, however. She'd been glad she'd managed to shoot Kevin Porter before he'd killed her, after all, but she'd regretted having to do it. Likewise, she was glad whenever she closed a case and managed to obtain some justice for a person whose life had either ended or been torn apart because of the carelessness or cruelty of another human being. But she regretted the necessity of obtaining that justice in the first place.

What she didn't like was that her regret often mingled with guilt.

In this particular case, the guilt wasn't necessarily pinpointed at herself so much as society in general. What failing had caused Odell Bowers's madness to spiral out of control? To push him to the point of feeling so utterly rejected by those around him that he had to escape inside a dark and deranged mind to find comfort? At exactly what point did someone cease to be the angsty teen she'd told Jase she'd been, or the troubled teen who took drugs and joined gangs like Kevin Porter had been, or a cross-dressing boy who loved his sister like Odell Bowers had been, and become something monstrous?

But it didn't matter. Guilt was guilt, and frankly, Carrie was sick of feeling it.

Wasn't it wrong to celebrate someone's death, even if the death you were celebrating was a serial killer's?

Maybe, but right now, that's what Carrie and her teammates were doing. At the very least, they were celebrating the fact she'd found a serial killer and closed the case. What that meant in the grand scheme of things she'd just have to figure out later.

No one outside DOJ or SFPD was celebrating Bowers's capture, however. Or his death, for that matter. For now, they'd decided to keep the circumstances of his death a secret. Amongst his things, they'd found Kelly Sorenson's green business card, but that was the only evidence they'd found linking Bowers to her murder. And, of course, because he'd likely been murdered himself, they didn't want to give his potential killer more information than he or she already had.

She glanced at Jase, and from the relaxed but slightly distant expression on his face, she wondered if he was thinking and feeling exactly what she was, including a hint of disappointment that there was no longer a reason for them to be working 24/7 together on the same case. With a small smile, she extricated herself from Commander Stevens, Simon and DeMarco and made her way to him, where he was sitting by himself at the bar in McGill's.

"Hey," she said softly.

"Hey yourself," he said. "What are you doing over here? You should soak up more accolades. You deserve it."

She shook her head, not in denial or false humility, but...well, she wasn't quite sure why. "I meant what I said back at his house. Before we went in. We solved this case together. I wouldn't have been able to work out all the details and come to any sort of conclusion but for you."

He took a drag from his bottle and winked at her. "Right. The fresh air and drive cleared your head and got you thinking creatively. I remember."

But despite his teasing tone, there was a somber cast to his mood that matched her own.

"What we do, it never heals us, not completely, does it?" she asked him. "Not the victims. Not society as a whole. Not whatever demons are chasing us, pushing us to do this job in the first place."

"Nope," he agreed. "Not completely. But no one escapes life unscathed, Ward. That just isn't how it works."

His words rang true. And the way he looked at her, intense, deep, caring...it reminded her of the last time she'd truly felt safe and content. When they'd made love.

They'd managed to ignore that little incident while tracking down The Embalmer, but now that he'd been caught...now that their official partnership was over, what would happen? Would they continue to ignore it? Pretend it never happened?

Instinctively, she knew Jase was through pushing her. That he was waiting for a sign from her about how to proceed. As they always did where he was concerned, her desire warred with practicality.

She wasn't what he needed. He needed a woman to balance out his job, and since she *was* part of the job, she couldn't give him that. He'd realize that soon enough, which meant she needed to be smart. As it was, she'd barely survive Jase walking away from her, but she would survive. So long as she stayed realistic and remembered who and what she was.

But that didn't mean he had to walk away *tonight*.

It didn't mean she couldn't have one more taste of the pleasure and safety he'd shown her. After everything they'd been through and witnessed in the past few days, she deserved that much, didn't she?

"That's how life works," she agreed. "But even so... we have to take our pleasure where and when we can. Isn't that what you said?"

Surprise flickered across his face before his heated gaze pinned her in place. "That's what I said."

Clearing her throat and looking around to make sure no one would overhear her, she said, "Are you all talk and no action? Or do you feel like taking me back to your house—back to your bed—and proving your point to me one more time."

He considered her words, and she knew it wasn't the offer he was actually contemplating, but her deliberate reference to making love to him one last time. As in, never again. As in, now that the case was over, things were going to go back to normal between them, with him dating his women and her...well, her dating no one.

"That depends," he finally said.

She raised a brow. "On what?"

"On whether you're still planning on leaving SIG for greener pastures. Are you?"

"Why does that matter?" She tried to inject a teasing note into her voice. Anything to break through this odd, tense mood that was coursing between them, but her attempt at humor failed. Neither of them was smiling.

"You know, the last time I went to bed with you, I woke up alone in a cold bed. You might not know this about me, but I'm a big cuddler. If we do this, if I prove my point to you, one last time," he emphasized, "I'd like to think you'd stick around for at least that."

The lump in her throat was as huge as the sudden compulsion to burst into tears. But nothing came close to the anticipation she was feeling. To the desire that pounded through her. She wanted Jase. She wanted to make love to him. To wallow in pure physical sensation with him.

And damn straight that included cuddling with him afterward.

She nodded.

That was all.

Just nodded.

He rose, took her hand and together they walked out of McGill's.

SHE TOOK HIM BACK to her place despite the refurbished living room and accompanying new paint smell. They'd already made love in his bed, and she wanted to savor holding him in her own. It would also help imprint the next few hours into her memory, something she'd cherish in the years to come when she no longer had him.

Slowly, Jase tugged off his jacket and tossed it onto

a chair. Next, he removed his holster and gun and laid it on the bed. Carrie stared at the gun and felt the sturdy weight of her own against her side.

"Come here, Carrie," he said, his voice low.

When she stood in front of him, he tugged her jacket back. Obediently, she moved her arms, enabling him to ease the jacket off. With the same precise movements he'd used to remove his own holster, Jase unsnapped hers, sliding her piece off her body. Instinctively, unused to another person removing her holster, she almost reached for it, but she just managed to stop herself. Jase picked up his own holster from the bed and put both of them on the nightstand table. Within reach if they needed them, but to the side. Business making way for pleasure.

It was still a concept she wasn't used to, but she was beginning to learn. Because of Jase.

He unbuttoned her shirt while she continued to stare at him, unmoving. Jase looked grim, his eyelids heavy with desire and intent. Their breaths were loud in the quiet room. She should be saying something, shouldn't she? Doing something? But instead she was just compliantly letting him undress her. Why? And more importantly, as she had the first night they'd had sex, she asked herself why it felt so good to give him control. To let down her guard and be completely vulnerable to a man again. Vulnerable in a way she hadn't allowed herself to be with a man since…

Dark memories threatened to intrude, and ruthlessly she pushed them away. Jase knew she'd been raped, and as far as his theories on nature and nurture were concerned…she knew the rape had stained her belief in men. It had, in fact, stained her view on life in general, but she wasn't going to let her past ruin this moment.

He unbuttoned her pants and tugged them down along with her lilac panties. Obediently, she stepped out of them until she was completely naked in front of him.

His eyes traveled over her body, and every inch of her warmed, as if his gaze was the lit match and her body the kindling. But still he didn't touch her.

Why wouldn't he touch her?

But she knew. He'd taken the lead, but he still wanted full participation from her. He wasn't going to let her be passive, after all.

Swallowing loudly, Carrie reached out. Swiftly, she unbuttoned his shirt, then, without removing it, unfastened his pants while her mouth trailed kisses against his hard muscles. She inhaled, taking in his intoxicating scent. He smelled good. Right.

He hissed when she licked him. The evidence of her effect on him filled her with excitement, and she slipped her hand into the front of Jase's open pants to cup him. He groaned, lifted his hands and cupped her breasts.

She jumped.

"Cold?" he whispered, his voice strained.

She shook her head. "With your hands where they are? Not at all. You?"

He barked with laughter. "With your hand where it is? Hardly."

She smiled against his warm skin, then moaned when he lightly tweaked her nipples.

"Come up here," he urged. "I want to kiss you."

Obediently, she rose up, and his mouth lowered to hers.

At first, she couldn't lose herself in the kiss. Instead, she made note of his technique. Like a good detective, she analyzed for clues based on angle, pressure and speed. How good was he? Off the charts. A world-class expert.

He pulled back, breathing hard, and narrowed his eyes at her. "What are you thinking? *Why* are you thinking?"

"Just that you're a good kisser. Must be all the practice you've had," she joked.

He tilted his head and frowned. She wondered if she'd made him mad.

"If you can still think that, I obviously haven't practiced enough." He cupped her neck, stroking it lightly. Making her feel even more vulnerable than before. "Let me in, Carrie."

"I am. You're here. Soon you'll literally be inside me."

"Not enough. Let me *in*. Even if it's only for now. For as long as we're making love. Let me past your guard."

She blinked rapidly against the entreaty in his voice. Against the wash of tears she felt in her eyes. "Will you let me past yours?"

"Don't you know? I lowered my guard where you're concerned a long time ago."

She swallowed hard, sensing the truth in his words. He'd been revealing tidbits about himself over the past few days. Not just to support his opinions, but to truly let her see him. She remembered how easily he'd shown her the knife scars at his side. And how natural it had felt when she'd kissed them. Touching someone never came that naturally to her. Being touched was even harder for her. "It's not easy for me," she whispered.

"I know."

She pulled his head down and kissed him. This time, she focused on how she felt and how he felt against her. Warm. Hard. Pleasurable.

Safe. Just like before, she felt safe with him.

And that was so intoxicating to her that she felt the exact moment it happened. She lowered her guard and completely let him in.

Jase seemed to sense the difference in her immediately and responded in kind. With a ragged groan, he angled his head and kissed her deeper, while at the same time he hoisted her up so her legs tangled tightly around his waist. She pushed at his open shirt, wanting to be rid of any type of barrier between them, but he thwarted her by trailing urgent, sucking kisses down her throat and lower. With his shirt still half-on, her hands dove into his hair and guided his mouth to one aching nipple. He drew it into his mouth, sucked softly, then harder until she whimpered and arched in his arms.

"That's it," he whispered against her. "Give me all you've got, Carrie. I want it all."

He carried her to the bed and laid her out on it, twisting himself away from the grip of her clinging legs in order to wrestle off his clothes. When she realized what he was doing, she relaxed and enjoyed the view. Against the soft, feminine backdrop of her bedroom, his muscles rippled and he thrust out heavily, eager to be inside her.

She held out her arms. "Now. Please. I don't want to wait."

"But you're going to wait," he said even as he leaned down to kiss her again. "I haven't had a chance to taste you yet and I can't go another second without it."

She gasped when he grabbed her behind the knees and tugged until her legs dangled off the bed. Kneeling between them, he kissed her stomach then tickled her naval with his tongue. The protest she'd been about to utter drifted away. As much as she ached to be filled by his hard length, the idea of him pleasuring her with his mouth was enough to have her flinging her arms above her head and closing her eyes with anticipation.

Given everything she knew about him, she expected him to be the best she'd ever had.

She wasn't disappointed.

He used his tongue like a lethal weapon, destroying every preconceived notion she'd ever harbored about her body or its ability to feel pleasure. The lightest of licks made her tremble, while a nip of his teeth or a firm dragging motion with the flat of his tongue had her hips arching desperately off the bed and her stifling a moan by biting her lip.

He didn't like that. "Don't hold back. I said I wanted

everything and that includes hearing your pleasure, Carrie."

He gave her no choice but to grant him what he wanted. His fingers dove between her legs, assured but gentle. Curling his tongue around her clitoris, he filled her channel with one thick finger, then two. He pursed his lips and sucked her. The stimulation blasted her to another time and place where only pleasure existed. Crying out, she gripped at the sheets for dear life, certain that she was going to shake apart but not caring. Whatever remained of her when this was over was his anyway.

How had she ever thought she could resist this man?

When her climax eased, she was panting and Jase was laying curled over her with one hand cupping her and one cheek resting on her stomach. Drowsily, she lifted her fingers and ran them through his hair.

"Now that you've tasted me," she croaked out, "can I have you? Please?"

Slowly, he lifted his head. His eyes burned with desire and intent. *Hell, yeah,* they said. *You can have me and then some.*

Oh, my, she thought, licking her lips.

Slowly, he rose, placed his palms on either side of her head, then paused. "Take me in your hand. Guide me inside you," he whispered.

His words had her going from sated to something else entirely. Greedily, she wrapped her hand around him. Though she intended to slip him inside her right away, she couldn't resist sliding her hand down his length then up again. Down. Then up.

He closed his eyes and hissed. But he bore the torture she administered for several minutes before finally gasping, "Now, Carrie. Before it's too late."

She guided him to her entrance and he'd already pushed partly into her when she cried, "Wait. You're not wearing a condom."

He froze.

"Do you have one?" he said. "Please tell me you have one."

"You don't?" she asked, trying to tease him.

He got a desperate look in his eyes.

"It's okay," she said quickly. "I have one. It's old but…"

With a grimace, he pulled out of her and she scrambled to the bathroom. When she returned, he was laying on the bed, his arm covering his eyes. He was shaking.

Vibrating with his need for her.

"Stay there. I like that position," she said.

Quickly, she knelt beside him, rolled the condom on, then straddled him.

Before she knew what was happening, he flipped her over, gathered her wrists in one hand and stretched her arms over her head. Startled, she stared up at him.

"You'll have to wait your turn. Right now, I need you like this. I need to ride you hard, Carrie." But he paused, obviously waiting for her permission to continue.

She opened her legs wider. "Please" was all she said.

He thrust, cleaving into her and filling her so thoroughly that she cried out.

Again, he froze, but this time he released her wrists. "Are you—"

She clasped his ass. "Move, damn you," she said. "Take me. Hard, just like you said."

With a groan, he let go. Over and over again, he pulled out of her then pushed heavily back inside. Their hips slapped together, their chests rubbed, their lips caressed and their hands cherished. They were all over each other, inside each other, no part left unexplored. "Oh, God, Carrie, I'm coming," he yelled just before she felt him release inside her.

With a final lunge, he embedded himself inside her as deep as he could go, arched his back and, with teeth clenched, groaned out his pleasure. As he did, he cupped her breasts and tweaked her nipples between her fingers. It was the final stimulation she needed before being thrust into her own earth-shattering release.

JASE HELD A SLEEPING Carrie as he caressed her hair. She looked peaceful. Relaxed and content in a way he rarely saw her. Of course, that might have something to do with how charged up and tense he normally felt around her. Just like his parents, they were two live wires constantly sparking off each other. It kept things interesting, but how long could that kind of intensity survive before it turned dangerous?

Before their impassioned natures turned their relationship into something like the one his parents had once shared?

Yet there was no denying they worked well together. That his laid-back manner complemented her more in-your-face style. Look at the huge progress they'd made on The Embalmer case in a relatively short time.

Plus, Carrie had been right when she'd reminded him he'd never raised a hand to her, not even when she'd bitten him. He couldn't imagine striking her in anger; in fact, all he could picture using his strength for was protecting her. From anyone and anything that made her feel sad or not good enough. Because she was more than good enough. For the job. For him.

But she'd made it abundantly clear that she viewed last night as a not-going-to-happen-again kind of thing.

He just wasn't ready to give her that. But it wasn't as if she was going anywhere. Not yet. They wouldn't be working the same case, wouldn't see each other nearly as often, but they'd still see each other plenty. He'd have time to adjust to his own feelings for her, and time to get her used to the idea of them together, too. He wasn't exactly sure how he was going to accomplish either. All he knew was that the longer he held her in his arms, the less he wanted to let her go. Ever.

His thoughts were interrupted by her ringing phone. He swiftly picked up before it could wake her. She shifted and moaned, but didn't open her eyes.

"Hello?"

There was a long pause followed by a sigh. "Agent Tyler?" It was Commander Stevens.

He winced and glanced down at Carrie again. Probably wasn't the best idea he'd ever had to answer her phone. "Yes, sir. Can I help you?"

"I'm assuming Agent Ward is with you?"

"Yes," Jase said.

"Just as well. I need to talk to both of you anyway. How long until you can be at my office?"

Not missing the tension in Stevens's voice, Jase gripped the phone tightly. "Is there a problem?"

"Several. But at the moment, the most pressing one is a new victim. It looks like we were wrong. The Embalmer didn't kill Kelly Sorenson. At least, it doesn't appear so. There's a copycat, and he's not ready to call it quits just yet."

CHAPTER TWENTY

SAFETY IN JASE'S ARMS. That and a whole lot of pleasure were what Carrie had been seeking. Despite the darkness and danger that had forced them to work together on The Embalmer case, she'd wanted to end that partnership with something sweet and life-affirming. And for a few precious moments she'd gotten it.

She clearly remembered that moment when she'd opened her entire heart to Jase. Soaked him in. Her fear had vanished. All her insecurities and doubts had gone with it. In his embrace, she hadn't been planning a future with him, exactly, but she hadn't been quite so focused on the impossibility of one, either.

Until Jase had woken her and told her about Commander Stevens's call.

She replayed Jase's words from the night before.

No one escapes life unscathed, Ward. That just isn't how it works.

The safety she'd felt in Jase's arms had been exactly what she'd thought it was.

Illusory. Temporary.

Bowers was dead, but another killer was still on the loose.

Again, the murder victim was a woman. Again, she'd had her eyelids cut off. But again, the method of her death and the disposal of her body were completely different from any that came before. This time, her skin had been peeled from her in wide strips. Given what she knew about Bowers and his fascination with horror movies, Carrie couldn't help thinking about the movie about a serial killer mentoring an FBI agent, enabling her to find another killer who starved hostages in a pit and ultimately took their skin for transformation purposes. She hadn't watched it herself, but it had been such a blockbuster hit that her cop friends had talked about it for months.

Unfortunately, despite their initial theory that the killer had targeted both Cheryl Anderson and Kelly Sorenson because of their connections to Sequoia College, Tammy Ryan had no apparent connection to the college at all. They'd immediately backtracked and returned to McGill's with Ryan's photo, but no one could recall seeing her, whether in Kelly Sorenson's company or otherwise. According to family and friends, including Susan Ingram, Ryan and Sorenson hadn't known each other. And no one they'd talked to, none of their friends and acquaintances, none of the strangers they'd managed to track down and none of the other employees who'd worked at McGill's, could remember seeing Kelly Sorenson at McGill's past eight o'clock the night she'd been killed.

That's what currently troubled Carrie the most. Susan Ingram had said Kelly had called her around nine that night. It was at that time that Kelly had said she was leaving with her charity-case client. The timing of Kelly's call had been verified by the caller ID on Ingram's phone. Yet even though many people could remember seeing her that night, most of them recalled her leaving at about eight.

Carrie had contacted Kelly's cell-phone company to get the records of incoming and outgoing calls from Kelly's cell-phone number on the night she'd been murdered. However, it would take upward of two days before they could get her that information. Now, she was also waiting for phone records from Tammy Ryan. When she had both, she'd cross-check them for duplicate numbers to see if the same person, the same killer, had called both of them.

Still, despite the fact Sorenson had been dismembered and Ryan hadn't, it was a logical assumption that they'd been killed by the same person, someone who, whether it was coincidental or not—and they were all betting not—had decided to cut off his victim's eyelids around the time Dr. Bowers was doing the same to his victims.

Even with the frustration pulsing through her, Carrie quietly closed the file she was reviewing and kept her voice calm. She didn't have to explode for Jase to know how on edge she felt; he likely felt the same way. "This has to end. We have to figure out how he's picking them. Why he's picking them."

"The eyelids are a clue," Jase said. "They have to

be. And that means he's probably leaving other clues behind, as well."

"How? He's changing his method of killing them. Of disposing of them."

"Maybe that's a clue in and of itself. The variety. He dismembered Sorenson's body. Left her head posed on a stump. With Tammy Ryan, he strangled her, then stripped her of her skin, leaving her body intact. In both cases, however, he did things to them that damaged their exteriors. Could that mean anything, coupled with the eyelids? Because unlike The Embalmer, this killer—"

Carrie nodded. "This killer wanted their eyes to stay open *while* they were alive. But why? According to the coroner, he didn't actually start taking Tammy Ryan's skin until she was dead. If that was true for Sorenson, too, then unlike The Embalmer, who supposedly embalmed his victims while they were still alive, this second killer didn't necessarily want his victims to feel pain."

"If he wasn't hurting them while they were alive, what else could he have been doing? Talking to them? But if talking to them was so important, why cut off their eyelids?"

"He didn't want them to hear him. He wanted them to *see* him," Carrie guessed, adrenaline rushing through her veins as they talked and, in her mind, got into the head of a killer more and more. "Maybe they knew him. Or maybe not. Maybe the point was they hadn't recognized him? Hadn't seen him the way he thought they should?"

"That makes sense. But what was it they didn't see?"

"You know," she said slowly. "The second victim. The way she was killed. It's like the victim in that horror movie that's so ingrained in pop culture right now. The one about the cannibalistic doctor. Given that Bowers's crime was based on a horror movie…"

They went on the internet. Minutes later, Jase nodded. "It makes sense. The eyelids? Horror movie. Stripping the skin off your victim? Horror movie. And as we now know, dismembering a body and propping a head on a tree stump?"

"Also a horror movie," Carrie said softly. "So he's a horror-movie buff, too. He's not copying The Embalmer so much as he's copying horror movies. The eyelids are just a component of that."

"Was he copying Bowers or is it just complete coincidence? What are the chances that two serial killers could be killing based on the same horror movie at the same time and not be connected somehow?"

"I'd say it would be possible but for the specificity of the eyelids. I'd never heard of that movie. It's too obscure. With that detail in common, I think it increases the chances that they knew each other. Or, at the very least, that this second killer knew of Bowers's crimes and decided to copy them for his own sick reasons."

"Right. If you're a horror-movie buff, it would only take that one detail getting out to catch your attention. The Embalmer kills his victims, somehow it gets leaked to the second killer that he's cutting off eyelids, he decides to do the same thing for whatever reason, but because he doesn't know the full M.O. of The Embalmer's killings, or because the embalming doesn't hold the same significance for him, he decides to wing it and use methods of killing from horror movies. Let's run with it."

"Run with it how?"

"Do some word searches on the internet that are related to the horror movies we've identified so far. See if there's any kind of connection with other movies. Or if anyone is talking about murders duplicating horror movies. Do some searches for classified ads. Anyone soliciting actors to act out scenes from horror movies. That kind of thing."

She nodded. As much as she'd resisted the idea at first, working with Jase was a huge benefit for her. He was smart and was teaching her to think outside the box. Again, she had no doubt she would have eventually thought to do the same things on her own, but who knew how long it would have taken her to do it? They were clearly at their most optimum when they were working as a team, bouncing information off each other.

"So you think the victims might be wannabe actors? I didn't pick up on that in any of the background information."

"Could be that we just haven't asked the right questions. They might not have been actively pursuing acting, but maybe they have some kind of interest in the theater. Some secret passion that someone could have taken advantage of. Since Tammy Ryan was a relative recluse, we should probably start with Susan Ingram. Find out if Kelly Sorenson had an interest in horror movies. And we need to contact the FBI. See if we can get any of their profilers to look over what we've got and give us any suggestions."

Carrie had another thought. "We also can't forget that Bowers invited his staff to watch movies with him. Who else might he have invited? His patients? We need to talk to his entire staff again. Get a warrant for his medical records and talk to his patients, as well."

Hours later, Commander Stevens heard back from the FBI. "They agree the horror movies might be a key piece of evidence in the case. They're happy to help out in any way they can. But I can tell the FBI's very impressed with the two of you. If what you wanted was to make a good reputation for yourselves and our team, you're definitely doing that. Good work. But let's keep the focus on our local victims and stopping the person who's killing them."

"Unfortunately," Jase responded, "we haven't found out much more. None of the victims are movie buffs. Sorenson enjoyed the occasional horror movie, but she liked a wide variety of genres. It doesn't show a link between Sorenson and Ryan."

"I'm sure you two will figure it out. Just keep working it. But you can't continue to work it alone. You both look exhausted. I know you've been burning the midnight oil for days straight. You need to take a break."

"We can't take a break, sir. Not with a second victim just having turned up."

"It's not a suggestion, it's an order, Carrie. You know the protocol. We give our detectives several days to get a jump on these cases, but you're not superhuman. You've already solved one complicated serial-killer case. You need to pace yourself if you're going to solve this second one. We'll bring in a couple of detectives from SFPD who'll work under you, following up on the leads that you've already set in motion. It'll be just enough downtime so you can actually get some sleep and some food into your bodies. I don't want to hear another word about it, do you understand?"

Carrie nodded. Jase said, "Yes, sir." However, they looked at each other, plainly not happy with the turn of events. When Commander Stevens left, Jase turned to her. "It'll take him a couple of hours to get a team of detectives in place and ready to roll. In the meantime, I've been thinking of a few things and wanted to run them by you."

"Go ahead," she said. "I'm all ears."

"Remember when you mentioned the eyelids earlier? The fact Sorenson's killer cut them off while she was still alive? That the killer wanted her to see him? On the outside. Maybe he picked them for the same reason, something to do with their exteriors. Something we've missed. The Embalmer picked women with light brown hair. What do Sorenson and Ryan have in common? We're missing something."

"Let's look at their 'before' photos again."

They did. And once again came up empty.

Frustrated anew, Carrie stood and began to pace. "The only thing I see is that Kelly Sorenson was gorgeous, and, even though I wouldn't have thought it was possible, Tammy Ryan was even better-looking. Also in her favor was that she was a competitive athlete. How helpful is that?"

"Maybe more helpful than you'd think," Jase said slowly.

"Really?" she asked doubtfully.

"Let's go with it for a second. He's picking them for how they look. No resemblance at all, but the second even more beautiful than the first."

"It might just mean he was attracted to each of them."

"But with the eyelids, with the idea of him wanting them to see him, when they hadn't before, I think it increases the chances that the person we're looking for isn't as good-looking. Or at least, is someone these women wouldn't be interested in."

"So that means what? That we're looking for someone who isn't attractive?" Carrie asked. "Isn't that a huge stretch?"

"Think about it. Remember what I told you? That my childhood affected why I date the women I do? Serial killers usually have some trauma in their background that they're trying to deal with through the murders. Something about beautiful women ignoring him plays a part in this guy's M.O. And I'm betting it's not just them ignoring him because that wouldn't trigger the type of rage that would warrant slicing off someone's eyelids."

"So if they didn't ignore him, they rejected and ridiculed him?" she clarified. It really did make sense, she thought. "According to Susan Ingram, Kelly Sorenson described her client that night as a 'charity case.'"

"Maybe she wasn't the only one to think so. Maybe he's been ridiculed his whole life. For some kind of physical defect?"

"Bowers was a plastic surgeon. Someone who'd be contacted to fix a physical defect."

"Right. But what if this defect was something he couldn't fix?"

"How long until we get that warrant to look at Bowers's medical records?"

"Not long. So we need to look for records of someone with a physical disability?"

"Not just any disability. Something on the outside. Something that would make others react violently to him, and as such make him take out his resentment in a violent way, as well."

BRAD TOUCHED HIS FACE, which felt smoother than it had in years. Tammy Ryan had been the right choice. The rush of power he'd felt when he'd begun to cut her had been exhilarating. The end result miraculous. His scar was almost gone now.

He wasn't crazy. He was just smarter. Smarter in ways that most people couldn't understand. Smarter than even Dr. Bowers.

Of course, Bowers hadn't seen it that way. He'd been arrogant enough when he'd just been a doctor, but a doctor who was killing women and evading the police, too? Hell, he'd thought he was some kind of God.

Yet, that's exactly how Brad felt now. And if Brad was a God, if he was smarter than Bowers, who was smarter than the police, then that meant that Brad was smarter than the police, too. So why not have a little more fun with them? Amp up the ante even more. After all, perhaps that was to be his final test. Who was stronger and more powerful than a bunch of cops?

Him, that's who.

That's why he'd started planting his clues on the internet. He wanted to give them a fighting chance. If they were smart enough to discover his clues, it would make things more exciting. It would be an ultimate challenge. Proof of his superiority. That he could so easily evade the police. Dupe them. Just like he was duping them now.

People thought they knew him. Everyday, they saw him. Talked with him. Probably dismissed his importance without thought. That wouldn't happen for much longer. Not anymore.

He didn't care about his own physical perfection. That was just a means to an end. But she cared. And she was all that mattered.

Brad's blood rushed through his veins in anticipation of seeing her again.

Maybe he'd be merciful with Tony Higgs. Forget the fact that Nora fawned over him.

Brad turned to look at the container that held the eyelids of his first two vic—donors. Instantly, he imagined it filled to the brim.

No, he hadn't had mercy on them. He couldn't have mercy on anyone else.

Mercy was for the weak.

Tony Higgs had to die.

CHAPTER TWENTY-ONE

HOURS LATER, EVEN AFTER Jase and Carrie had thoroughly instructed their replacements on the facts of the case and what they should be following up on, Jase asked Carrie to stay at the office for a little while longer to talk things out.

"We believe he picked Tammy Ryan because she was even more beautiful than Kelly Sorenson. If we forget the movie that involved the eyelids for a minute, the other two movies, the ones he incorporated into his murders, explore the theme of beauty, too. That's not coincidental. So he enjoys subtext. Layers. Riddles. Someone like that is going to think he's smarter. Smarter than us. Smarter than the whole damn world. What's the best way to prove that? By playing with the whole world. Taunting them with clues."

Carrie nodded in understanding. "You're talking about the internet."

"Exactly. I'm suggesting he might be leaving clues on the internet. But not just any clues. The horror movies are significant to him. Someone who's a movie buff would be interested in sharing that interest with others. Making the movies part of his riddles. So I asked Larry

Tanaka to do some searches on the web. He's been looking for anything having to do with horror movies, but in particular horror movies that have a common theme of beauty."

Larry Tanaka was a computer forensic tech for DOJ. One of the best they had. "And he's found something?"

"He thinks so. He's on his way up to tell us right now."

"Carrie! Jase! You're not going to believe this."

Carrie glanced up. Tanaka rushed toward them, several papers clutched in his hand. The compact Japanese American always moved as if he'd had one too many cups of coffee, which was hilarious considering he didn't touch the stuff. Or refined sugar. Or meat. Larry referred to his body as a temple and treated it that way.

"We found your guy on the internet."

"What?" Both she and Jase exclaimed at the same time. They'd been hoping for some good news, but this?

Tanaka shook his head. "Sorry. Didn't mean to get you so excited. We don't know who he is, but he's been bragging about his crimes. The guy's a fucking nut job. You know Michael Miller, down in Vice?"

She didn't blink at Tanaka's abrupt change in topic. It was typical for him, but the information he often found was well worth the tangents everyone had to endure to get it. "Sure."

"He's been working a child-porn case, searching for predators on the net. Came across an interesting blog. You know, it's like the other social networks out there, only for freaks. Do you know there's an organization called the Kevorkian Clan? They advocate 'voluntary population reduction.' Altruistic suicide. God, people are twisted."

"I'm interested in one twisted person, right now," Carrie prompted.

She and Jase looked at each other, and the amused glint in Jase's eyes suggested a shared joke between them. She was so tempted to smile back but forced herself not to. He was dangerous to her in more ways than one. She couldn't forget that.

"Right, right. Anyway, Miller came across this site. Didn't know if the guy was just another nut but didn't want to take any chances. He started looking for word patterns and figured out a code. Based on that, he deciphered a whole bunch of gobbledygook words into blog posts that actually made sense. He compared the dates of his blogs to our homicide reports, and presto, they matched up. Kelly Sorenson and Tammy Ryan."

A rush of excitement and hope slammed into her, and she greedily latched onto it. It had been devastating for her to think that she'd stopped The Embalmer only to realize that another killer had taken his place and was proving to be just as elusive, if not more so. With the long hours they'd been putting in, she wasn't sure how well she and Jase could stay at the top of their game before something had to give.

This could be the break they'd been waiting for. But a blog? Why would the killer be stupid enough to blog about his kills? As a general rule, serial killers were smart. They had to be to get away with multiple crimes. But most of them did get caught. Eventually. It was only a matter of how many victims had to be sacrificed before that happened.

For half a second, Carrie's mind went somewhere she rarely let it. To memories of a man who'd thought he could get away with raping her. She hadn't let him. She'd done the right thing by turning him in, but she'd been shocked by how their friends had turned on her. She'd somehow become the bad guy, and it had changed her life enough to make her want to start over. To leave. To prove that she didn't need him or anyone else. Not so long as she had herself. Her strength. And afterward, she'd continued to do the right thing regardless of what it cost her.

Just like shooting Kevin Porter had been the right thing to do.

"—we can use to track him?" Jase finished asking.

"We don't know yet. In terms of the content, he doesn't give much away. In fact, he was obviously trying to be careful, never giving away the type of information that could be used to track or identify him. He's been blogging about movies, in the guise of movie reviews, but see how his blogs have used the key phrases you had me look for? Things like the movie titles. And other words having to do with beauty. Beauty and strength."

"Strength?" Carrie asked.

"Yes, apparently that's what floats his boat. Not only beauty, but being the strongest. You know, the whole

Darwin survival of the fittest philosophy. Does that fit with your victims?"

"It does," Jase confirmed. "The two women he's killed have been gorgeous. Sorenson was a runner. Tammy Ryan was a competitive softball player."

"Then I'm betting the guy will be an athlete, too," Tanaka said.

"What guy?" Carrie and Jase asked at the same time.

"His next target. If we've decoded his blogs correctly, he's already got his sights on a another victim. A man this time."

"Show us," Jase ordered.

Maybe it was simply Tanaka's certainty that the killer had already picked out a third victim. Or maybe it really was because she was tired and hungry and feeling burned out. In either case, even though he wasn't even talking to her, the sound of Jase's authoritative voice rankled Carrie. As much help as he'd been, she couldn't forget she was the lead on this case. She needed to act like it. "Wait," she said to Tanaka. "Before you show us the blogs, tell me what we're doing to track him down."

Beside her, Jase shifted impatiently, but listened as Tanaka talked.

"Tech just called me with the results on the ISP search. They'll keep working on it, but it looks like Darwin's using proxy servers, which makes him even harder to track."

Darwin? So this second killer had finally earned

his own moniker. "And you said the blog entries themselves were useless?"

"Right. Other than a possible motive, he doesn't reveal much."

Carrie remembered Sorenson and Ryan's ravaged bodies. Murder she could understand. Focusing on them because of their beauty made sense, too. But what kind of motive was Tanaka talking about? "What hints?"

"Not sure. Again, it has something to do with power. And beauty. The commander wants Dr. Hudson to look it over. If she can't come up with anything, he's going to send things over to the FBI."

Carrie nodded. Of course, Commander Stevens would want to keep things internal if at all possible before asking the FBI for any more help. Despite his confirmation that she and Jase had "impressed" some people at the FBI, there was still that ever-present sense of autonomy and competitiveness separating the state and federal agencies.

Besides, Lana was good at her job, Carrie conceded, even if she sometimes pushed when Carrie didn't want her to. In truth, she and Jase probably should have consulted with her as soon as they began to link the murders to movies involving beauty. She'd make sure they did so as soon as they could. Lana might be able to give them some insight into this killer.

"What about Lana?"

Carrie looked up. Simon had walked into the room, and she knew immediately that the tension in his broad shoulders had nothing to do with the job so much as the mention of Lana's name. He was careful not to let the emotion show on his face, but she knew it was there.

"Stevens has asked Lana to look over some blogs that might have been written by our serial killer." She finally looked down at the blogs Tanaka had handed them. There were three pages.

Three. For three victims.

Knowing that Tanaka had his own work to get back to, Carrie thanked him.

"Sure thing," he said. "Keep me posted. I want to know when you nail this creepy fuck."

"Same goes for me," Simon said before stalking off.

"You think he's going to see Lana?" Jase asked her.

"I'd bet on it. Now, let's sit down and read these blogs."

The first one was short and dated right around the time Kelly Sorenson had been killed. According to the code that Tanaka and Miller had put together, the blog read:

I killed last night. A prostitute who'd probably been too high on meth to show me a decent time anyway. She'd thought she was doing me a favor. Laughed at me. Kept yapping until it hurt my ears. I wrapped my hands around her neck to shut her up. She died and that's when I knew.

By killing her, I'd made her see my power. My beauty. I'd had the last laugh. And liked it. Fate had led me to her.

She was the first. But she won't be the last.

"He calls her a prostitute," Carrie murmured. "So he

knew Kelly Sorenson was an escort. And that he was going to be her 'charity case' for the evening. Obviously he didn't like that."

"Can't blame him for that." Jase jerked his chin, indicating she should flip to the next blog post, which she did.

Killing the prostitute had been easy. A snap. LOL. Anyone could have done it. Last night I proved I can do better.

Better prey. Stronger prey. It makes killing all the sweeter.

Survival of the fittest.

In eradicating the strong, I will grow stronger. In eliminating perfection, I will become perfect.

Beauty is in the eye of the beholder.

The strong shall inherit the Earth.

Death is the ultimate equalizer.

"You were right," Carrie said. "He's not only killing to punish people for how they treated him, but because he thinks it's curing some kind of defect he has."

"But now he wants to amp things up? He's getting tired of killing women who weren't posing enough of a challenge for him?"

"Right. So he's going to kill a man. Assuming that Tanaka is right."

"Flip to the next one." He moved closer to read over her shoulder. His chest brushed her shoulder, and his breath tickled her neck, but for the first time his presence comforted her rather than rattled her.

Carrie flipped the page to the next entry.

She sucked in a breath. "He wrote it today. This morning."

He thinks he's a God but he's not. She adores him, but she shouldn't. He's nothing. Less than nothing. When I kill him, however, his power will become mine. His strength will make me stronger. My scars will finally be gone and finally, I won't be alone. She'll see how much time she's wasted on him and she'll be mine. My angel. Together we'll thrive, and make those who've mocked us regret it.

"Oh, God," she whispered. "Tanaka's right." She turned to once more meet Jase's gaze. "He knows who he wants to kill. Not just a random man but someone specific."

Jase stared at her grimly before speaking. "But who's this angel he's talking about being with once he kills his next target? And afterward, is she going to be with him voluntarily or not?"

Jase stared into Carrie's horrified eyes.

He wanted to reassure her. To tell her they'd find the bastard before he killed again.

He couldn't.

Even so, the connection that had been between them had only grown stronger as a result of the work they'd been doing together. He felt steadied by her very presence, and he prayed that he offered her the same kind of strength in return.

He rolled his shoulders, trying to loosen the tightness that radiated up his neck and into the base of his skull. This case was going to explode in the press soon. They'd tried to keep things under wraps, but he knew it wouldn't stay that way for long, especially not with these blogs on the internet.

Darwin, as Tanaka had dubbed him, clearly wasn't done yet.

CHAPTER TWENTY-TWO

THEY GOT THE CALL about Darwin's third victim the very next day.

Tony Higgs had been twenty-two-years-old, his whole life laid out ahead of him. Handsome. Popular. Well-liked. His girlfriend, Ashley Hartford, swore he was a nice guy who'd been willing to help anyone out. Unfortunately, what he'd gotten in return was a vicious death, one involving a chain saw. Like the two before him, however, his eyelids had been cut off.

Jase was right in the middle of interviewing Ashley. He hadn't been able to get much else from the crying girl, and Jase tried to temper his impatience with compassion. The girl had just learned her boyfriend had been brutally murdered. She had a right to grieve. Still, he had a job to do. He needed to find out as much as possible about Tony Higgs. His friends. His routine. Especially his school habits.

While Tammy Ryan hadn't attended Sequoia College, Tony Higgs had. That meant that next to the horror movies, the college connection was still the best chance they had of solving the case. Maybe they'd missed something before. Something that could lead them to Darwin.

"So there was no one who had a grudge against Tony? You're sure?"

Ashley looked up, her perfect makeup smeared across her face, all thought of looking good forgotten in her grief. "No. No one! Everyone loved Tony."

Jase doubted that. According to Darwin's blog, Higgs hadn't been the perfect man Ashley thought he'd been. He'd pissed Darwin off. For some reason or another, imagined or otherwise. And it had definitely had to do with a girl. Could that girl have been Ashley?

"Could someone have been jealous of him? Has anyone shown an inordinate amount of interest in you?"

She just started crying again. Shaking her head. Jase bit back his frustration. Out of his periphery, he saw someone enter the interview room. He sighed.

Carrie. She walked in, nodded and took a seat next to him. Ashley glanced up at her but then started crying again. Jase waited a few minutes until she'd calmed down.

"What about girls? Someone who liked him? Someone who was jealous of you?"

She nodded her head. "There were all kinds of girls who liked Tony. I mean, he is…" Her voice cracked. "He was the college quarterback. Water-polo captain. Gorgeous."

"But anyone specific you can think of?"

She shook her head. "He never talked to other girls. He was very respectful of me."

Jase closed his notepad, ready to leave her to her mother who was waiting outside.

"Wait." Ashley reached out and touched his forearm, catching him off guard. Her grip seemed strong for such a slight person. "There was one girl. A girl who's been tutoring him. But she's a total nerd."

Jase opened his pad again. "What's her name?"

"Nora. Nora Lopez."

"She's a student, too?"

Ashley nodded. "He was prepping for his chem final on Friday. She was meeting him every afternoon. At a café across from campus. It's called Steam. She must have been the last one to see him." Ashley dissolved into hysterical tears again, but Jase barely heard her.

A campus café. They'd have to check it out. Maybe it was a place that Sorenson and Ryan had frequented. If so, it could be where Darwin was picking out his victims.

Nora had greeted Brad warmly when she'd arrived at Steam. Just like always, she took the time to ask him how he was doing and what he had planned for the day. She found a table in the back and watched the door eagerly. Five minutes went by. Then ten. After twenty minutes, she looked annoyed. After forty minutes, sad.

In about another ten minutes, when she realized Tony had stood her up, Brad would be there to comfort her. He practically rubbed his hands together with glee.

She got up and headed toward the restrooms. Probably to cry, Brad thought with annoyance. For a moment, he felt angry. Higgs had been a loser with nothing going for him but his looks and physical strength. Didn't she realize that? He took several deep breaths, trying to calm himself. Telling himself she'd soon be his.

Eager to talk to her, he rushed to stock the open display shelf in front of the cash registers. He was almost done when the café's front entry doors opened and two people walked in.

Brad recognized the police officers instantly. The badass detective with the fancy clothes and the redhead from McGill's Bar. Brad's heart almost leaped out of his chest, and panic caused him to clench his fists so that he mangled the packaged pastries he'd been handling.

Shit. Had they somehow traced the blog to him? But that was impossible. He'd been so smart. So careful.

He forced himself to remain calm. He put his hands in his pockets, turned and started to walk toward the back room. Toward the back exit. He stiffened when he heard a voice call out to him.

"Excuse me."

It was the woman.

He stopped abruptly, his hand tightening on the blade in his left pocket. He wondered if he could outrun her.

"You work here?" she asked.

Brad half turned toward her, making sure he remained in profile. "Yeah. Can you hang on a second?"

"Turn around and face me, please." The command was spoken politely, but it was still a command that she clearly expected him to obey. With no other choice,

Brad slowly turned the rest of the way and raised his head.

Would they see it? The scar? The blood on his hands?

She frowned. "Do I know you?"

"I don't think so." But she'd seen him before, just as he'd seen her. She obviously just couldn't place him. Which was good, really, but it made him mad. Was he that unimportant to people? How could she help but notice him with the damn ugliness on his face?

When the man she was with turned and looked at him, there was no recognition on his face, either. What a hoot. Although the woman's eyes flickered to his hands, which were still in his pockets, they found nothing about him or his appearance surprising.

Which meant…they couldn't see his scars.

They were finally gone.

After all the years of suffering. After killing not just Sorenson and Ryan, but Dr. Bowers, too, he'd struck on the winning combination.

Killing Tony had worked. The terror that had coalesced inside him just moments before transformed into something else.

Arrogance.

Survival of the fittest.

He was better than the police. Smarter. Stronger.

Brad let out a silent sigh of relief and took his hands out of his pockets, noticing how each of the detective's shoulders subtly relaxed when he did so. The male detective scanned the crowded café, obviously looking for someone else.

Brad's nerves skittered as he realized the man must be looking for Nora. That they'd made the connection between her and Tony. Shit, he didn't want the police anywhere near her. Stay in the bathroom, he silently commanded.

When he brought his gaze back to the female cop, she was studying him carefully, but not necessarily with suspicion. She really had no clue who he was. His nerves transformed into delight.

Just as Brad had the thought, Nora exited the restroom, and he could see the detectives' eyes light up. Brad's confidence stuttered like a car running out of gas.

"THAT'S HER," Jase said. "I'll talk to her."

Carrie turned her eyes back to the good-looking kid in front of her. She could swear she'd seen him before, but from where? She flashed her badge and identified herself as a police officer. "What's your name?"

"Brad. Brad Turner."

"Brad, were you working yesterday afternoon?"

"What's this about, officer?"

Carrie smiled, albeit impatiently. It's what everyone asked, and she understood that anyone would be nervous when being questioned by the police.

"We're investigating a crime. Please just answer the question. Were you working yesterday afternoon?"

"Yes. I work the night shift. Two to ten. Just like today."

Higgs had been killed sometime between 11:00 p.m.

and 2:00 a.m. Carrie studied him more carefully. This boy was barely older than the students he served. And far from being scarred, he was the picture of all-American charm and good looks. He looked a bit like Lance Reynolds, the bartender from McGill's.

"Tony Higgs. Do you know him?"

"Sure, I know Tony. Everyone does. Nice guy."

"Did you see him in here last night?"

Uncertainty overtook his face, and he furrowed his brow. "Gosh, I'm not sure. I think so. We were really busy last night. It's finals, you know. Lots of kids cramming for exams."

Carrie looked around. The café was indeed crowded. She saw Jase talking to the girl, who was now crying and visibly shaking.

"That girl. Do you remember seeing him with her? Nora Lopez? Someone told me she tutors him here every afternoon."

The boy looked where Carrie pointed, and seemed upset when he saw her crying. "Yeah, I know Nora. What's happened? Why is she crying?"

Instead of answering him, Carrie pulled out several photographs. "I need you to look at these photos and tell me if you remember seeing any of these people before."

He looked at the photos she handed him. Kelly Sorenson. Tammy Ryan.

He pulled out the one of Sorenson. "I think I remember seeing her in here before. But I don't recognize the other."

A wailing came from the corner. Carrie looked over

and saw Jase motioning her over with a look of panic
on his face. Nora Lopez had obviously been more than
Tony's tutor. The girl was hyperventilating and looked
ready to faint. Carrie pulled out her card and Jase's card
and handed them to Brad Turner.

"This is my card, as well as my partner's. If you remember seeing these people or think of anything suspicious, will you call us, please?"

"Sure."

But she was already hurrying toward Jase.

BRAD WATCHED THE FEMALE cop rush over to the table
and escort Nora outside. They sat with her at one of
the tables there, the male detective looking impatient
at Nora's hysterics.

He hated to see Nora upset, but she would've found
out sometime. It was better this way. The faster she put
Tony Higgs out of her mind, the sooner they could be
together. He finished stocking the pastry case and then
kept an eye on Nora while he wiped down some tables.
A few minutes later, he saw the officers rise and hand
Nora their cards before walking away. He straightened
tables and chairs as Nora walked back into the café
alone, went back to her table and started to put her stuff
back into her backpack. Midway through the process,
she stopped and simply slumped back in her chair, a
dazed look on her face.

He shook his head again. Poor girl. She just didn't
realize how she was wasting her time, grieving for such

a weakling. But she'd get over him. He'd make sure of that.

He glanced at his watch. Soon, the police would catch their killer. He'd made sure that everything was already in place. Pleasure filled him at the thought of the police breaking into his foster father's house and putting the drugged degenerate out of his misery. He was a worthless piece of shit who'd fostered an abandoned freak of a baby simply because he and his druggie wife had wanted the cash. He wouldn't be expecting Brad to take his revenge. Revenge for years of abuse and neglect. Revenge for years of being made to feel like an ugly beast that needed to be hidden away.

He thought it was fitting that the foster father he hadn't seen in years would be the one to complete his transformation. He shivered with impatience, liking the fact that the police would be going from him to his next victim all in less than twenty-four hours.

Anticipation filled Brad, and he struggled to control his impatience. He knew he should wait until the police thought they'd found their killer. That was the plan. He'd planted the evidence. All he had to do was call the station and tell them where to find it. Once they did, he'd be free. Free to pursue Nora and share his life with her.

It had only been an hour since the police had left, but the longer he looked at Nora, the more excited he became. He'd waited so long to be with her, and now that his scars were gone, now that Tony was gone, there was nothing keeping them apart.

What harm would it do? To talk to her now? To declare his love, so she wouldn't feel so alone.

There were only a couple of stray customers left in the café. Walking up to Nora, he saw the ravages of grief on her face. Her face was splotchy, her eyes red and glazed with moisture. When he said hello, she stared at him in confusion, as if she didn't even recognize him.

Still, he maintained his confidence. He sat down next to her and took her hands in his. He marveled at the opportunity to finally touch her. "What happened?" he asked softly.

She said nothing and he leaned closer.

"What is it, Nora?"

"Tony...Tony is dead." Her mouth quivered at the last word.

Brad feigned shock. "The boy you study with? Oh, my God. How horrible! What happened?"

She shook her head. "Murdered. They said he was murdered. By some psychopath."

Brad held back his snarl of anger. Of course the police would call him a psychopath. They had to account for their incompetence somehow.

"They gave me their cards...the card of a shrink they work with...." Nora motioned to the cards that she'd placed on the table. "Said I should call them if I think of anything..." Her face collapsed again, and she began crying quietly. "I can't believe it. I can't believe he's gone. He was so...beautiful. Such a beautiful person."

He thought of the last time he'd seen Tony. How he'd

cried and whimpered as he'd sliced him up. The terror had indeed been beautiful. He squeezed Nora's hand. "You're so much more beautiful than him, Nora. I've always thought so. I'll make you forget him."

Nora stared at him uncomprehendingly. Then she flushed and pulled her hands back. Stiffness transformed her features, and she stood, stuffing books into her backpack with violence.

"Don't be scared," he said. "I love you. I'll never hurt you the way he did...."

Nora stopped and looked at him with confusion. "Hurt me? Tony never hurt me! He was perfect. A wonderful person."

Jealousy overwhelmed him. "Perfect?" He scowled. "You think so? Is that why he laughed at you behind your back? I'd never do that. I appreciate who you are. I've been waiting for you. Watching you."

Nora paled, and he felt ashamed of himself for lashing out at her. He reached out for her hand, but she flinched away as if he'd slapped her.

"You've been watching me? What—what does that mean? What do you mean Tony laughed at me behind my back? Why are you saying that?"

"It's true. He thought you were a joke. He didn't love you the way I do."

Nora's eyes bulged. "Love me? You're crazy!"

Brad stared at her and clenched his fists. "Don't call me crazy." Shaking his head, he reached out a hand to her, trying to ignore the fact it trembled. "I'm not crazy. I love you—"

"Don't touch me!" She flinched away, grabbed her things then spied the business cards on the table. She picked them up and threw one at him. "Here. You need this a lot more than I do. Get some help!"

Nora ran away, and that's when he noticed the stunned silence in the café. All of the remaining customers looked at him with varying degrees of shock and amusement. Brad flushed at their stares, mortification overwhelming him. He touched his face, feeling the skin that suddenly felt rough. Distorted.

Bending over, he picked up the card Nora had thrown at him. Once he straightened, he backed up, stumbling over a table and chair. Rushing to the restroom, he slammed the door and locked it. His heart threatened to pound out of his chest, and he looked in the mirror fearfully.

It was faint, barely visible, but he could see it. The once smooth skin had started to ripple. His complexion was no longer pure.

Pain filled him at Nora's rejection.

How could she reject him after all he'd done for her? For a moment, he imagined punishing her. Stripping her naked and torturing her. Telling her how he'd tortured Tony and how it was all her fault.

He whimpered. No. He loved her. She was his angel. It was Tony's fault. Tony must have seduced her. Turned her against him.

Someone knocked on the door, the sound jolting through him and making him flinch in fear. Had the police returned?

More knocking. "Come on. I've gotta use the can, man!"

Tony turned on the water and splashed some on his face. He opened the door, kept his gaze down and walked out. He sensed the young man waiting to use the restroom looking at him before he shut the door behind him.

He tried to ignore the people in the café, but he sensed the snickers and stares directed toward him. They were mocking him again. Just like before.

As he passed the table where Nora had sat, he noticed the card that she'd thrown at him. He bent down and picked it up.

It was a card.

A card for a Dr. Lana Hudson.

The shrink Nora had mentioned.

Calmness descended upon him like a hazy cloak.

He smiled.

He understood now. He'd thought Tony was the final victim. The one who would complete him. Obviously he'd been wrong. His transformation wasn't complete yet.

He remembered the way the cops had shaken his confidence. He'd shown weakness, however brief. No wonder Nora had turned from him. Females gravitated to the strongest male because they wanted to be protected. She must have sensed his weakness and run from it.

He needed to reassert his power. And quickly.

He rubbed his cheek again. It was still there, under

the surface. He wouldn't allow it to come back. Not the scar. Not the fear. Not the powerlessness.

He caressed the card he held. He'd go ahead with his plans. Send the police on the hunt for his foster father. And while they were doing that, when they thought they'd won, he'd hunt down one of their own.

Then he'd be back for Nora. One way or another, she'd realize she was his.

CHAPTER TWENTY-THREE

AFTER MEETING WITH Nora Lopez and doing a bit more investigative work at the college, Carrie and Jase reported what they'd gathered to Commander Stevens. Subsequently, Carrie took a detour to Lana's office. She'd wanted to discuss their theory about Darwin being scarred, but Lana wasn't there. She was heading back to SIG to meet Jase when Carrie caught sight of a familiar face. Bo Havens, her friend from the SFPD SWAT team.

"Well, look at you, girl. How are you doing?" Bo gave her a hug. "You should stop by McGill's and say hello to the boys tonight. It's been a while since we've seen you."

Carrie smiled. She really liked Bo and almost all the other men on her former SWAT team. But she felt drained by the events of the past few days. By witnessing the incredible grief on Nora Lopez's face when she'd learned that her friend Tony Higgs had died.

She shook her head. "No. I won't be able to make it. But you have a great time. Tell everyone I said hi."

"Even Pete?" Bo smirked.

Carrie's stomach contracted at the mention of the

SWAT sniper's name, but she simply smiled wider. "Even Pete."

Bo winked at her and waved. Carrie turned the corner, then came to an abrupt stop when she saw Jase. The affection she'd felt for Bo was suddenly replaced by something more intense. More primitive. More alive.

She didn't know why, but each time she saw Jase, she felt her heart expand just a bit more, until it was in her throat.

He sat slouched in his chair, his hands shoved into his pockets and staring up at the ceiling. He looked up when she walked up next to him.

"Hey, Ward. Did I hear you talking to someone?"

"Someone from my old SWAT team," she confirmed. "Both of them, actually. He was with the Austin SWAT team with me, too, and we both ended up working for SFPD. Bo Haven. A good guy. He was inviting me to stop by and see the team at McGill's and I…" With the name of the bar echoing in her head, Carrie suddenly thought of Brad Turner, the young man who'd worked at the college café. The one who looked a lot like the bartender at McGill's. Was it possible that she'd seen him there, too? And if she had, could that mean anything, especially since Kelly Sorenson had been at McGill's just before she'd been killed?

"What is it?" Jase asked.

Carrie automatically shook her head, not wanting to give her thoughts too much credence before she could actually confirm what they meant. "The guy at the college café earlier today. His name's Brad Turner. I thought I recognized him. I suddenly wondered if it could be because I saw him at McGill's. I mean...he looks a lot like the bartender, Lance Reynolds. But he knew Tony Higgs. Maybe he knew Kelly Sorenson, too? Her picture seemed to ring a bell with him but maybe there's more to it."

"That would certainly be a relevant connection. But you can't be sure you've seen him there?"

She shook her head. "Still, I want to go to McGill's and check it out."

"I'll meet you there. I'll swing by the café first. See if I can talk to him."

"Okay. Thanks, Jase."

Less than thirty minutes later, Carrie stepped into McGill's. She was immediately greeted by several people, including some of the guys from SWAT.

After making brief small talk, Carrie headed straight to an older woman tending the bar. "Hi, I'm Special Agent Carrie Ward. I'm looking for someone I've seen here before. Tall. Blondish hair. Dimples. Sound familiar?"

"Sounds like a dozen kids I see in here every night. It even sounds like a bartender that works here."

"Right. Lance Reynolds." She was right. Both Brad and Lance had similar looks to a few guys at the bar right now. So maybe she hadn't seen Brad Turner here. Maybe she'd only thought she had.

"You know Lance?" the female bartender asked her.

"We've talked. But I'm looking for someone else.

I'll probably come back tomorrow with a photo, just to make sure you haven't seen him before, okay?"

"Sure, hon. Whatever you say."

"Thanks." She turned and caught sight of a glass bowl sitting on the bar. It was filled with business cards that would be entered into a drawing for a free this or a free that. It was a common marketing tool, one she'd seen at many delis and restaurants. Even cafés.

She turned to the female bartender. "Do you mind if I look through those business cards?"

"Help yourself," she said before turning to fill an order.

Carrie walked to the bowl and rifled through it. Then she dumped the whole thing out onto the bar before sorting through the cards. One—a green one—caught her attention, and she swore. She picked up another one. And then another. Three of Kelly Sorenson's business cards. Not the purple one she'd given Jase, but the kind that DeMarco had gotten from Lance Reynolds.

The minute she saw Jase walk into McGill's, Carrie moved toward him. She handed him one of the green cards she'd found.

He read it and frowned. "Kelly Sorenson. Her business card."

"Yes. The same kind Susan Ingram gave us. There's two more of them in the bowl by the bar."

"So?"

"So anyone could have seen her drop her card in there and taken it. Or jotted down her contact information and given her a call. Maybe that's why we can't verify she left with anyone in particular that night. Maybe she didn't leave with someone per se, but maybe someone called her after she left. And told her he got her card from McGill's. That's what Susan Ingram said. That Kelly met a client from McGill's. Not that she actually left McGill's with one."

"Okay. So it's a distinction. But what does it mean?"

"It means maybe no one saw her leave with someone from McGill's, but she still met up with someone from McGill's. Someone that was here that night. Someone I saw."

"Someone, meaning the guy from the café?"

"Maybe. I don't know. But we need to push for those records from Kelly's cell-phone company."

"I swung by Steam, but the place was shut down."

"Damn. And I haven't had any luck verifying whether Brad Turner's been here, not without a photo. But we can rectify that tomorrow. Maybe even see if Steam has a bowl filled with business cards, too."

"Right. If Sorenson dumped her cards here, why not there, too? And if she did, why not Tammy Ryan? Maybe we can connect Darwin's vics that way. But until then...it's late. What now?"

What now? Now she wanted to take some aspirin. Her head was beginning to pound and she suddenly remembered Stevens's orders to get some rest before she broke. It was now sounding like very sound advice. "Should we head home?" she asked Jase, noting that he looked pretty shot, too.

Then she realized what she'd said.

Home. As if they had a common home to go to. Except for the one night they'd spent together at her place, she'd been sleeping at his place. Even after they'd discovered Ryan, even though her house was habitable once more, she'd crashed on his sofa. She'd left her stuff at his house. *His*. Not hers. Never hers.

"Our respective homes, I meant," she clarified, trying to hide her embarrassment, as well as her disappointment. She didn't want to go back to her place. Not without Jase.

"I know what you meant," he said quietly. "Listen, I know your house is fine now, but how about—"

"Hey, Carrie! You decided to join us. Awesome."

Carrie stared at Jase, willing him to complete the offer he'd been about to make. But he didn't, leaving her with no choice but to turn toward the man who'd called out to her. "Hi, Bo. This is Special Agent Jase Tyler. Jase, this is Bo Haven."

"Hi, Bo. Carrie thinks highly of you."

"Wish I could say the same, Tyler, but I haven't heard of you."

Jase just grinned. "Doesn't surprise me a bit. Carrie tends to be closemouthed about what's really important to her."

Bo laughed and Carrie blushed. "We were just about to leave," Carrie said.

"Come on over and say hello to the rest of the guys first."

"I don't know, Bo. We're both tired."

"Too tired to say a quick hello? Come on, girl.

You're not on the team anymore, but we're still friends, aren't we?"

She looked at Jase. "You can go ahead—"

"No. I'd like to meet your old team."

The way he said that had her frowning, but it was too late. Bo led them to a table in the back.

As Jase watched, the group of men greeted Carrie warmly.

She, in turn, seemed to take genuine pleasure in see- ing them all. Jase remembered what she'd said about feeling more like a team member on SWAT than she did on SIG. But he also remembered what she'd said about SWAT not being fully ready for a female mem- ber. He saw no sign of that here and wondered what she'd meant. Hoping to get some insight into her past, he decided to stay awhile. "I'm going to get us a drink. Beer?" he asked her.

She frowned slightly, then nodded her head. "Sure. A Bud Light, please."

Jase winced and the guys groaned at her wimpy choice in alcohol. She shrugged her shoulders. She could barely stomach the taste of beer anyway, but she'd learned to adjust while she was hanging out with guys. And since that's pretty much the only gender she spent time with...

As Jase walked away, Carrie followed him with her gaze until he got to the bar. There, an extremely short and feminine-looking waif of a woman with long blond hair and lots of cleavage started talking to him. Jase smiled, and the sight made Carrie both happy and sad. He looked good, when he smiled. He always looked good and that was something that women would forever be drawn to. Jase would never lack for female company. As soon as they caught Darwin, he'd remember why he'd dated so many of them before getting involved with Carrie.

Rich Andrews spoke up. "Good-looking guy, Carrie."

Carrie couldn't help it. She laughed at his exaggerated drawl. Andrews was gay, but the only people who knew that were sitting at the table with him.

Luke French and Bo groaned again, and Bo hit Andrews in the arm. "Shit, man. Cut that crap. You need to get your gaydar fixed. There's no way that guy's gay."

"So?" Andrews laughed, shrugging. "I can still enjoy the view. Besides, no one would think I'm gay, either, dude. Gaydar is a myth." He had something there. Andrews looked about as alpha-male as one could get without scaring little children on sight.

Bo turned to her. "Heard you closed a big case. Good for you, gal. A serial killer, huh? Man, you've got balls."

She winced inwardly. Cojones. Courage. She remembered what Mansfield had said to Jase at the Sorenson crime scene. Something about her being made of steel. If only they knew. She just shrugged. "Someone has to work them. Why not me? What have you heard about it? Anything about the guy's M.O.?"

Something bumped her in the shoulder, and she

turned to find Jase standing behind her with a couple of beers, noting that he'd chosen a dark pilsner for himself. She took her light beer and sat in one of the vacant seats. Jase joined her.

"Nope," Bo said. "I figured you guys were keeping that on the down-low for a reason."

"We were," Jase said. "But someone's been talking. Now we have a copycat on our hands."

"Shit. Talk about double trouble. You close to finding him? Or her?" he said with a playful glance at Carrie.

Jase shook his head. "We're still knee-deep in interviews and link analysis. Trying to find a connection between the victims. If he could have targeted them from a single location. We haven't come up with anything solid yet."

"Copycat, huh? I wonder if the first guy knows about it? If he didn't like being copied, well, that would be one way to draw both of them out, don't you think?"

She sensed Jase stiffen next to her. "What do you mean?" she asked.

Bo shrugged. "Even stone-cold killers, maybe *especially* stone-cold killers, have their pride. If someone was going about methodically killing people, he probably wouldn't like it if he knew someone was passing off the killings as his, you know?"

Jase nodded. "That makes sense."

Carrie agreed. "It does. And it would go both ways, wouldn't it? Maybe the copycat wouldn't want the competition being dished out by the killer he was copying. What if—"

"Well, well. If it isn't Wonder Woman," came the voice of the last man Carrie wanted to hear.

JASE WATCHED THE TALL, muscular man with the blond buzz cut walk up behind Carrie and grab her shoulders, kneading them roughly for several seconds. He tamped down his immediate desire to cut the guy's hands off and instead studied Carrie's face. She looked like she was bracing for battle.

"Hey, Ward. Good to see you," the man said to her before turning to Jase. He held out his hand. "I'm Pete Taylor. SWAT sniper." He said it like it was an official title.

Jase looked at Carrie, then back at Pete. Raised his right hand, which still held his beer. "Jase Tyler. Not a sniper."

Pete looked at him for a moment, confused. He then laughed, obviously not getting Jase's sarcasm. High-fiving the other men, Pete sat down on the other side of Jase. He rubbed his hands together.

"Shit, did you guys check out the Grade-A tail that's in here tonight? Look at the chick in the red miniskirt. We are going to get some serious action tonight."

Jase almost choked on his beer at Pete's crass words. He looked at Carrie, but she avoided eye contact. Silence descended while all the men sitting at the table glared at Pete. He pretended not to know why. "What? What'd I say?"

"Dude, you are such as asshole."

"Yeah," Andrews said, agreeing with Bo.

Grinning, Pete leaned back in his chair, raising his hands in a gesture of appeasement. "I'm just saying, if you boys want some tonight, there's prime meat to be found."

Jase couldn't take it anymore. "Why don't you shut up?"

Pete rose to his feet, looking ready to pound Jase into the ground. "What did you say?"

Pushing back his chair, Jase rose, as well, aware that he was a good two inches shorter than Pete but not giving a shit. "In case it slipped your notice, there's a lady at the table."

Pete frowned in confusion, apparently not sure who the "lady" was that Jase was referring to. Then his mouth dropped open when he realized Jase was talking about Carrie. "Ward? Oh, get over it, Romeo. Carrie's been around cops for a long time. She's one of the guys. Right, Carrie?"

She nodded her head. Smiled stiffly. "That's right, Pete. Just one of the guys."

"Who the hell are you anyway? Her guard dog?"

"If you don't get your mouth out of the gutter, you're going to find out, aren't you?"

She grabbed his arm. "Just drop it, Jase. It's fine. Pete didn't mean anything by it. Did you, Pete?"

Pete remained mutinously silent.

"Did you, Pete?" Carrie glared.

Still glowering at Jase, Pete finally shrugged. "Nope. I didn't mean anything at all." He sat down and looked up at Jase, who hadn't taken his chair. "Come on, dude, sit down. We're all friends here."

Jase slowly took his seat.

"Great," Carrie said. "Now, if you two he-men are through marking your territory—"

"Excuse me," a soft, feminine voice interrupted. "Jase, right? I was wondering if I could talk to you for a second."

It was the blonde woman he'd been talking to at the bar. From the look Carrie shot him, however, you'd think she'd just introduced herself as Jase's long-lost wife. "Carrie," he began, but she pushed to her feet.

"Excuse me for a second. I see someone I want to say hello to. I'll be right back."

As soon as she was out of earshot, Jase stood and addressed the woman who'd introduced herself as Sandy. "Did you need to talk to me about anything important, Sandy? Because I'm here with my girlfriend and we're probably going to be leaving soon."

Sandy's face fell, but she recovered quickly. Forcing a smile, she shook her head. "No. Never mind. But it was nice meeting you, Jase."

"You, too, Sandy."

Jase sat down. The other men were looking at him with shit-eating grins on their faces. Pete whistled. "Look at you, man. You had that little girl panting for a piece of you. And Ward—"

Before he could finish his sentence, Jase leaned closer to Pete and got right in his face. "Listen, asshole, I don't care how you talk the rest of the time.

But if you ever talk like that in front of Carrie again, I promise I will hunt you down and make you sorry."

Pete's shocked face was almost comical. He pushed back his chair and towered over Jase. "Are you shitting me? You're threatening me? Did you not hear me when I said I'm a SWAT sniper?"

"Believe me, I heard you," Jase said, but didn't get up. He took a sip of his beer. "And it's not a threat. Maybe your mother didn't teach you better, but you don't talk that way in front of a woman."

Pete looked at the other men at the table, watching the interplay between them. "Did you hear this jackoff? He actually threatened me."

Bo leaned back and shook his head. "Nope. I didn't hear anything. You, Andrews?"

When Andrews shook his head, Pete appeared completely befuddled. "Whatever," he said and walked toward the bar. Jase started to go after Carrie when Bo stopped him.

"Hold on there, Jase. Why don't you sit down? I want to ask you something." He turned to Andrews. "You mind making sure Pete doesn't get into any more trouble?"

"Not at all." As Andrews and Luke walked off, Jase took his seat again.

Bo took a drag of his beer and leaned back, studying Jase with veiled eyes. "I'm getting the impression Carrie means something to you."

Jase held Bo's gaze. "You're a smart man."

"Good." He nodded. "I'm glad. Few men have seen what she has to offer."

"But you have?"

"At one time. But she's not really my type."

Okay, so he wasn't planning on claiming Carrie. Which was good, because it meant he wouldn't have to beat the shit out of him.

"But? 'Cause I figure there's a but in here somewhere."

"But she's kind of Pete's type, if you know what I mean."

"Pete? She went out with that asshole?"

"When she first joined SFPD SWAT. It didn't last long and when it ended, it went downhill really fast."

SWAT. Jase still had trouble wrapping his mind around it. Oh, not because he didn't think she could do it, but because she was such a contradiction. A ferocious cop, but also a woman with long silky hair who decorated her house in girly fabrics and soft wispy watercolors. It was subtle, but she compartmentalized her life. As if she couldn't believe that the different sides of her could coexist. "She wasn't on SFPD SWAT for very long. She said you worked with her on the team in Austin?"

"That's right."

"Did she ever say why she became an MP in the army? Why she wanted to join SWAT?"

Bo smiled. "I think it started out as a challenge for her. You know, never been a woman on the SWAT team, so she wanted to do it. She had an edge. Her shooting skills are amazing. Do you know her history?"

Remembering the scrapbook, the ribbons and newspaper articles, he nodded. "Olympic shooting team."

"Yeah. And she also had an edge physically. She's stronger than most women. When she set her eye on SWAT, she was already fit, but not nearly fit enough. She worked with a personal trainer for a year. She asked for my help to get ready for tryouts, which mirror the FBI's. Extremely rigorous. But she did it. Ranked third out of the eight that made it."

"So you're a sniper, too?"

"Not like her. I'm cross-trained for entry and perimeter work. I can shoot. We're all trained to use the AR 15 rifle. But nothing like Carrie. Or Pete."

At the mention of the man's name, Jase stiffened. Bo laughed. "Pete's an okay guy. He just can't stand the thought that she's a better shooter. Sometimes he lets his pride get the better of him."

"She deserves more respect."

"I won't argue with you there," Bo said. "You going to make sure she gets it?"

"What the hell does that mean?"

Bo shrugged. "Just that I sense something between the two of you. And I hope you don't fuck things up. She needs someone who can handle her strength."

"I'll try not to disappoint you." Jase drained his beer and stood, putting his glass down with a thud. "You sure you're not just warning me off?"

Bo laughed. "Believe me, man. I'm helping you. But

as far as warning you off, I think it goes without saying that if you hurt her, you're going to be sorry."

Carrie waved to him from the front door. "Looks like we're moving. Thanks." He held out his hand, which Bo shook amiably.

As he started to walk away, a man called out to him. Jase turned around, thinking it was Bo, but it was actually Pete.

"Word of advice, dude. Carrie likes things rough. But not too rough. You might want to remember that if you have any hopes of keeping her."

Jase frowned. Incredibly, it sounded as if the guy was giving him relationship advice. As if he didn't want Jase to repeat some mistake he'd made with Carrie. Jase didn't need or want the guy's help. "I give Carrie everything she needs," he said. "I always will. And if it ever turns out what she needs is to kick your ass, I'll be right beside her making sure it gets done."

CHAPTER TWENTY-FOUR

JASE DROVE STRAIGHT to his house.

"Jase, there's no reason for me to stay with you any-more. My place is fine now, remember?"

"It would be hard for me to forget being in your bed, Carrie." He glanced at her. "On the other hand, you seem to have forgotten that's where we were be-fore Commander Stevens told us about Tammy Ryan. Or is it just that you'd like to forget?"

"I'm not forgetting anything. But I—I left some stuff at your place anyway. I'll gather it up and then get out of your hair."

Like he was going to make things that easy for her, he thought.

She must have sensed his determination to talk. Once they got to his house, she said, "You know what, Jase? I think I'll take a run before I head out. You don't have to wait up."

Despite his increasing impatience, Jase let her go. He had some thinking to do, and a lot of it had to do with what he'd witnessed back at the bar with Carrie's old team. As he often did when he needed to hammer things out, Jase slipped into his own tank top and shorts and took advantage of the home gym in his garage.

Even as he pumped iron, his thoughts were all about Carrie. He could tell she frequently worked out with weights herself. She was by no means bulky, but she definitely had the type of muscle definition that one only got with regular workouts. He wasn't intimidated. And he wanted her to know that. But he also couldn't get Pete's words out of his head. Jase had already experienced the complexity of Carrie's sexual needs and desire, and certainly wasn't surprised by them. Obviously, Pete had run across the same issue—the fact that Carrie's needs ran a wide spectrum. But had he learned the lesson too late? Had Pete been too rough with her? And what, exactly, did that mean? Because Jase was forming a picture in his head, and it was one he didn't like. Not in the least.

Although she'd said she'd been raped by a college boyfriend, that didn't mean it had been the only time it had happened. Had Pete, Carrie's own teammate, raped her? Is that why she'd left SWAT? And if it turned out to be true, what was Jase going to do about it? Other than kill Pete with his bare hands, which is what his instincts demanded.

An hour after she'd left, Carrie returned and walked into the garage. She'd worn a tank top and sweats, and both were stained with sweat. She'd obviously pushed herself hard. She was flushed. Panting. And despite his fearsome protectiveness and his suspicions about Pete, seeing her like that made him envision the last time they'd been in bed together. Jase felt himself harden and dropped his weights on the floor.

"You ready to stop running now, Carrie?"

LAUGHING SHAKILY, Carrie held up her hands and took several steps back. "Whoa, there. What the hell are you doing?"

Jase kept walking toward her. "I've stopped running, too. I'd much rather run to you, and since tomorrow is going to involve another busy day working the case, I'm thinking we should take advantage of what little downtime we have left."

"All I want now is a shower and to head home. Not necessarily in that order."

"I think we can give you a little more than that."

She bumped up against the wall and scrambled away from it so she had room to maneuver. "Look, Jase, I thought we established that the nights we spent together were a mistake. You've certainly acted like you've agreed. And regardless, I'm just not in the mood right now."

"What's the matter, Carrie? We were getting along so well, even after Stevens's call. You didn't have a problem staying here after that. So what happened? Was it seeing your old friend Pete that has you out of sorts?"

She frowned, trying to keep him in her sights as he circled around her. "Maybe it was seeing you flirt with the bimbo at the bar that was the turnoff."

At first he looked confused. Then he laughed, obviously pleased by her admission. Which made her fume even hotter.

"Is she what you think my type is? Why? Because she's not a cop? Hasn't any man ever been strong enough to handle who you are? A strong, capable woman with a generous, soft soul? Do you feel you have to hide your strength for a guy to want to make love with you? Is that what you had to do with Pete?"

She saw red. "Is that what he told you? Were you comparing notes with that bastard?" She shoved him in the chest, making him take a step back.

"No. I don't need to compare notes with him. He volunteered more than I could ever expect but it was enough to know you probably were tempted to kick his ass a time or two."

She turned to leave, but he grabbed her arm and whirled her around, then backed her into a wall, crowding her with his body and the determined look in his eyes. "So, did you?" he demanded. "Have to kick Pete's ass? Was he one of the guys who needed to beat his chest after he'd taken you to bed?"

She refused to struggle with him and instead lifted her chin. "He didn't realize that's what he was doing, but, yeah, he was. And, yeah, I ended it. Fast. I wasn't going to let history repeat itself. But I guess I never learn. You obviously enjoy flexing your muscles with a woman, too. Maybe you were right about that whole nature and nurture thing, after all."

He flinched and the sheer degree of hurt and shock

on his face was enough to make her flinch, too. Instantly, he let her go.

Just as quickly, she reached for him. "Jase, I'm sorry—"

He shook her touch away. "Well played, Carrie. But don't worry. That kind of history is never going to repeat itself with you. You wouldn't allow it. And believe it or not, I wouldn't, either."

He tried to turn away, and this time she was the one who grabbed his arm, refusing to let him leave. Refusing to let him turn away from her.

"I'm sorry, Jase. Please believe me. I was mad, that's all. And you're right. I was jealous. Am jealous. So many women want you and I'm nothing like them. I'm not even sure why you're interested in me when you can be with someone like that woman at the bar. But I know you'd never hurt me. I trust you. I trust you out of bed and in bed, too. I just don't think sleeping together is the smart thing for either one of us."

His expression remained frozen. Distant. "Yeah. So you've said. Numerous times. I'm beginning to think I might have to start listening."

Deliberately, he pulled away from her and went inside. She followed him, but only after she blinked back the flood of moisture in her eyes.

She'd used what he'd told her about his parents to push him away, and she'd never forgive herself for that. She couldn't expect any more from him.

But to her utter shock, Jase didn't stay mad at her. When she approached him, he didn't storm into his bedroom and slam the door. With a weary shake of his head, he walked up to her, caressed her cheek with his knuckles then bent to give her a light, sweet, lingering kiss before pulling back.

"This is my last invitation, Carrie. No games. No pretenses. And if you refuse, that's fine. I'll give up gracefully and never bring it up again. So here goes. You're welcome to sleep on the couch, but you don't have to. Just so you know, I'd love to share my bed with you again if it's what you want, too."

With that, he walked into the bedroom, leaving her to stare after him.

It took her several minutes of thinking of all the reasons she shouldn't walk into his bedroom before she gave in gracefully and did what she really wanted. She followed him. He was standing by the bed and when she walked in, he shot her a smile that made her heart melt.

The last time they'd made love, they'd reveled in each other's bodies with a kind of desperation, as if they'd been afraid they'd be snatched out of each other's arms. This time, they were determined to give each other what had always been between them anyway— trust. Trust to be everything they were and trust that each would welcome the other with not just open arms, but an open heart.

The events of the night and her own confession of jealousy had wiped Carrie's mind free of worry. Jase knew how she felt about him and she was incapable of hiding it anymore. Being exposed emotionally made it only fair she expose herself physically, as well. Unembarrassed, Carrie stripped off her clothes. With each article of clothing she removed, she grew stronger in her belief that she was gifting Jase something precious, something she'd never given anyone before. When she was done, he stripped just as precisely. Just as slowly. Until they were both naked and basking in each other's admiration.

She led him to the bed and asked him to lie down. She took her time reacquainting herself with every inch of his body. The rounded, bulging muscles of his shoulders. The hard, ripped planes of his torso. The long, elegant framework of his legs and feet. She kissed and stroked and licked him from head to toe, then turned him over and did it all over again. And the whole time, she gave his hands and mouth free access to any part of her he wanted.

He sucked and molded her breasts. He dipped his fingers into the warm wet heat between her legs. He buried his face there and feasted on her.

There was no hurrying this time. There was no desperation.

There was only the night. Their bodies. United and inseparable.

And when they climaxed, they climaxed together, then remained wrapped tightly in each other's arms until sleep claimed them.

THE NEXT MORNING, Carrie heard Jase come out of the bathroom and finished up her phone call with Commander Stevens. After what Bo had said about killers being competitive, an idea had formed in her head. She'd left Jase and the woman who'd approached him to call Stevens. Commander Stevens had been open to her suggestion from the start, but he'd become even more receptive after Carrie had talked to Lana earlier that morning and told Stevens what Lana had offered.

"What time do the cameras start rolling?" she asked.

"Ten sharp."

"And that'll give them enough time to air it tonight?"

"That's what I've been told," Stevens said. "They're going to play the spot on all their sister channels. Please don't be late. I hate reporters."

"We'll be there."

Carrie closed her cell phone and thought of Jase.

He wasn't going to like what was about to go down, and she understood why. But as wonderful as their intimacy last night had been, its magic had disappeared with the light of morning. It hadn't changed who she was. She was a cop first and she always would be. As such, she needed to do whatever she could to get the job done. What she and Lana had come up with might be a long shot, but right now it was the only avenue they had.

Turning, she jumped guiltily when she saw Jase standing behind her. He was bare-chested and wearing flannel pajama bottoms. He looked so good she smiled and stepped closer to kiss him.

But he frowned and evaded her touch. "What cameras, Carrie? What's going on?"

Carrie sighed. There was no denying it. She felt guilty. She should have run her idea by him, and she'd been going to, but then that woman at the bar had approached him and she'd been too rattled from seeing Pete and she'd known Jase would try to talk her out of her plan....

He probably still would, but he was her partner. He had a right to know. "Bo said something last night and it gave me an idea. Serial killers are proud. They think they're smarter than the cops. Probably think they're smarter than each other, right? The Embalmer was methodical. Patient. Unlike Darwin, who seems to be escalating his murders without any clear plan. We've been keeping the details of both cases under wraps, but maybe that's not how we should play it. The Embalmer's dead. Darwin might be responsible or he might not be. But what if we pretend we don't know? That we think The Embalmer's alive? That we think it's The Embalmer who's been committing these latest murders, not Darwin?"

"What do you think Darwin would do with that information? Besides move against another victim to make a better impression on us?

"That's definitely a risk. But he's going to move against another victim anyway. This way, we play the odds and swing them a little in our favor. Hope that Darwin will contact us directly to set the record straight. Do something to poke his head above water, and give us a chance to catch sight of him."

"And the way to do this is to put your face on national television?"

"We're a team, Jase. I'd be addressing him myself,

but as to what I'd be saying? I'd want your input on that, of course."

"I actually play a role in this grand plan? Good to know. So how come I'm just now learning about it? Why did you go to Stevens without discussing this with me first?"

"You know why. It involves a certain amount of risk. I'm the lead on the case and I'm willing to take the risk. But I was afraid if I told you that you'd try to talk me out of it. Because you—because you—"

"Because *I care about you,* Carrie," he said quietly.

"Yes, Jase," she said. "Because you care about me."

"But you won't let that stop you."

She shook her head. "I can't. This may be a long shot, but it's something. It gives us a chance, if nothing else."

"Yeah, well, the last long shot you played led us to The Embalmer, so I'd say you have a pretty good track record. But that's no surprise. Gambling isn't anything new to you. You gamble with your life all the time."

"*We* gamble with *our* lives, Jase. You were right beside me when we entered Bowers's home."

"That was different. We had no choice. This television spot will paint a target on you. But maybe that's exactly what you want? Let me ask you something. When did you phone Stevens about this plan? Was it when you left me sitting with Bo and the rest of the SWAT team? After that woman came up to talk to me at McGill's? Did you come up with this plan in part to prove how *not* my type you are?"

"I don't have anything to prove."

"Bullshit. You're constantly trying to prove how tough you are. Tough enough to be a cop. Tough enough not to need me or any man."

"I don't need you, Jase. I don't need anyone. And it looks like you, just like Pete and every other man I've ever met, have a problem with that. Good to finally get it out in the open."

"Why didn't you tell me you're a sniper?"

Carrie blinked and raised her brows. "Like I told you before. It wasn't a secret. Why do you keep going back to that?"

"Because being a sniper is pretty damn badass, but it wasn't enough for you. You left SWAT, but you say it wasn't because you were forced out by Pete or anyone else. So, why? I'm beginning to think even being a sniper wasn't enough for you. Why? Because you had the protection of your rifle? Distance? It wasn't risky enough for you?"

Carrie's face immediately tightened, and she narrowed her eyes. "I'm trying to find a killer. And I know my limits."

"Obviously not. We don't need to do this. We haven't even had a chance to go back to Steam and determine whether Brad Turner is the man you think you saw at McGill's. You're jumping the gun. Trying to prove something, just like you have your whole damn life."

"Of course we'll still follow up with that, but I can't be certain I saw him at McGill's. And what the hell do you mean I've been trying to prove something my whole life?"

"I mean you chose a profession based on some crock-of-shit theory that the only thing you had going for you was your strength. And God forbid that anyone forget that."

"That's not true. I'm good at what I do. I'm a good cop."

"But that's all you allow yourself to be, and as such you're also a lonely cop."

"You are full of shit!" She tried to push past him, but he blocked her with his body.

"Oh, come on, Carrie. A cop, sure. But a cop in the army? The SWAT team? How much more of a male-dominated job could you have picked? And you did it because you'd be good at it. But you also did it because it was easier. By being one of the guys, you didn't need to worry about being a woman."

She reeled back at his accusations, but only because they hit so close to home. She hated the knowledge that he saw through her that easily. That he knew deep down inside her most private self, the thing she feared most wasn't failing as a cop, but failing as a woman. And yet she'd allowed herself to be more of a woman with him than she'd let herself be with anyone else....

Not good enough. Never good enough.

She shoved hard this time, so hard that he retreated a few steps. She took a breath and held up her palm, trying to stop the stream of words with that and a shaky laugh. "Look, Jase. I don't need your pop psychology. You're wrong. I'm completely satisfied with…"

"I can give you what you want, Carrie. I can see you as both a woman and a cop and never forget either one. But I can't let you endanger yourself because you have something to prove."

"Listen to me. This is a good plan. What are the chances that I really saw Brad Turner at Steam and McGill's? Last night, the bartender told me I was describing a lot of guys she's seen, including her fellow bartender, Lance Reynolds. Remember him? Remember how similar he and Brad looked? It's far more likely I simply got them mixed up. Besides, we agreed Darwin is killing good-looking people because he has a physical defect he's ashamed of. Lana agrees with us and she supports my plan."

His head jerked back in surprise. "Lana?"

"She's going to do the spot with me."

He laughed with no trace of humor, only bitterness. "Of course. If Darwin doesn't take the bait with you, why not try your polar opposite? You're a tough cop and have red hair. She's blonde and a whole helluva lot softer. Bad cop, good cop, right? Interesting since I'm the one that's actually your partner."

"You don't have to agree with the plan. You don't have to come with me. I don't need your permission. Remember that, Jase? Sleeping with me doesn't give you any right to protect me or tell me you know better."

"No, I thought being your partner gave me that right, Carrie. But I guess that doesn't matter jack to you, now, does it?"

CHAPTER TWENTY-FIVE

CARRIE, COMMANDER STEVENS and Lana met at the SIG building to film the television spot. The TV crew wired each of them for sound with a microphone that had its own transmitter. Commander Stevens was the first person to be interviewed. He gave a brief statement about The Embalmer's initial crimes. Next, the TV anchor, Liza Montoya, introduced Carrie by giving a rundown of her credentials, heralding her as one of the best detectives on the SIG team. Carrie gave a brief statement in which she deliberately named Kelly Sorenson, Tammy Ryan and Tony Higgs as The Embalmer's latest victims. She mentioned that the killer's M.O. had changed, becoming decidedly less sophisticated, but that they believed it was a deliberate ruse to throw off the police. She asked anyone with any information about her to call the police at a special number.

Finally, Lana spoke. Her voice was calm. Soothing. Her message brief but sincere. Although she pretended she was speaking to The Embalmer, her words were meant for Darwin.

"I'd like to address The Embalmer and offer my help. I've read your thoughts about your victims. I know why you're killing. Not out of hatred. You've felt powerless. Rejected by the world. And for something that wasn't your fault at all, but simply a twist of fate." She raised her hand and touched her own cheek. "Some marks on your face. But those marks don't make you a monster. And you can control what you do. I'll see you for who you really are. I'll help others see that person. Let me help you. You can contact me, Doctor Lana Hudson, at the California Department of Justice."

When Lana finished, she turned and caught Carrie's eye. Her compassionate words made Carrie feel uncomfortable. Jase's words about her and Lana playing bad cop and good cop suddenly came back to her.

Lana was the good cop. The one who played to the criminal's humanity.

And Carrie was the bad cop. The one who played to the criminal's darkness and depravity. What did that say about her place in the world? she wondered.

When someone functioned best in the dark, didn't they eventually reject the light?

SIMON FOUND OUT about the television interview about forty-five minutes after the fact. He was so angry at being kept out of the loop—and he was betting that had been deliberate—he knew he should avoid Lana until he cooled down. But that didn't stop him from looking for her an hour after the shoot. He found her in the department conference room, talking to a group of rookies from SFPD. He took a seat toward the side of the room, noting how she straightened her back and avoided looking at him.

She walked in a circle around the room, trying to make eye contact with the half-dozen recruits as she discussed hostage negotiation strategies. "Remember," she said, "any language that stimulates conflict is unprofessional."

One recruit interrupted her. "So, what, we need to be polite when we ask a suspect to put down his gun? Seems like that puts us in a position of weakness. Aren't we supposed to project power and authority?"

Simon wanted to smack the cocky young recruit for challenging Lana, but she didn't seem to take offense to the question. Eventually, she finished up her training, and Simon waited while she answered a few more questions. When the last rookie left and she was gathering her papers, Simon shut the door with an audible click. Lana walked toward him and stopped several feet short.

He cut to the chase. "What the hell did you think you were doing, Lana?"

She didn't even try to pretend that she didn't know what he was talking about. "I've reviewed his blogs, Simon. I know why he's killing. He's acting out of pain. I can help him. He's been scarred...."

Simon stalked toward her and thrust his face close to hers, speaking through clenched teeth. "I don't care how he looks, his ethnic background, his religious preference, if he came from a broken home or if his dog got run over when he was kid. I want him to stop killing."

Lana looked at him impassively, not flinching at his

aggressively physical behavior. "That's what I want, too."

"And how are you going to accomplish that? By appealing to his better nature? The guy's a murderous psychopath."

She shook her head. "We have the same goal, Simon. But you admitted it yourself. You don't care what brought him to this. I do. Because in understanding that, we can prevent other people from becoming the same thing. Maybe help him to change."

"He can't change. He's a fucking monster."

She hitched her bag higher on her arm. "He has that element, yes. I wrote that in my profile." She quoted from it: "'Well-educated, manipulative, self-centered sociopath; Likes being looked at, thinks he's unique, wants people to study him. He probably wouldn't mind being caught. He wants attention because he's never had the attention he needs.'"

He snorted. "Please, stop. You're making me sick."

"Almost four percent of the population are functioning sociopaths. Did you know that? They don't have a conscience, and I don't believe they were just born that way."

Simon stepped away, pacing in front of the door, still blocking her way out. "Oh, please. Not that old song and dance. Nature versus nurture. The average person knows right from wrong."

His sarcastic tone finally got a reaction from her. "Oh, really? How many Americans watched the televised replays of Sadam Hussein's execution, and reveled in his death? Somehow, conscience no longer applied. He was no longer a human being, but evil personified. And he isn't the first person the American public has vilified: gays were to blame for the AIDS epidemic, blacks were so inferior the Constitution refers to them as three-fifths of a person, and prisoners deserve to be raped in prison. Even the government trains its soldiers to ignore their own moral conscience, to follow orders in wartime, to kill without thought to who they're killing or why."

Simon stopped pacing, understanding hitting him like a freight train. "So that's what this is about. You think by helping Darwin, you'll somehow be one step closer to your antiwar sentiments."

Lana frowned and shook her head. "No, Simon, that's not what I think. But it's easy to demonize someone to the exclusion of anything else. He's doing horrible things. He needs to be stopped. But something caused him to stray off the path of moral conscience, and maybe something can help him get back."

"So you want to save him? Since you couldn't save your husband, Johnny?"

Lana took in a deep breath and looked as if he'd spit in her face. He could almost see her distance herself from him. "This has nothing to do with Johnny. Nothing."

"Sweetheart, everything you do has to do with him. Which is a shame, being as he's dead and all."

She flinched. Simon knew he was acting like a bastard, but her determination to save Darwin, a cold-blooded killer, poked at the raw wound he'd been nursing since the night she'd told him she couldn't see him anymore. That he believed her to be motivated by the death of her husband only made things worse. He didn't like feeling jealous of young Johnny Hudson, but that didn't mean he wasn't.

Lana drew back her shoulders and faced him squarely. "I'm not talking about him with you, Simon. You have no business talking about him. None at all."

Simon kept step with her when she backed away. "Is that right? Well, let me tell you this, sweetheart. It's a damn shame when a woman as beautiful and warm as you spends her life trying to help sick bastards like Darwin just because her husband chose to blow his brains out rather than deal with what life dealt him."

Even before Lana slapped him, Simon knew he'd crossed the line. Her palm moved swiftly, and he didn't even try to block the blow. He deserved it. And maybe, just maybe, part of him was willing to take whatever physical contact she was willing to dish out.

Her body, her voice, her entire being was shaking, the vibration causing the tears in her eyes to spill down onto her face. "You macho bastard! How dare you judge him? You, who've never gotten a raw deal in your life. He fought for his country and what did it get him? He came back half the man he'd been, literally. With nightmares of killing. Innocent people. Women and children. Killing he should never have had to do." Lana's voice cracked, and she had to take several breaths before she could continue. "Maybe it's the same for Darwin.

Maybe he doesn't want to kill. Maybe he just needs a chance, someone to see the goodness inside him."

"Lana…" he began, needing to apologize. Needing to explain that bringing up Johnny had nothing to do with disrespecting the man but more about being jealous of him. And wanting the woman he'd foolishly left behind.

She shook her head. "You do your job, Simon, and I'll do mine. I'm going to help Darwin, either before he's brought in or afterward. I'm going to show you that compassion is just as valuable a weapon as a gun."

She raced from the room, leaving Simon with an almost unbearable desire to run after her. But knowing that was the last thing he should do. For either of them.

CHAPTER TWENTY-SIX

BRAD WANTED TO KILL that redheaded bitch. How dare she go on national television and pass off his work as The Embalmer's?

She had to know better.

The police had found Bowers; his house was surrounded by crime-scene tape.

Plus, there was the fact Brad's work was smarter. More layered.

Hadn't she read the blogs? Hadn't she figured out the connection between the murders and the movies? Obviously not, and her ignorance and stupidity were being played off as his.

When he'd first seen her at McGill's he'd thought she was interested in her good-looking partner, Jase Tyler. He'd thought Jase was interested in her, as well.

But that couldn't be right.

Special Agent Carrie Ward was nothing but a weakling posing as something more. A woman trying to survive in a man's world when what she should be doing is popping out babies and cleaning out toilets.

Special Agent Jase Tyler, the name on the other business card she'd given him at the café, wouldn't be interested in someone like her. No, he was too attractive. Too well dressed. If Brad looked like him, he'd go for someone like Lana Hudson, the cool blonde doctor who'd spoken to Brad with softness and sympathy, the one who looked a lot like the lady who lived in the apartment downstairs. Yes, he'd bet Lana would be attracted to Jase, too. Any woman would be.

Brad had seen the way Kelly Sorenson had wanted Jase Tyler, but when she'd handed him her card, he'd pocketed it without giving it a second glance. That was someone with confidence.

Power.

The connection throbbed triumphantly through Brad's veins.

He's the key, Brad thought. *Good-looking. Powerful and strong. A cop but also a playboy. Someone men wanted to be. Someone women wanted to love.*

Even Nora, his sweet Nora, had looked at Jase Tyler with something akin to worship when he'd talked to her at Steam.

She'd looked at Jase Tyler as if he was a fucking god.

The television interview, as much as it angered him, was another sign. He needed to look to the cops. Look to the blonde doctor. Look to them to defeat Jase Tyler, a man who would otherwise be undefeatable. Ideas began to spin through his mind.

To lay the trap, he needed to be smart. Smarter than the cops.

But that shouldn't be too difficult. The fools thought

their little television interview would sway or trap him; instead, it would lead to their own destruction.

He needed to pay a visit to the college's Audio Visual Department. If they didn't have what he needed, he'd pay for it. And he'd check out Bowers's house, too. The doc had had a lot of high-tech stuff there. Stuff that could help him.

As soon as Brad did what he needed to, as soon as he proved he was stronger than Jase Tyler, the only god Nora would be worshipping would be him.

CHAPTER TWENTY-SEVEN

AFTER THE TELEVISION SPOT and a full day at work, Carrie didn't return to Jase's home. He'd made it plain as day when he hadn't shown up for the filming that he wanted nothing to do with her any longer. She went back to her house, where she belonged, with no lover to distract her. Yet the whole time, she missed Jase. Her body and heart yearned for him. And that was only further proof of what a mistake it had been to get so close to him.

The following day, Carrie worked from home, then headed into the office at about 3:00 p.m. DeMarco was on the phone, but motioned for her to take a seat. "Okay, thank you very much. We'll check it out." He hung up and held up a handful of memo sheets. "We've been getting calls from everyone and their mother, either claiming they've seen The Embalmer or confessing to the crimes themselves. It's a toss up as to which one of you has gotten the most marriage proposals. Lana's pulled in front, but you're not too close behind."

She snorted. "Any promising leads?"

Shaking his head, he sighed and she felt his frustration. "No. None. But we're not taking any chances.

SHADES OF TEMPTATION

We're following up on every single one. We've got patrol cars checking out the most promising of the bunch."

An hour later, Carrie slammed the phone down in frustration, cursing the fact that she couldn't find one solid lead in the stack of messages she'd received. So far, two men had confessed to killing women and cutting out their eyeballs. Several other people had called saying they had information about someone who was digging up corpses and having sex with them. Almost all of them had asked about a reward. And none of them had provided any useful information.

What, had she thought Darwin would call her and set up a meeting as if it was a playdate? Carrie rubbed the back of her neck, but straightened when Simon walked up to her desk.

"Any luck?"

She shook her head. "No. You?"

"No. None." Simon looked at her closely, and she wondered if her eyes were as red and fatigued as his own. "It doesn't mean anything. It's probably too soon to tell. Something could still come up."

Carrie didn't answer, appreciating Simon's optimism but not really believing it. "Do you think he's going to do it again?"

He shrugged. "I don't know. We haven't picked up anything yet. But we can't just hang around waiting for it to happen. Why don't you get out of here?"

"No. I'll stay." When her phone rang, she picked it up. Simon walked away. "Carrie Ward."

"I...uh...I know about Tony Higgs," said an unfamiliar voice. "His car. Did you ever find his car?"

Carrie frowned. No, they hadn't. His girlfriend, Ashley, had said he drove a black Corvette. There was an APB out for it at this very moment.

"Who is this?" Carrie asked.

"I saw his car. It's outside a house in Daly City. 532 North Avenue. Watch out. The guy's dangerous."

Carrie frowned as the caller hung up. She pulled out a map and checked the address. It was only a few blocks from where the body of Darwin's first victim had been found. Carrie reached for the phone and dialed SFPD dispatch. Given the brevity of the call, she had no hope of tracing the location of her anonymous caller, but...

"SFPD. How may I help you?"

"This is Special Agent Carrie Ward with SIG. I need to do a title search. The address is 532 North Avenue, Daly City. I need it stat."

Five minutes later, she got a call back, which necessitated her making several other calls. One of those was a call to Jase, but she couldn't reach him at home or on his cell phone. She called Commander Stevens and told him the situation. "I just got a call from an anonymous tipster who says he saw Tony Higgs's car outside a house in Daly City. Property's owned by a James Fishburn, an ex-marine trained in chemical and impact munitions. He had a clean record until about five years ago, when he was convicted of several crimes ranging from drug use to assault."

"What are you thinking?"

"I checked and the SWAT team is handling service of a warrant at a crash pad known to house guns. I'd like to go in with a team from SFPD, one trained in munitions and entry. We can be there within the hour."

"Where's Jase?"

"I haven't been able to reach him."

"Any other SIG members available?"

"Simon. And me." She couldn't keep the challenge out of her voice, which was something Stevens didn't miss.

"That's enough for me, Agent Ward. Be careful."

"Thank you, sir."

Simon and Carrie arrived at Fishburn's house with several officers. She spotted the black Corvette and confirmed that it was registered to Tony Higgs. The other officers set up ballistic protection and evacuated neighboring houses. Carrie then attempted to make contact with Fishburn via a bullhorn.

"James Fishburn. This is the police. Come out with your hands in the air."

After several minutes with no response, Carrie ordered the officer to her right to begin entry. The officer shot several 12-gauge beanbag rounds at the upper corners of the windows to break the glass. He then shot several rounds of chemical munitions into the house. The chemicals would contaminate the interior and hopefully force anyone hiding inside out into the open.

Sure enough, within several minutes, the front door

slammed open and a huge man wearing a stained shirt and boxer shorts stumbled outside. Carrie noted the pockmarks on the man's face.

"Stop. Get down on the ground."

"Fuck you!" the man replied, stumbling down the porch steps.

"Down. Get down."

The man kept moving, coming at Carrie. "Fire baton rounds." The officer next to her complied, shooting off five KO1 baton rounds that hit him in the legs and torso. It should have been enough to knock him off his feet. With almost superhuman strength, he flailed back momentarily, but didn't fall. He screamed in pain and rushed even faster toward Carrie. Carrie Tased him. He fell to the ground as the two prongs hit him in the chest, his muscles contracting from the ongoing activation of the Taser.

Carrie signaled the arrest team to approach him with caution. The two officers neared Fishburn, covered by two other officers with their pistols ready. As they leaned over him, he heaved his body up and ripped the prongs from his chest. With one hand, he grabbed at one of the officer's guns and tried to wrestle it away from him.

The officers withdrew their batons, hitting Fishburn's arms and back in an attempt to force him down. Carrie ran to assist but heard the gun explode before she could get there. Fishburn's body flopped backward as a red stain spread across his chest.

LANA DRAGGED HERSELF out of her office and toward the
front lobby. Because of her confrontation with Simon
yesterday, she'd been feeling decades older than she actually was. Guilt and desire weighed her down. Desire
for him and guilt because of it.

On her way out, she waved at the receptionist, who
was talking to an irate woman holding a screaming
toddler. Stepping into the cool night air, she'd walked
only a few steps when she heard someone crying. She
stopped and looked around. Saw a man sitting on a low
retaining wall, his shoulders visibly shaking. She approached him hesitantly.

"Excuse me. Do you need help?"

He looked up, and recognition seemed to flare
briefly in his eyes. So quickly she thought she must
have imagined it. But he did look familiar to her. Did
she know him? For a moment, she struggled to remember. Then it struck her. He reminded her of Johnny. He
had the same type of angelic baby face not in keeping with his tall, muscular body. Unlike Simon, whose
face seemed carved out of granite. Thinking of both
Simon and Johnny within the span of seconds made
her feel dizzy with renewed confusion and guilt. She
still missed Johnny. He'd been her friend since grade
school, her lover since high school. When they'd married, she'd thought it would be forever. But she'd been
so young and naive then. Lana paused for a moment,
twisting her wedding ring back and forth.

Doubt twisted in her gut. Maybe she was doing the
wrong thing by walking away from Simon. But what

other choice did she have? She couldn't live in constant fear that one day he'd kiss her and never come back. She'd had enough of that when she'd waited for Johnny to come home from battle. Even when he had, he wasn't the same. Death had claimed him long before he'd shot himself. She couldn't become involved with another man whose life revolved around death. She just couldn't.

She turned her attention back to the young man in front of her. He tried to compose himself. "I...I came to see Special Agent Tyler. Do you know where he is? He said I could talk to him about my friend...Tony... he's dead." The boy broke down again, sobbing.

Yet another victim. And he was here to see Jase. "I'm sorry. He's not here."

He held out two cards to her. "He gave me his card. And the card of a doctor if I wanted to talk to her. Someone named Lana."

Feeling more comfortable knowing that Jase had given this boy her card, Lana walked closer. She saw her card in his hand next to Jase's. With a sigh, she sat next him, wanting to help him. Hoping to spare Jase grief. "My name is Dr. Lana Hudson. I'm sorry about your friend. I'm a psychiatrist. I'd be happy to talk with you for a while. Would you like that?"

The boy looked at her, grief plainly etched onto his angelic features. "Yes. Please."

Lana nodded tiredly. She wanted nothing more than to go home. But something about this grieving boy called out to her. What harm would it do to have a cup of coffee with him and let him talk about his friend?

"There's a place across the street. Why don't we go there?"

He nodded and stood. For a moment, he loomed over her, and she instinctively stepped back. He simply looked at her. "Is something wrong?"

She shook her head, shaking off her unease. He was a grieving boy. And they were in public. She'd talk with him for a while. Send him home. It was the least she could do.

They walked the short distance to a café and talked for about an hour. Eventually their conversation shifted from Tony to his own dysfunctional relationships. He talked about his foster father, a drug addict and an ex-felon who, he said, was probably at this very moment getting what he deserved. He talked about how his mother had abandoned him when he was young. And how he'd never felt love or acceptance from anyone. Except Tony.

When they'd finished their drinks, she made him promise to call her if he needed to. But as she walked toward her car, she put the young man out of her mind. Her thoughts returned to Johnny. And Simon.

When she got to her car, she unlocked the door and opened it. She put her purse inside. A force shoved her forward on the seat, the gearshift jabbing her in the neck. She felt the cold press of a knife against her throat.

"What's up, doc?" a familiar male voice said, chilling her to her bones.

CARRIE WALKED OUT of Fishburn's house and watched as
the medics loaded his dead body into the back of their
cab. Jase ran up to her. Although he didn't hug her, his
gaze quickly ran over her body, assuring himself that
she was okay.

"Jesus, I got your voice mail. I was at the gym working out and I must have had spotty cell service. I didn't
even realize you had called until I was on my way to
Steam to talk to Brad Turner."

She looked just past his shoulder, trying to maintain
some of the emotional distance she'd managed to attain
in the last few hours.

"We searched the house," she said. "Fishburn's a
druggie. We found dippers, more than a thousand in
cash, crack and marijuana. He even owns an AK-47 assault rifle, something he was probably trained to use
when he was in the Marines." She pointed to Tony's
Corvette. "That's Tony Higgs's car. We found other
evidence inside. Pictures of Kelly Sorenson. Before
and after. A collection of bloody knives. It looks like
Fishburn's our guy."

"But?"

Now she looked at him. How could he read her so
easily? How could he know, based on what she'd said,
that she was feeling any reservations? "But I don't think
it is. It was too easy. It reeks of a setup."

"Wasn't that the whole point of the television spot?
It was a setup to lure the killer to you. And that's exactly what happened. Or at least, someone else saw the
spot and gave you the information you needed, right?"

"Yes, that's what we were hoping for. But I don't know. This seems more like a diversion than a victory for us. I just—I just don't want to wait until we have another victim to find out if I'm wrong or not."

Carrie's cell phone rang, and she checked the caller ID. "It's Commander Stevens. Let me get this."

"Is Jase with you?" Stevens asked.

She glanced at Jase. Dread pulsed through her. The last time Stevens had called looking for the two of them, Tammy Ryan's body had just been discovered. "Yes, sir."

"You both need to come in. He's got Lana."

Dread morphed into shock. Then horror. Then desperation. She couldn't have heard Stevens correctly. "Excuse me," she forced out. "Who has Lana?"

But she hadn't misheard. The anonymous tip. Fishburn. It had all been a diversion.

"Darwin," Stevens said. "I'm sorry, Carrie, but Darwin has Lana."

Her mind began to spin and she felt herself fumble her phone. Distantly, she heard Jase curse and take the phone from her. "This is Tyler. Yes. We'll be right in."

He ended the connection and gently gripped her arms. "Carrie, are you okay?"

"He has Lana," she said.

Grimly, Jase nodded. "Not for long. We need to go in. You going to be okay?"

He was still holding her. His touch, his steady gaze, his very presence seemed to infuse her with strength.

Things had just turned horribly personal, but now wasn't the time to fall apart.

Together, they got into Jase's car. On their way to the station, Carrie said, "You were right. You tried to warn us that taunting the killer on television was too dangerous. And now, because we didn't listen, a killer has Lana."

"Lana knew exactly what she was doing, Carrie. Don't you take responsibility for this, do you hear me?"

But she couldn't absolve herself that easily. "How can I not take responsibility? I knew there was risk involved. I'm the one who brought my idea to Lana."

"And she's the one who insisted she do the spot with you, right?"

"How did you know that?"

"Because you'd never ask someone to take that kind of risk, even if you did think it would help catch a killer."

She didn't know if she believed him. But she knew his belief in her eased her distress, if only a little.

When they got to the station, Commander Stevens told them, "It's Darwin who has her. Fishburn was just a decoy."

"How can you know that for sure? That Darwin took Lana?"

"He's posted her photo on the internet. Thrown down the gauntlet. Mentioned Jase's name specifically. Wants to do a trade of some sort."

Commander Stevens handed them the blog. As one, they read it.

You're trying so hard to find me, aren't you? But how can you, when I've never really existed. Not really. Not to you. Not to so many of you. Until now. My angel showed me the way. Taught me that I need to be bolder. Braver. Fearless. I must face my weaknesses and that includes the police.

Special Agent Carrie Ward. You were there when the doctor called out to me. You'll understand why I shed her blood.

Just like all the others. Just like Fishburn. And just like your partner.

Special Agent Jase Tyler.

I want him.

Only after I have him will you finally understand.

You'll all finally see who I am.

As Carrie read the words, rage and despair warred within her, muddying her thoughts. When she was done reading, she glanced at Jase. He'd paled slightly, and his features were grim.

She struggled to remain calm. At that moment, however, Simon Granger walked into the commander's office.

Just like Jase, his features were dark but even more intense.

Murderous.

She'd thought it before and she thought it again: this was personal now. Darwin had invaded their own turf, their police family, by taking Lana. And he actually thought he was going to get Jase, too?

Never.

"We'll get her back," Carrie said to Simon. But even as she said the words, she knew they were a statement of intent, not a promise. She couldn't promise they'd get Lana back. How could she?

"Where'd he take her?" Simon asked.

"We don't know," Commander Stevens responded. "We checked her house first thing. Looks undisturbed. But her car's missing."

Having read the blog and seen the photo attached, Carrie turned to Simon. "Simon, you need to know…"

"What is it?"

"He attached a photo to his blog this time. He's started to cut her."

Simon closed his eyes and cursed. "What does he want?"

"He wants me," Jase said.

"How?"

They turned as one to Commander Stevens, who said, "He obviously wants Jase to meet him for some kind of exchange."

"I'm going to do it."

Carrie whipped around to face Jase. "No, that's crazy. You can't."

"I have to. He's got us over a barrel, Carrie. It's our only way of getting Lana back."

She saw Jase and Simon lock gazes. Simon looked grim but said nothing. The same was true for the commander. No one was going to say anything to dissuade him? She damn well knew that if the tables were turned, if it was *her* the killer wanted in exchange, they

wouldn't be so quick to let her sacrifice herself. She'd
be damned if she let them sacrifice Jase.

"No. I won't let you," Carrie said.

Jase walked up to her. "Baby, listen to me...."

She pushed his hands away when he tried to take
her by the arms. He'd called her "baby." For the first
time. And in front of their colleagues. As if he didn't
care whether anyone, the commander included, knew
they were sleeping together. That they were more than
just colleagues.

She didn't care, either. In fact, she wanted the others to know. If they knew, they'd also know how serious she was about keeping Jase safe.

As quickly as she'd pushed him away, she reached
out and took his hands in hers. "The only reason you're
on this case is to assist me," she said with measured
precision. "I'm the lead. I'll take the risks."

"But he doesn't want you," Jase said gently. "He
wants me for some reason."

Her eyes filled with frustrated tears, but she furi-
ously blinked them back. "He wants you for the same
reason *everyone* wants you, damn it! Because you're
beautiful. You're perfect."

He pulled her into his arms, and she buried her face
in his neck, clasping him close, never wanting to let
him go.

Laughing shakily, he rocked her in his arms. "God,
do you know how long I've been waiting for you to say
those words?" he joked. At least he tried to. But she
knew he was being serious. That he cared about her

more than she'd ever imagined. And that he was trying to protect her and reassure even now, even as he proposed something that could destroy her. Because it would. If anything happened to Jase, if she lost him, her world would never be the same.

She loved him, she finally admitted to herself. She'd been so scared to let him in, to give him any power over her, because she'd known all along how much it would kill her to lose him. And now she was being forced to admit her feelings for him at the same time her worst fears were coming true.

"You can't," she whispered, shaking her head and grinding her forehead into his chest to emphasize her words. "You can't do this." *You can't leave me now that I know. I know I love you. You made me love you, damn it.*

Pulling back, he cupped her face in his hands. "You're the one who's always talking about the inherent dangers of being a cop. That when we come to work, we understand we're putting ourselves at risk in order to help others. Save others. We need to save Lana. She's a doctor. Not a cop. We knew the risks, she didn't."

"She knew the risks when she put herself in front of that camera," Simon said quietly. Reluctantly but honestly.

"And I let her do it," Carrie added. "It's my fault he has her."

"It's no one's fault," Jase said gently. "If he wanted you to make the trade, you'd do it, wouldn't you? You wouldn't even hesitate."

Knowing the trap he was leading her into, she remained stubbornly silent.

"Carrie," he prompted. "Wouldn't you?"

She wasn't going to lie. "Yes."

"And the last thing you'd want, the thing that you would hate most in the world is if we tried to stop you, especially if you thought it was because you were a woman and we were trying to protect you."

"It's not the same thing. I'm not trying to protect you because of your gender. I'm—I'm trying to protect you because—because I love you," she said.

Jase smiled, but it had a hint of sadness to it, as if he knew it was too little, too late. "Wow. This really is true confession time, isn't it?" In a flash, his expression grew serious. "I don't have to make any confessions, do I, Carrie? Because you already know how I feel about you. You knew why I didn't want you to put your face on television and talk to a killer. Because I love you, too, and I didn't want anything to happen to you. But you did it anyway. Because that's the only thing you could do. You thought that's what you needed to do to stop a killer and I understand that now. You need to let me do this."

She stared at him. Didn't want to concede his point. But she saw the resolve in his eyes. The acceptance in everyone else's. He was going to save Lana whether she agreed to his methods or not. "Okay," she whispered. "But we have to be smart about this. We don't even know if Lana's still alive. You can't risk yourself until he proves it. Comment on the blog. He either proves to us that Lana's alive or we have to assume she's not."

CHAPTER TWENTY-EIGHT

WITH DISBELIEF, Brad read the comment the police had made to his blog post. Jase Tyler was willing to make a trade with him, but not unless Brad provided them with clear and convincing proof that Dr. Lana Hudson was still alive.

"No!" Brad screamed the word. Turning, he smashed his fist against the mirror on the wall, cracking the glass so that it distorted his facial features even more.

The scars were coming back, he thought frantically. He hadn't meant to kill Dr. Lana Hudson, but he had. Was that the reason his scars had returned with a vengeance?

She'd been pretty. Smart. Even as terrified as she'd been, she'd kept her cool for quite a long time. He'd brought her to Dr. Bowers's house, the place he'd set up shop after watching that televised interview. It was amazing how little effort they'd put into securing the area, even after he'd finished with Tammy Ryan. Some police tape, an occasional patrol car in the area, but that was all. They'd obviously thought a copycat killer would be foolish to infiltrate the home of The Embalmer. But it wasn't foolishness that drove Brad. It was

boldness. And brilliance. He was smarter than them
all, and that was particularly true of the dead doctor.
Why shouldn't Brad enjoy the luxury of Bowers's home
given he'd been the one smart enough to track him
down and kill him?

After killing Kelly Sorenson, after discovering the
murders were the key to treating his scars, he'd visited
Dr. Bowers. He'd explained what he'd been doing. Told
Dr. Bowers they should partner up.

But Dr. Bowers hadn't been willing to share his secrets. As soon as that had become clear, Brad had had
no choice but to kill him. He hadn't listened to any of
Dr. Bowers's psychobabble bullshit when he'd begged
Brad for mercy.

And he hadn't listened to any of Lana Hudson's
when she'd tried to tell Brad he was sick.

He was acting out of pain, she'd said.

Expressing anger because his parents had rejected
him.

Because so many people had taunted him.

She'd told him he was a good person and only needed
help. Eventually, what she'd been saying had started to
make sense.

He'd started to wonder if maybe he was crazy. He'd
started to doubt himself. What he was doing. He'd
begun to wonder if his obsession with Nora was all
based on a fantasy.

Despite the camera equipment he'd set up and the
plans he'd made, he'd started to hurt the doctor just to
shut her up. But even when he'd started cutting her the

doc had shown an amazing tolerance for pain. So he'd started cutting her deeper, just for the joy of hearing her cry and scream, trying to regain that elusive feeling of power that he'd become dizzy with during all the other murders. But that feeling hadn't come.

Somehow, killing the doctor had tainted him again, accelerating the setback he'd experienced at the café with Nora.

He felt scared. Weak. Powerless.

Scarred. Deformed.

He screamed again, grabbed one of Dr. Bowers's vases and flung it on the ground. The movement and sound satisfied and calmed him, so he screamed again, grabbed another object and threw it.

It was only a matter of time before others saw it. Mistook his scars for weakness. And started treating him with disdain again.

Brad glanced wildly around him. The pretty blonde doctor was dead, but Jase Tyler wanted proof. Proof that she was alive. That was the only way to lure him in. To separate him from the redhead. How was he—

Wait. When he'd first seen Lana Hudson on the television, he'd thought she reminded him of someone. Who was it? Who—

His neighbor. The blonde woman with the dark-haired husband.

He'd thought she and Lana looked strikingly alike.

Maybe the cops would, too.

CHAPTER TWENTY-NINE

SEVERAL HOURS LATER, Jase was talking one-on-one with a cold-blooded killer. It wasn't the first time he'd done so in his career, but it was the first time he was truly scared. For Lana. For Carrie. For himself. For all of them.

He remembered when he'd first learned that Carrie, and not he, had been assigned The Embalmer case. He'd been disappointed at not being able to work another serial case because it would mean fewer kudos to list on his professional record. As if the number of complicated cases he closed was somehow a reflection of how worthy a cop he was. How worthy a man. He supposed because he played so hard on his off time, he'd felt he had something extra to prove when it came to his work. Now it all seemed like utter bullshit.

He had nothing to prove. The same way Carrie had nothing to prove. Yes, good cops liked a challenge. Even better cops had the stamina and ambition to go the long haul. But Jase and Carrie had been using the job as a measure of their self-worth, and that was never a good thing. It had taken working a case with Carrie for Jase to realize that.

When Jase disconnected the call with Darwin, he immediately looked at Simon, who was on a different phone.

Simon shook his head. "We couldn't trace him," he said.

"I'm not surprised," Jase said. "He's smarter than we thought. Lana's alive. He let her talk to me. It was brief but—"

"Thank God," Simon said, and the sentiment was evident in all the sighs of relief that resounded throughout the room. But Carrie was still skeptical. He could see it written all over her face.

"What did she say?" Carrie asked.

"She just said, 'This is Lana Hudson. I'm okay.'"

"How do you know for sure it was her?"

"It sounded like her," Jase said. Her voice had been low. Shaky. But he'd recognized her.

"That's not good enough," Carrie said. "We need more proof. We need to see her."

"That's what he figured," Jase said. "In thirty minutes, he's going to post a video of Lana to prove to us that she's still alive. In order to be sure it was taken after we talked, I told him to have her blow me a kiss, then curl the same hand she'd used into a fist. That way, if we see her do that in the video, we know she's really still alive."

"Which doesn't mean he won't kill her as soon as he takes the video," Carrie argued.

"No," Jase agreed. "It doesn't. But we'll take what we can get." She was thinking on her feet. Covering all the bases to make sure Jase didn't take any additional risks when he didn't need to. She wasn't going to like what he had to say next, but they had no choice. No choice, he reminded himself. "He wants me to get in my car and start driving right now."

Carrie's eyes widened. "Now? Before he posts the video?"

"He says the rest of you can verify that she's alive and call me. At that point, I'll already be at the meeting spot. The Ferry Building."

"I'm coming with you," Carrie said.

"He said for me to come alone. And before you can say it—" He held his hand up. "I know I'm not really going to go alone. Just like we discussed, you and the SWAT team will follow me from a safe distance, but only if you promise me—and I have to be able to trust you to keep your word, Ward—that you will pull back if I tell you to. Can you do that?"

He could tell she struggled with her answer. On whether she should lie. But she didn't.

"It will be hard, but I'll do it. We all will. We'll pull back if you really need us to. But only as a last resort. Promise me that in return."

"I promise," he said. "Are you going to bring your sniper's rifle?"

"You're damn right I am," she said.

"And are you really as good as I think you are?"

She nodded. "Yes. But for you? I'll be better, Jase. The best I've ever been."

He stepped up to her and cupped her face. "You're

already the best, Carrie. No matter what happens, I want you to remember that, you hear me?"

FIVE MINUTES LATER, they were on their way. Jase drove his Mustang toward the Ferry Building while Carrie followed him in her own car with her sniper rifle stowed in the trunk. Three SFPD SWAT team members, Bo, Luke and Andrews, followed in an unmarked van.

Throughout the drive, she and Jase maintained communication with a wireless transmitter. Simon called her on her cell.

"I watched the damn video," he said, his voice husky and shaking. "She—she was wearing the same clothes she'd been wearing when she disappeared. She blew the kiss and curled her hand into a fist just like Jase wanted."

"Was she—was she badly hurt?"

She heard him swallow hard over the line. "Her face was still bleeding from where he'd cut her, and he wrapped duct tape around her eyes, maybe to hide—"

As his voice choked off, Carrie imagined Darwin slicing Lana's eyelids while she fought him and screamed in pain. "Simon—" she whispered.

"Your shadows from SFPD followed up on the warrant for Dr. Bowers's medical records and did a search for the names you gave them. They found one."

"Who?"

"Brad Turner. He came to Bowers for a facial disfigurement. A port-wine stain."

"Brad—? Oh, God. The guy from the café. But he

didn't have a port-wine stain. He—" She shook her head. "I've got to tell Jase. Simon, will you be okay?"

"Just get her back, Carrie. Then I'll be okay."

"We will, Simon. We'll do everything we can."

But what if that wasn't enough? What if Darwin— what if Brad Turner—really was smarter than them? Stronger?

They couldn't lose Lana, but she couldn't lose Jase, either.

She called Jase and told him exactly what Simon had said. But even as she did, she suddenly remembered her previous conversation with Lana, when Lana had asked if the job always came first. At the time, Carrie hadn't been completely positive of her answer, but now she was.

The job was a priority, but it wasn't her only priority. It wasn't even her first priority. Not anymore.

There would always be bad guys. Those compelled to hurt others.

And there would always be good guys. Like SIG. Like Jase and Carrie.

But the only way the good guys could do their jobs and fight the bad guys was if they loved their own lives enough to truly live, and lived well enough to truly love.

Love was what was important. *Love.*

"Carrie. Carrie, baby, can you hear me?"

She jolted at Jase's insistent voice in her ear and came back to herself. She'd been speaking her thoughts out loud, she realized.

"Love *is* the most important thing, Carrie, and we

have it. You and me, it's going to give us strength. We will beat him, do you understand?"

She forced herself to respond firmly. "Yes. We will beat him." She couldn't have him worrying about her. He needed to keep his focus on what was coming. It was almost time.

She saw her turnoff and maneuvered the car toward the exit. The SWAT van was right behind her, its headlights shining in the twilight. They were positioning themselves on a roof about forty yards away from the spot where Darwin had said he'd be waiting for Jase. Ten minutes later, they were in position. "We're in place, Jase. Do you see him?"

"He's here," Jase said. "It's not Brad Turner."

"Not Turner? But that can't be right…. The coffee shop, Tony, the connection to Dr. Bowers. It all made sense."

"We'll deal with Turner later, but this isn't him, Carrie. He's a couple of inches shorter than me. Dark hair. Slim. He's holding Lana in front of him."

"Fine. Maybe Turner and this man are working together. Lana, is she wearing the red jacket and gray skirt?"

"Yes. And she's got the duct tape on her eyes. And blood. Damn it, there's lots of blood."

"Wait. Let us look. Does anyone see him?" she asked.

"Negative," Bo responded, who was looking through a pair of binoculars, as were Luke and Andrews.

"Where is he?" she muttered. "Wait!" She moved

her scope back to the left until she saw them. "Damn it, he's holding her in front of him as a shield. He keeps moving behind a tree, and I can't quite get a spot on him. But I will. As soon as he lets her go, I'll have a shot. Hang back a bit."

"I can't. He's seen me. I'm going in."

"Jase, wait—"

"It's okay, Carrie. I know you have my back."

"Jase. Damn it." But he was already walking toward Darwin. When he stopped, he partially blocked Carrie's view of Darwin in her scope.

"Jase, you need to move to the right," she said. "Two steps."

Jase obeyed her instruction, but then something completely unexpected happened.

The man holding Lana dropped her and held up his hands in surrender. Lana dropped like a dead weight, making no effort to catch herself with her hands. The man who'd dropped her was talking. Screaming actually.

She could just hear the man's frantic words through Jase's mic.

"I'm not him. Don't shoot me. Please! I didn't kill her. He has my wife. He has my wife."

Jase cursed and snapped, "Hang back, Ward," he said. "Hold your fire." Through her scope, she saw Jase bend over Lana's prone body. "Lana's dead. She's already dead. And this isn't Darwin. Hell, the guy's pissed his pants. He says his name is Mark Nelson and that Darwin has his wife, Maria. We need to—" Carrie raised her head to look at the rest of the team and—

A gun fired. Over her transmitter, Jase screamed.

And Carrie screamed, too. "Jase!"

Heart thundering wildly, she looked through her scope again. Jase was on the ground, and the man he'd called Mark Nelson was standing over him with a gun. "No, no," Carrie muttered at the same time she automatically aimed. She was just about to pull the trigger and shoot when Nelson dropped the gun and fell to his knees. He covered his face with his hands and sobbed. Once again, his voice drifted toward her over Jase's mic.

"I'm sorry. I had to. He's watching. I had to shoot or he'll kill her. He said he'd kill Maria."

EVEN AS JASE KEPT REASSURING them that he was okay, that Nelson had shot him in the leg, Carrie and the others scrambled to get to him. When they finally got there, she dropped to her knees beside him. Only after examining the gunshot wound to his leg was she reassured that he'd be okay; the bullet had passed clean through his outer thigh and hadn't hit any major arteries. She threw her arms around him. "Thank God you're okay," she breathed.

While the other officers detained and dealt with Nelson, Jase hugged her tightly. "I'm okay, but Lana— God, Carrie, she's dead."

She pulled back and glanced at Lana's body, where Bo was bent over her. Bo met her gaze and shook his head slightly. Grief for the other woman rained down on her, but she turned to Jase and said, "You did everything you could. You were willing to die for her, Jase. It's not your fault."

But his expression was one of devastation and pain, both physical and emotional, and she knew her words weren't a comfort to him.

Within minutes, backup and an ambulance had arrived. In the commotion, they confirmed Mark Nelson's identity. He was just another one of Darwin's victims. He'd kidnapped Nelson and his wife shortly after Jase had demanded proof that Lana was alive.

"He taped up my eyes so I didn't see where he brought us. But he told me he has video equipment set up here," Nelson sobbed. "He's watching us right now. It's the only reason I shot you," he said, looking at Jase. "He has my Maria…. God, I'm sorry. I'm so sorry."

Although Carrie knew the man had been acting under duress, it took everything she had not to go after him. Thank God he'd shot Jase in the leg and not to kill. Jase would be okay.

Lana, however, had been dead for a while. It had been Maria wearing Lana's clothes in the video. And the fact Jase had heard Lana's voice on the phone? Probably a recording spliced together from the TV interview they'd done. Darwin was proving himself to be smarter and more ruthless than they could have ever anticipated.

Carrie was watching the medics dressing Jase's wound when her cell phone rang. Thinking it might be Stevens or Simon, she answered. "Special Agent Carrie Ward," she answered.

"I'm watching you right now. I can see you standing next to the woman in the blue shirt. Look up and blink three times if you understand."

With fear paralyzing her, Carrie did as he'd ordered. To her right was a female EMT in a blue shirt, jotting down some notes. Carrie scanned the area, but there were too many places to hide cameras. They hadn't found any of them yet. She gave three exaggerated blinks.

"Good," he said, confirming he indeed had his sights on her. "Now listen to me very carefully. No more games. You know how smart I am. I'll know if you disobey me again. I want you to come to me. Alone. Turn around. Throw your cell phone and your gun into the trash can to your right. Make sure no one sees you. Get in your car and drive to Dr. Odell Bowers's house. Do you know where that is?"

She nodded slightly.

"Good. Normally, the drive would take you ten minutes. I'm giving you seven, just to make sure you don't have time to make any stops along the way. Don't say a word. Don't hesitate. Don't do a thing to make me suspicious. If you do or if you're not here in the seven minutes I'm giving you, I swear I will slice Mark Nelson's pretty wife up the same way I did the doctor. And this time, I won't be nice about it."

He hung up.

Carrie took in a shuddering breath. Jase was lying back on the stretcher and talking to Bo. Andrews had begun looking for Darwin's cameras while Luke stayed with Nelson. Slowly, carefully, Carrie turned. At the same time, she removed her gun from her holster. Covertly, she dropped her gun and phone in the trash, made her way to her car and left.

Her mind was spinning with questions. What did Darwin want with her? What was she doing, going to meet him alone? He wouldn't have placed a camera in her car, so she could call for backup, right? She reached for her radio but...Darwin had been two steps ahead of them all along. Hell, he'd gotten to Lana. How did she know he hadn't wired her car? That he wouldn't know immediately she'd called for backup and kill an innocent woman?

She withdrew her hand from the radio and made it to Bowers's home in just over seven minutes. She threw open her car door, bolted outside and ran up the stairs to his front door. She reached for the doorknob, praying that Darwin hadn't started hurting Maria Nelson.

Pain exploded through her head as someone hit her from behind.

WHEN CARRIE CAME TO, the world was pitch-dark. A sharp, insistent throbbing drummed at her temples where she'd been hit, as well as in her neck, back and shoulders. Her arms were pulled back tightly and tied to her feet. She couldn't open her eyes and knew they'd probably been taped shut with duct tape. Her mind was muddled and she was confused. Where was she? Where was Jase? What had—

Suddenly, memory returned. She remembered everything. How Darwin had kidnapped Lana and bartered for a trade. How Jase had gone to meet him, only to discover that Lana was dead and the man they'd thought was Darwin was a bystander desperate enough to shoot Jase. How Darwin had called her and ordered her to come to him.

How in her drive to get inside and save Maria Nelson, she'd let him get the jump on her.

Just like Kevin Porter had gotten the jump on her that first time. But she'd had a second chance to take Porter down, she reminded himself. And she still had the chance to take Darwin down. Because she was still alive.

Alive but freezing.

She lay on a cold surface and she was guessing it was the tile Dr. Bowers had installed in his basement. The rest of his house had carpet or hardwood floors. At first, she couldn't hear anything, but then a door opened and she heard the sound of scuffling and a woman whimpering.

Maria Nelson, she thought.

Helplessness washed through her, escalating into terror. Suddenly, she struggled to breathe.

Stop it, she commanded. She couldn't have a panic attack. Not now. She needed to be strong. Needed to be ready.

She forced herself to take deep breaths. Told herself she might be the only chance Maria had. The woman sounded so frightened. So—

"Shut up!" A man yelled.

Carrie heard flesh striking flesh. A moan of horror and pain. And then things went quiet again. But not for long.

"You're going to feel so stupid, Special Agent Ward," a man said from behind her. "You had me right in front of you but weren't smart enough to realize it."

No, they hadn't been. They'd just figured out Brad Turner's connection to Dr. Odell Bowers.

Brad Turner. The man from Steam. He was Darwin.

Carrie recognized his voice the moment he spoke, and she wanted to curl up and howl with fury and self-disgust. Stay calm, she told herself. Don't panic. Eventually, Jase and the others would have noticed she was missing. Granted, they wouldn't know where she'd gone, but they'd figure it out. Somehow, they'd figure it out.

"As for your good-looking partner?" he continued. "He was the one I needed all along. Beautiful. Perfect. Now that I have you here, he'll follow, right? And I'll have him where I need him. I'll kill him and claim his perfection. I'll be perfect and Nora will see that."

Nora. The girl who'd grieved for Tony Higgs. She was the one. The angel he'd talked about. The one he'd believe he'd gain once Tony Higgs was out of the way.

He was right. They'd had him right in front of them and they'd failed to see him.

Now she and Maria Nelson were going to pay the price.

"WHERE'S CARRIE?" Jase asked Bo as he was being loaded into the ambulance.

Bo put his hand on his shoulder. "I'll go get her." He was back in minutes, a concerned frown on his face. "I can't find her."

"What do you mean you can't find her?"

"She's not here, Jase. She took her car. No one saw her, and we don't know when she left."

"Damn it," Jase said. "Help me up."

Bo looked at the EMT, shook his head. "Jase," Bo began. "She might have gone for backup. Or food—"

"Without telling me? Without seeing for herself that I made it to the hospital? No, Bo. Listen to me," Jase gritted out. "Carrie is missing. Help me get the fuck up so I can find her. Please."

Bo helped Jase stand.

"The cameras," he gasped. "He was watching us. He got to her somehow."

"But why? Why would she gave gone without telling us?"

"Because he had cameras on us. Because he has an innocent woman held hostage. And because she's Carrie. She—"

Jase abruptly stopped talking when he saw the flashing light on his phone. He had a text message. He looked at his screen.

Looking for someone? She's at the scene of the crime. Guess which one. Come alone. If I see anyone else, she's dead. Just like the doctor.

DARWIN GRABBED HER by her bindings and dragged her up. A small tremor of hope shook her when she felt him cut the rope holding her hands and feet together, releasing the tension in her neck and back. She prepared herself to move as soon as he untied the rest of the rope, but he never gave her the chance. With her hands and feet still bound, he lifted her up and into a straight-backed chair, smashing her hands behind her before securing her to the chair with more rope around her chest. She felt him kiss her cheek softly, and his warm breath puffed against her.

"You'll be the first thing the woman sees when she wakes up. For a second, she'll feel hope. Wonder if you're here to save her. Then she'll realize it doesn't matter. That I'm going to kill you both. She'll see what I really am then, just the way you will." Without further warning, he ripped the duct tape from her eyes, not caring that he took flesh and hair with it. She let out an involuntary gasp, but then bit her lip hard, refusing to make another sound.

She slowly blinked her eyes, adjusting them to the light, and focused on the man standing in front of her. He wiggled the fingers of one hand and smiled tauntingly.

"Hello again."

It was him, all right. Brad Turner. The same baby-faced, handsome boy whose complexion was completely unmarred. Unscarred.

The man she and Jase had both failed to see for what he was.

Had they been wrong about why he was killing, as well? After all, he'd come to Bowers with a disfigurement, but it had been one Bowers had cured. At least, that's how it seemed.

She did a quick scan of the room. Saw a woman that looked startlingly like Lana crumpled in the corner. But since Carrie could see her breathing, she was alive. At least, for now.

She returned her gaze to Turner.

They'd thought he was killing because of his scars.

But he had no scars. None that she could see.

No scars, so no motive.

Had his talk of beauty and power all been a diversion? "You're very handsome." She obviously didn't mean it as a compliment, but he took it as one.

He laughed. "Thank you. It's come with a price, I must tell you."

"So all your talk about scars was bullshit?"

He grabbed at his heart as if she'd wounded him. "Of course not. Don't you see? That's why I've been killing. I was born with a port-wine stain. It covered half of my face and caused me terrible grief growing up. Do you know what it's like? Being the freak that everyone stares at? Being the one that your own parents give up because they can't stand to look at you?"

Carrie snorted unsympathetically. "I know exactly what it's like to feel like an outsider. It doesn't give you a right to turn psycho and start killing people."

He walked up to her and slapped her hard. Then visibly tried to control himself. He laughed again, the sound high and jittery. "Don't be condescending. It's hardly the same thing. My defect wasn't a choice. I tried everything. Paid thousands of dollars for laser surgery. One painful procedure after another committed by that damn crazy quack Odell Bowers. None of it worked. I even followed him from Fresno to San Francisco, but the stains kept coming back. Ruining my life. Ruining my chances to be with Nora. It wasn't until I killed the prostitute that I found the cure. Found the way to get rid of my scars and Tony Higgs, once and for all."

Understanding gripped Carrie. Understanding and despair. He'd called Odell Bowers a quack, but he was just as disturbed. Maybe even more so, if that was possible. So delusional that he didn't even realize the surgeries had worked.

Suddenly, she remembered where she'd seen him before. Why he'd seemed familiar to her. It hadn't been at McGill's Bar, at least not exclusively. If she'd seen him there, it had been in passing, just as she'd seen him at the medical clinic where she had her P.T. appointments. She must have seen him coming to or leaving his appointments with Odell Bowers. She looked away, not wanting to give him the satisfaction of seeing any kind of emotion on her face, be it compassion or disdain.

She concentrated on where he'd brought her. Dr. Bowers's basement. It wasn't as clean as it had once been because it had been processed ten times over, but the room still contained the steel operating table. Counters with lots of storage space inside for who knew what.

He looked around, as well. "It's nice, don't you think? Have you seen the upstairs? Dr. Bowers liked to live large."

"I know," she said. "I was the one who found him. I didn't realize it at the time, but you killed him, didn't you? Did you dress him in the women's underwear and apply the makeup, too?"

Turner giggled. "I did. But it was all his stuff, so I'm sure it wasn't anything new for him. Can you imagine? What a fucking psycho."

"Yeah. A psycho. So did you work together? Before you decided to—what?—go off on your own?"

"I wasn't involved with Dr. Bowers's crimes, but I was smart enough to figure out what he was doing. As soon as I heard about the serial killer that was cutting off eyelids, that he'd committed crimes in Fresno, too, I knew it was him. Dr. Bowers was a huge fan of horror movies. I've spent practically half my life listening to him talk about them, in particular his favorite one, one where the killer cut the eyelids off his victims. Such a small thing but unique enough to be memorable, don't you think?"

She remained silent, which he didn't appear to like.

"Oh, come on. You have to admit, it was clever of me. Once I knew what he was doing, I thought, why not try it myself? Afterward, I knew exactly why he'd been doing it. It gave me the beauty and the power of my victims. Can you imagine what an intoxicating rush that would be?"

He lifted his hand, and for the first time Carrie noticed the knife he held. He watched her closely and began twirling it between his fingers. "My victims were beautiful and strong, but not strong enough. Nature took them out the way it's supposed to be. To give way to the stronger and more beautiful of us."

She tested the ropes again, noting that they had very little give. He'd made sure she wouldn't be able to escape. She couldn't remain silent any longer. "So that's how you justify killing Kelly Sorenson. Tammy Ryan. Tony Higgs. They deserved to die because they weren't strong enough to live?"

Walking up to her, he laid the cool flat of the blade against her cheek. Carrie refused to be cowed and continued to stare at him. He pressed harder and began to rub the flat surface in circles. "What do you think?"

"I think you're weak enough to kill others because it's the only way you can feel powerful."

Fury glittered to life in Turner's eyes. He raised the knife, and she waited for him to strike her in the face. The blow never came.

Carrie heard something outside at the same time Turner did. They both turned their heads and watched as Jase Tyler limped down the basement stairs toward them.

"Ah, Special Agent Tyler. Right on time," Turner said.

CHAPTER THIRTY

JASE STRUGGLED TO KEEP his footing as he made his way down the stairs toward them. Immediately, he spotted the woman who looked a lot like Lana Hudson crumpled in the corner. Was she still alive? His stomach clenched at the memory of discovering Lana's death. However, terror nearly overwhelmed him when he saw Carrie tied to a chair. He recognized the man from the college café immediately. Maybe in his early twenties. Tall, with light hair and an angelic face. He looked like the boy next door, except for the insane glint in his eyes. Seeing Jase seemed to stoke the fire there.

Thank God he'd guessed correctly given Darwin's vague reference to a crime scene, Jase thought. He'd immediately dismissed the places where they'd found Kelly Sorenson, Tony Higgs and Tammy Ryan; none were isolated or contained enough to give Darwin the advantage. So what crime scene had he been talking about? The more Jase had thought about it, the more Carrie's theory about competing serial killers had made sense. After all, her televised ploy had brought Darwin out in the open. There'd been every reason to believe that Darwin had killed Bowers to get rid of the competition, which meant Bowers's home was a crime scene and, hopefully, the one where he'd find Carrie.

Just to be sure, however, he'd told Commander Stevens to keep the others away from all the known crime scenes.

"You can't go in alone, Jase," Stevens had said. "You're injured. You need backup. You don't even know if he has Carrie. If she's still alive—"

"She's alive," Jase had snapped back. "And he has Carrie. She went to him alone in order to protect a life. And that's why I'm going to him alone, too. To protect hers."

"You know I can't let you—"

Jase had almost fallen to his knees at that point. "I'll beg if I have to, Commander. You know this is the only way. He's played us at every turn. He sees you coming, and Carrie's dead. I can't—I won't—let that happen. And you know we don't have time to argue about this. Please."

"If I let you go in alone, you're both dead," the commander had replied, but in the end he'd done the only thing he could do. He'd given Jase an hour. After that, he was surrounding all the known crime scenes full force. Jase didn't have much time left.

It looked like everyone knew it, too.

Darwin, aka Brad Turner, swiftly took position behind Carrie's chair and held his knife to her throat. As soon as Jase stepped onto the basement's tiled floor, Turner tensed, tightened his hold on Carrie's hair and pierced her neck with the blade. Her face contorted with pain. A streak of red appeared and ran down her throat.

Jase froze. "No. Stop!"

Turner stared at him and laughed. "I knew it. I knew you'd make the right choice. I assume the police have given you some kind of deadline before they rush in? Call right now and tell them you've found her. Tell them you're on your way to the hospital and for them to meet you there."

Jase's gaze once again flickered to Carrie. "Listen to me," Jase began. Instinctively, he took a step toward them. Again, Carrie flinched. Again, Jase froze. Again, a small stream of blood ran down her throat from where Turner cut her. Rage and panic bubbled inside of him, cutting off his breath and, combined with his recent blood loss from the shooting, making him feel perilously close to passing out.

"I don't want to hurt her, but you have what I need, Agent Tyler. You *are* what I need and if hurting her gets me what I need, I'll do it."

Carefully, Jase pulled his cell phone out of his pocket and called Commander Stevens.

"I've got her, sir. She's okay. I'm driving her to the veterans hospital near Geary and 40th right now."

"Thank God. What about Darwin? Did you—"

He hung up before the commander could say anything else.

His cell immediately began to ring.

"Silence it and then toss it over there," Turner said, jerking his head to indicate the far corner of the room.

Jase did as he said.

"Now your weapon." Of course he had one. Tucked into the back of his pants. But he couldn't give it over. Not yet.

"I don't have one with me."

"Liar," Turner screamed, spittle spraying from his mouth. "Take off your shirt. Now."

Jase unbuttoned his shirt and shrugged it off. It fluttered to the floor. He wasn't wearing a holster, so at first he couldn't understand why Darwin's eyes widened.

"You bastard. Your body. What did you do to your body? You're scarred."

Turner's hands were shaking now, jerking against Carrie's throat, sprinkling cuts and nicks across the smooth surface that Jase had showered with kisses just two nights ago. She held herself still, trying to stay calm, but Jase could read the terror on her face. Jase prepared to lunge for Carrie, to try and knock her chair down, knowing that if he waited much longer the man would kill her anyway.

Turner raised his hand from Carrie's throat and slammed the knife handle into the side of her head. Jase could tell the blow dazed her. She blinked several times, trying to focus her vision.

Jase wanted to kill him. Strangle him with his bare hands. He tried to move toward them, but Turner returned the knife to Carrie's throat.

Helplessness washed over him. He stared at Carrie, trying to gather strength from her presence. She needed him to be strong. To help her. But how was he going to get the bastard away from her?

Turner continued to rant. "You're worthless to me. I need someone perfect. Someone perfect, do you hear me?" He paused, looked down at Carrie again.

Jase felt bile rise in his throat. Shook his head. "No."

Ignoring him, Turner grabbed Carrie's chin and shoved it up for his inspection. He stretched her neck up, causing the wounds there to weep even more. Then he roughly pushed her away.

He shook his head. "She's pretty. Not beautiful. I need something more."

"Wait!" Carrie spoke this time, jarring him. "I'm perfect. A perfect shooter."

No. "Shut up, Carrie," he growled.

She kept talking. "I'm a sniper. Best of the best. I can shoot a dime from a hundred yards away. I won a gold medal in the Olympics."

Jase knew that it had been a silver medal, but Turner probably didn't.

"Plus I'm strong. I'm probably even stronger than you. What do you think of that?"

Turner looked down at her. "You're bullshitting me." But Jase could tell her boasting had caught his attention.

"I'm not."

Jase felt dizzy and closed his eyes, trying to get back his equilibrium. When he opened them, Turner was grinning. "How are you feeling, Jase? You're not looking good at all."

He swayed on his feet. He didn't know how much

longer he could hold on. Bracing an arm against a wall, he steadied himself. "You don't want to hurt her, Brad. You hurt her, and the whole police force will be after you."

Turner laughed. "Like they aren't already? Come on, Tyler. I'm not a fool. Give me the gun."

When Turner moved the knife threateningly close to Carrie's eyes, Jase reached into the back of his back waistband and pulled out his gun.

Turner smiled. "Nice and easy. That's right. Kick it toward me. Now, Tyler. Or she's dead."

Jase put the gun on the ground and kicked it toward Turner. It stopped about two feet away. His muscles bunched in anticipation. When Turner leaned down to pick it up, Jase lunged toward him.

CARRIE SCREAMED when she saw Jase rush Turner. She'd seen the way Turner had smiled and kept an eye on Jase. Knew that he'd laid a trap for him. Like her, he had known that Jase wouldn't go down without a fight. Even as weak as he was, even as hopeless as things seemed, Jase wouldn't give up. He'd die first.

Even as she had the thought, she saw Turner pivot to meet Jase's tackle. Saw the way he lifted the knife and held it aloft so that it would meet Jase's forward momentum. Saw the blade sink into Jase's torso with sickening ease.

Someone was screaming. Crying. Howling Jase's name in grief and rage. It was her. She stopped. Watched

Turner rise and pull his knife back. The blade was covered with a shimmery layer of blood.

Jase fell to the ground. He shifted and tried to move, grabbing the bottom of Turner's leg to pull himself up. Turner tsked. "Give up, man. You're going to lose." He kicked Jase in the face and then stomped on his bad leg. Jase moaned and then went still.

He shook his head in disgust. "Weak. I don't know why I ever thought he was perfect."

Carrie was crying again, throwing her weight around in her chair, trying to get loose so she could kill him. "You bastard. I'm going to kill you. You bastard." She repeated the words over and over again, the whole time looking at Jase, who no longer moved.

Turner picked up Jase's gun. He opened the barrel, apparently satisfied when he saw it was loaded. He flicked it shut and grinned at her.

"Is that so? I didn't know he meant so much to you. You said you could shoot a dime from a hundred yards away? Prove it to me. All you have to do is shoot something." Keeping Jase's gun trained on her, he loosened the bindings on her feet, not completely, but just enough that she'd be able to work her way out of them. He looked around, grinned then crouched down next to Maria Nelson's unconscious form and put something small on her shoulder. Something so small Carrie couldn't even see what it was.

Rising, he once again stood directly next to her. He motioned to Carrie with the gun. "Work yourself loose. You're going to stand on that side of the room and shoot that fragment of glass from her shoulder. You do that. You prove to me how perfect you are. And I'll let him go. I'll let both of them go. I promise."

She calmed at his words and sat absolutely still. This was it. This was her chance.

It took her five minutes to work her feet free. Stumbling to her feet with her hands still tied, she shot a quick glance at Jase. Blood pooled from beneath his body, and she prayed he was still alive.

As Turner followed, she moved to the side of the room he directed her to. Then she waited for him to untie her and hand her his gun. When he didn't, she frowned. "Well? Are you going to untie me? And I need something to shoot with, don't I?"

"The rifle from your car," he said, gesturing with his chin. She turned and saw her sniper rifle leaning against some cabinets. Seeing the rifle gave her strength. She gathered her fear for Jase and bundled it inside her heart, knowing that it would overwhelm her if she let it. Right now, she needed to focus on Turner.

She'd kill Turner. She'd save Maria Nelson. And she'd save Jase. And if she failed? Well, only then would she let the grief out. Let the grief consume her and swallow her whole. And take her to a place where she'd never feel pain again.

AT FIRST, JASE THOUGHT he was being eaten alive. That a thousand carnivorous bugs were crawling on him and feasting on his body. He struggled to get away from them and forced himself to open his eyes. The world came into slow focus, and he could barely make out Carrie standing with Turner across the room from him. He saw the vacant chair in which she'd been sitting and various lengths of rope lying nearby.

Why wasn't she trying to overpower him? What was going on? Because he didn't know, he remained quiet. Quiet but watchful. He did everything he could to fight off the pain, sharp razors that sliced through his leg. His vision wavered, and he feared he was going to pass out again.

No! Gritting his teeth, he took several deep, silent breaths. No. He could hang on.

Remember what you told Carrie. Rowing and sports aren't just about strength. They're about creativity. Upward motion. Overcoming your fears. Stamina.

He pictured Carrie as she'd been that night at the restaurant. A little tipsy on wine. More open than he'd ever seen her.

You're certainly strong, she'd said to him.

And he was. Strong enough to push back the approaching darkness.

Carrie would make her move. When she did, Jase would be ready.

CHAPTER THIRTY-ONE

CARRIE WAITED AS Turner sawed through the ropes binding her hands, taking care to keep the muzzle of the gun pressed directly to her scalp. Sharp pain danced through her hands as blood rushed to her fingers. She shook them out. He handed her the rifle.

"I need a second. My hands are numb."

He hit the back of her head with Jase's gun, and she choked back her instinctive gasp of pain.

"You have one shot," he snapped. "Do it now."

Carrie lifted the scope of her rifle to her eye and focused it on the fragment of glass on Maria Nelson's shoulder. It was the exact size of a dime, she thought with grim fascination. The bastard had taken her literally.

She took several deep breaths and gathered her strength. She tried not to think of Jase, bleeding and dying, if not already dead. Once she fired, Turner would look to see if she'd hit her target. That would give her a second, maybe two, to catch him off guard.

Carrie took another calming breath and focused. Focused on the small object that wasn't more than fifty feet away. Focused on the feel of the rifle in her hands. Focused. And squeezed the trigger.

Nothing. Nothing happened. She squeezed again. Still nothing.

Understanding and then horror overtook her.

Her rifle didn't have any bullets.

BEHIND HER, TURNER LAUGHED. "You really thought I'd be stupid enough to give you a loaded gun? But, shit, you're gutsy. You really could have done it, couldn't you? Perfect."

He leaned down and kissed her ear. She didn't even pull away. He'd won. He'd kill her. Then Jase. Then Maria Nelson. Three for the price of one.

A rush of movement, then Turner was off her. She twirled and saw Jase.

The two men struggled, their bodies flaying back and forth as each tried to topple the other. Carrie ran toward them, ready to bludgeon Turner with her rifle. But their bodies were a writhing swirl of movement, practically indistinguishable. She saw Jase's gun lying close by and scrambled toward it, praying that Jase could hold on just a couple of seconds longer. She grabbed his gun and turned. Ready to fire.

Only she couldn't. Turner had Jase in front of him, using him as cover as he held the knife to his throat. Unwanted images swirled through her head. Images of Kelly Sorenson, Tammy Ryan and Tony Higgs's bloody remains. The way Kelly's roommate and Nora Lopez had wept upon learning those they loved were dead. Carrie had watched with compassion but an emotional detachment necessary to do her job. Now she was forced to watch as a madman held a knife to the throat of someone she loved.

Anxiety. Fear. Panic. The emotions hit her in the face with the force of a heavyweight champ landing a knockout punch. Her breath spiraled out of control, and she feared she was going to faint.

She took in a deep breath. Then another. She could do this. Suck it up, she told herself. Focus on what she needed to do.

She needed to keep Turner talking.

Talking was a distraction. Plus, he had a habit of gesturing with his knife hand to make his points. The movement was subtle, but it could be enough to give her an opening.

If Jase was strong enough to help her.

She stared into Jase's eyes, communicating her belief in him. *Hold on, Jase. Just a little longer. Hold on.*

Injecting a tone of command in her voice, she aimed her gun. "Drop your weapon."

For a moment, Turner looked nervous. Then he started to laugh. "Drop my weapon? I don't think so. I, unlike you, have a hostage. I think dropping yours sounds like a better suggestion, don't you?"

Again, panic threatened to overwhelm her. She'd frozen the first time she'd tried to shoot Kevin Porter. What if she froze now? What if she failed? What if Jase died because of her?

She looked at Jase. He wobbled on his feet, barely

able to stand. Blood covered his shirt, and she knew he wouldn't last much longer. He'd die if they didn't get help soon.

And she'd die, too.

She knew that. Even if she managed to kill Turner. Even if she physically survived. If Jase died, Carrie wouldn't be able to go on. That couldn't happen.

"You won't get away, you know. The cops will find you. They won't rest until you're behind bars. And for what? Because some idiots made fun of you? Because you didn't have the guts to believe that Nora would like you just the way you were?"

Turner frowned. "She did like me. But she liked Tony more. And the ones I killed were shallow. Too involved in their own beauty to care about anyone else."

"What about Lana?"

"I just... You'd gotten too close...made me feel weak.... I needed to prove myself...."

"By killing a woman who wanted only to help you?"

He looked as if he was going to argue with her some more. But then he smiled evilly. "Hey, maybe I'm getting used to it. Maybe I'm starting to like how it feels to be the one with power. With the control. You know all about that, don't you? Isn't that why people become cops? Because they get off on controlling others?"

As Carrie looked at Turner's angelic face and mocking smile, she felt a veil of confidence settle over her. No. She'd chosen to be a cop because she thought she'd be good at it. Because she wanted to do good.

Like Jase.

Turner had shifted his knife when he talked. Only a few inches, but it was no longer pressed against Jase's throat.

She remembered how Lana had spoken to Turner in that television interview. How she'd thought of him as a victim. A product of a cruel world.

It no longer mattered.

Victim or not. Sick or not. Youthful or old. She'd thought it before, but until now, she'd never truly believed it.

She locked eyes with Jase. And said his middle name. "David."

Simultaneously, she fired her weapon.

Jase wrenched himself to the side. The bullet lodged in Turner's brain before Jase even hit the ground. Turner stumbled back, his eyes flickering with disbelief before going blank. He tumbled down like a building detonated with dynamite. Right on top of Jase.

Carrie raced over and pushed Turner off Jase. Jase's eyes were closed, and he was breathing shallowly. She ripped open his shirt, shredding the fabric so she could hold it firmly over his bleeding wounds. He grimaced at the pressure, but she didn't back off. His eyes were open now, and he was looking at her. Unbelievably, he had a slight smile on his face.

"Carrie…" he said. He coughed, his lungs wheezing noisily when he tried to catch his breath.

She shook her head. "Shh. It's okay. You're going to be okay."

"You did it."

She nodded. "We did it, Jase. We. I couldn't have done it without you. I love you, Jase. Please hang on."

He smiled again. "I love you," he responded quietly before his body went limp and he closed his eyes.

CHAPTER THIRTY-TWO

JASE PUT THE FINISHING touches on the table. His table. Not theirs. Even though they spent virtually every night together, Carrie still hadn't agreed to move in with him.

Not yet.

The bouquet of peonies he'd gotten her spilled out of a crystal vase that reflected the light of the fire. He set down two bottles of beer. A dark pilsner for him and a Bud Light for Carrie. He always stocked up on both. Not that they spent a lot of their time together drinking.

But tonight was a special occasion.

At least, that's what Carrie had told him on the phone.

He was really hoping the specialness of this occasion included the frothy piece of lingerie she'd worn a few nights back. When he'd seen her in the feminine little number, it had just about destroyed him. Not just because she was sexy, though God knows that was a given, but because it showed him how far they'd come. Slowly but surely, she was showing him the individual facets of herself. The strong parts, and the vulnerable ones. She was also becoming more secure in her feminine appeal and he couldn't think of anything sexier than that.

It made all his patience over the past two months worth it. No, he hadn't pushed her to move in with him, but it hadn't been easy for him to refrain from doing so.

She'd told him she wanted them to start working a normal routine again—together yet independently, not as partners glued together in a crisis situation. They loved each other—there was no question about that—but she wanted to be sure he knew exactly what he'd be "getting into" by making a life with her. While it bothered him that she still had insecurities, he understood why his stubborn warrior-woman wouldn't allow herself to fall blindly even if that's what she wholeheartedly wanted to do. Sooner or later, she'd accept what was so patently obvious to him: he loved her and he wanted her and that wasn't ever going to change.

He heard a sound behind him and turned, watching as Carrie walked toward him, her gait smooth. Sometimes, depending on how hard they pushed themselves, they walked with identical limps. Healing was going to take time, but at least they had each other to speed things along.

Her gaze sought his and the love he saw there caused his battered heart to dance.

They'd stopped not just one killer but two. Although they hadn't saved as many lives as they'd wanted to, they'd saved Maria Nelson and had stopped Odell Bowers and Brad Turner from taking more lives.

Lana's funeral had been a somber occasion, one that

had cast a seemingly permanent pal over the SIG team. Simon walked around grimmer than ever and Jase could only hope that, with Mac's return, he'd take some time off to heal.

In a few nights, both Jase and Carrie would be recognized for their outstanding service at an awards banquet put on by the mayor. It would obviously help Carrie and the department oppose Martha Porter's civil suit. As far as their careers were concerned, they'd have opportunities now that they hadn't had before.

But nothing was as important as what they'd found with each other. Not even the job that had made it possible.

As Carrie walked toward him, all he could think was, *My God, she's beautiful. Beautiful and brave. Strong and compassionate.*

The woman of his dreams.

The partner of his heart.

Together they'd survived the worst kind of monsters, and although there would be more of them in their future, there'd also be pleasure. Happiness and joy.

For him, there'd be Carrie.

Always.

* * * * *

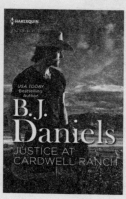

REQUEST YOUR FREE BOOKS!

2 FREE NOVELS
FROM THE SUSPENSE COLLECTION
PLUS 2 FREE GIFTS!

YES! Please send me 2 FREE novels from the Suspense Collection and my 2 FREE gifts (gifts are worth about $10). After receiving them, if I don't wish to receive any more books, I can return the shipping statement marked "cancel." If I don't cancel, I will receive 4 brand-new novels every month and be billed just $5.99 per book in the U.S. or $6.49 per book in Canada. That's a saving of at least 25% off the cover price. It's quite a bargain! Shipping and handling is just 50¢ per book in the U.S. and 75¢ per book in Canada.* I understand that accepting the 2 free books and gifts places me under no obligation to buy anything. I can always return a shipment and cancel at any time. Even if I never buy another book, the two free books and gifts are mine to keep forever.

191/391 MDN FEME

Name	(PLEASE PRINT)

Address	Apt. #

City	State/Prov.	Zip/Postal Code

Signature (if under 18, a parent or guardian must sign)

Mail to the **Reader Service:**
IN U.S.A.: P.O. Box 1867, Buffalo, NY 14240-1867
IN CANADA: P.O. Box 609, Fort Erie, Ontario L2A 5X3

Not valid for current subscribers to the Suspense Collection
or the Romance/Suspense Collection.

Want to try two free books from another line?
Call 1-800-873-8635 or visit www.ReaderService.com.

* Terms and prices subject to change without notice. Prices do not include applicable taxes. Sales tax applicable in N.Y. Canadian residents will be charged applicable taxes. Offer not valid in Quebec. This offer is limited to one order per household. All orders subject to credit approval. Credit or debit balances in a customer's account(s) may be offset by any other outstanding balance owed by or to the customer. Please allow 4 to 6 weeks for delivery. Offer available while quantities last.

Your Privacy—The Reader Service is committed to protecting your privacy. Our Privacy Policy is available online at www.ReaderService.com or upon request from the Reader Service.

We make a portion of our mailing list available to reputable third parties that offer products we believe may interest you. If you prefer that we not exchange your name with third parties, or if you wish to clarify or modify your communication preferences, please visit us at www.ReaderService.com/consumerschoice or write to us at Reader Service Preference Service, P.O. Box 9062, Buffalo, NY 14269. Include your complete name and address.

VIRNA DePAUL

77635 SHADES OF DESIRE   ___ $7.99 U.S. ___ $9.99 CAN.

(limited quantities available)

TOTAL AMOUNT	$ _____
POSTAGE & HANDLING	$ _____
($1.00 FOR 1 BOOK, 50¢ for each additional)	
APPLICABLE TAXES*	$ _____
TOTAL PAYABLE	$ _____

(check or money order—please do not send cash)

To order, complete this form and send it, along with a check or money order for the total above, payable to Harlequin HQN, to: **In the U.S.:** 3010 Walden Avenue, P.O. Box 9077, Buffalo, NY 14269-9077; **In Canada:** P.O. Box 636, Fort Erie, Ontario, L2A 5X3.

Name: _____
Address: _____ City: _____
State/Prov.: _____ Zip/Postal Code: _____
Account Number (if applicable): _____

075 CSAS

*New York residents remit applicable sales taxes.
*Canadian residents remit applicable GST and provincial taxes.

HARLEQUIN® HQN™
www.Harlequin.com

PHVDP1012BL